D0090254

IGNITE

IGNITE

⇥ A DEFY NOVEL ⇤

SARA B. LARSON

SCHOLASTIC PRESS
New York

All rights reserved. Published by Scholastic Press, an imprint of Scholastic Inc.,
Publishers since 1920. SCHOLASTIC, SCHOLASTIC PRESS, and associated logos
are trademarks and/or registered trademarks of Scholastic Inc.

Library of Congress Cataloging-in-Publication Data

Larson, Sara B.
Ignite : a Defy novel / Sara B. Larson. — First edition.
pages cm
Sequel to: Defy.
Summary: King Damian and his trusted guard, Alexa, focus on rebuilding Antion
after years of war and strife, but the citizens are reluctant to trust their new king,
and when a new threat arises, including an assassination attempt, Alexa must
protect the king she loves and uncover the enemy before it is too late.
ISBN 978-0-545-64474-7 (jacketed hardcover) [1. Magic — Fiction. 2. Kings,
queens, rulers, etc. — Fiction. 3. Conspiracies — Fiction. 4. Adventure and
adventurers — Fiction.] I. Title.
PZ7.L323953Ign 2015
[Fic] — dc23
2014017067

10 9 8 7 6 5 4 3 2 1   15 16 17 18 19

Printed in the U.S.A.   23
First edition, January 2015
Book design by Abby Kuperstock

For Brad, Gavin, and Kynlee
You are the sparks that ignite my desire to be the best I can be.
I hope you will always know how much I love each of you.

⊰ ONE ⊱

*T*HE HEAT IN the hallway was stifling, even though it was well past midnight. Thick humidity lingered from a storm that had passed earlier in the evening, coating my skin with moisture. I couldn't smell the wet leaves and mud of the jungle here, outside King Damian's room, but I knew the rich scent well enough to conjure it on my own. I was only halfway through my night shift, and I was already drooping. Willing myself to stay alert, I began to pace.

There hadn't been a single threat since Damian's coronation almost a month earlier, but Deron, the captain of the king's guard, wasn't about to take chances with Damian's life, and I couldn't agree more. Especially after how hard we had all fought — and how much we'd lost — to stop Damian's father, King Hector, and put Damian on the throne. My brother, Rylan's brother, almost half the guard, and countless others had died in the fight to free Antion from the evil vise in which Hector and his black sorcerer, Iker, had held the kingdom for almost my entire lifetime.

As I marched up and down the hallway, forcing the blood to move in my tired limbs, the side of my face and neck began to throb. The pain from my scars had eased over the last month, but it was still there. A constant reminder of the battle I'd fought against Iker.

1

Damian, too, had fought and lost so very much. He and I were alike in more ways than one — we'd both had to play parts to protect ourselves, and we'd both seen our families wiped out. I'd watched my parents and brother die at the hands of our enemies, but Damian . . . He had been forced to kill his own father in order to protect his people. Those scars were the type that no one could see, but would never truly heal.

The lit torch propped in the bracket across from Damian's door flickered suddenly, as if a gust of wind had blown past it, although I felt nothing. My hand dropped to the hilt of my sword. As I peered into the darkness to my right, there was nothing to see except a long stretch of empty hallway.

I crossed in front of Damian's door again, my thoughts turning to my king, as they often did. Though I'd made my choice, and convinced Damian that I didn't have any feelings for him, it was yet one more buried wound that I carried with me. I could never let him uncover the truth — that not only did I have feelings for him, but I was still in love with him. I would do whatever it took to keep our new king safe and to help him rebuild his kingdom and be the best ruler he could be, even if it meant causing him pain now. It was the right thing to do.

That dedication to his safety and well-being was why I never complained about taking the night shifts like some of the other guards did — usually the new ones. I was still unaccustomed to their faces and voices, rather than those of my old friends: Jude. Kai. Antonio. So many others.

"Alexa." A familiar voice called out my name — my real name — making me jump. I turned around to see Deron striding toward me from the other direction. Maybe someday I would get used to the captain of the guard calling me Alexa, rather than Alex, as he had for years when he thought I was a boy.

"Deron, what is it?" I asked as he closed the gap between us, his own lit torch chasing more of the shadows away.

"There's a man at the gate who's demanding entrance to the palace. He claims to be from Dansii, acting as a runner to warn us that a delegation has been deployed by King Armando and will be arriving within a day or two."

"A *delegation*?" I repeated in disbelief. "Has Dansii ever sent a delegation before?"

"No. Not so much as a political emissary, as far as I know."

A cold chill skittered down my spine. "Why send one now?"

"He claims they have come to celebrate the coronation of the new king." When his eyes met mine, I could see my own nervousness reflected in their dark depths. A number of different scenarios ran through my mind in quick succession — reasons why the king of Dansii, Hector's brother, would send a delegation now. Each was worse than the last.

"We should increase the watches and guards in the palace while they're here," I said. "No matter what, we can't trust Dansii. And we need to alert the king."

"That's why I came up here."

"Alert me to what?"

I spun around to see Damian pulling open his door, wearing nothing more than a pair of pants, his hair mussed by sleep, his jaw shadowed with stubble. My heart jumped into my throat, and my fingers tightened around the hilt of my sword. But he wasn't looking at me; instead, he gave the captain of his guard a questioning look.

3

"We didn't mean to wake you, my liege." Deron inclined his head.

"You didn't. I couldn't sleep." Damian's voice was clipped. He still wouldn't look at me. "Now tell me what's happening."

"Your uncle, King Armando, has apparently sent a delegation that will be arriving at the palace shortly. A runner has preceded them to warn us of their coming." Deron kept his voice level, indicating no response to this news.

Damian lifted one eyebrow, his gaze finally flickering to mine, then quickly away. It lasted less than a second, and yet the brief connection sent a wave of awareness through me. I'd been guarding him, standing next to him all day long, but for some reason — possibly because he was half naked — standing only a few feet away from him now, in the middle of the night, felt too intimate. In the low light, his shockingly blue eyes were shadowed. I couldn't read his expression as I forced my eyes to stay on his face, rather than letting my gaze stray to his chest or abdomen.

"*Alexa*," Deron said, with a hint of exasperation as though he were repeating himself.

I quickly straightened my spine as I turned away from the king to look at Deron.

He gave me a sharp, questioning look. "Do you still agree that we need to increase the watches and guard presence in the palace for as long as the Dansiian party is here?"

"Yes," I said. My heart beat unsteadily in my chest, but I hoped that my expression remained neutral. "Yes, I do."

"And where do you suggest we recruit the extra help? The army is already short staffed," Damian pointed out.

Shortly after being crowned king, Damian had released the orphan boys from their forced enrollment in the army. Many stayed, as they had nowhere else to go, but there was a significant number who had quit, returning to their ravaged villages and homes to try to put the horrors of the war — and Hector's reign of terror — behind them. Even Nolan, Damian's former "handler," had chosen to leave the palace. Damian had done the right thing, letting them choose, but it left Antion with a diminished army.

I answered without looking at the king to see if he was watching me or not, gazing just past him instead. "Now that there is no threat of attack from Blevon, we could pull some of the soldiers assigned to the outer patrols into the city and pull the city patrols into the palace."

"But that would take weeks, and the Dansiians are almost here," Deron pointed out.

"There isn't a threat of attack in Tubatse any longer; those soldiers are helping with rebuilding efforts more than anything," I said. "If we pulled just one man off each squadron in the city, we could double the watch numbers without impacting the rebuilding efforts significantly."

Damian nodded, steadfastly keeping his eyes on Deron. "Are you sure this is necessary? I don't want to cause a delay in the housing project."

"Taking one man off each group shouldn't slow it down much. Your safety is of the utmost importance — even more so than finishing the new homes," Deron said.

"My safety won't be in question. That's why I have you — isn't it?" Damian lifted his eyebrow. Before either of us could respond,

5

he continued. "The women and their babies need places to live. They can't stay in tents indefinitely."

I shuddered as I thought about the building that had once been the focal point of so many horrors. Damian's very first act as king, even before releasing the boys from their involuntary servitude in the army, had been to move the women and babies out of the breeding house and tear it down. I still remembered the night that it had crashed to the earth through a targeted attack by both Eljin's and Damian's sorcery; some had cheered but others hadn't been able to do anything except stand in the falling dusk and sob. Now there was a small tent city situated in a section of the courtyard, as far away from the former breeding house as possible, where the girls and women were relocated. The hard ground was preferable to the nightmarish hovel where they had been forced to reside for so many years, but it was no way to live — especially for those women who were pregnant or had new babies who hadn't been taken away. Yet another project Damian had spearheaded was to try to reunite mothers with children who had been taken after they were weaned and then put in the orphanage to survive until they were old enough to join the army themselves — or to take their place in the breeding house. It was a heartbreaking and, in some cases, futile process. The wounds from King Hector's rule ran deep, and many were still slashed wide open with little hope of healing.

"I know you are worried about those women, and rightfully so, but if there is a threat to your safety, that has to take precedence," Deron said.

"We don't know that there is any threat," Damian argued. "And I refuse to do anything that will make my people think I care more about myself than their welfare."

"Sire, I understand your concern," I began haltingly, still staring at the wall past Damian's bare shoulder, "but it would be unwise to assume that this is a friendly delegation. King Armando is the one who sent Iker to your father. What if there is another black sorcerer with them?"

He stiffened when I used the word *sire*. He hated it when I didn't call him by his name. But I'd made my choice — I'd led him to believe I didn't love him anymore, that I didn't trust him. I'd done it for his own good, and for the good of the kingdom. Even though I knew I'd made the right choice, that didn't make it any easier to live with the consequences. The only way to survive my self-imposed torture was to force up some kind of barrier. "If there is a sorcerer of any sort, I'll know it and so will Eljin," Damian said, his voice matching the frostiness of his expression. "But we can't assume that their intentions are malicious. Armando *is* my uncle."

Did Damian hope that his uncle had benevolent intentions toward Antion, even though he'd been the one to send Iker, a black sorcerer, to his own brother — Damian's father?

"And if they attack us?"

Damian finally looked directly at me. When our eyes met, the hardness of his gaze sent a jolt through me. The stonelike mask on Damian's handsome face was my fault. The hurt that lurked in the bright blue depths of his eyes was because of *me*.

It tore me apart inside to see all the love, all the passion I had once inspired in him wiped away, replaced by the same facade he'd presented to the world for years to protect himself from his father's machinations.

"Then we'll fight them — just like we fought Iker," Damian finally said.

"Alexa was barely able to beat Iker," Deron pointed out, his voice gentle. But however kindly he said it, it didn't ease the pain of his words. I fought the urge to touch my scarred cheek again as the memories of that horrible day threatened to surge up. "What if there's more than one black sorcerer this time?"

Something inside of me clenched when Damian's gaze flickered down to my cheek, then back to my eyes. "Black sorcerers are not common," he said after a pause. "I doubt they'll have one with them."

Deron shook his head. "I'm sorry, Sire, but it's our duty to assume the worst. And then try to prepare for it. We can't take risks with your life."

At Deron's words, my fingers tightened around the hilt of my sword. "I won't let them hurt you," I said before I could stop myself, my voice low. Damian tensed, his eyes widening slightly — a tiny crack in his veneer. I forced myself to tear my eyes away from the king, to stare at the floor instead, lest he see the emotions I'd spent the last month suppressing.

"We've kept the man waiting too long," Deron said suddenly, before Damian could respond. "We need to bring him inside; we can discuss the details of what we should do in the morning."

There was another long pause before Damian spoke. "Fine, but I would like you to come up with a solution that won't slow down the building project." Damian stood there for a moment longer, but when I wouldn't meet his gaze again, he turned on his heel and stalked back into his room, slamming the door shut behind him.

I flinched but didn't move, waiting for Deron's orders.

"Stay here and finish out your shift. I'll take care of the runner." Deron turned away but then paused. "Alexa . . ." he spoke hesitantly. "Are you . . . and the king . . ." He trailed off uncomfortably, and my stomach clenched. The last thing I needed — or wanted — was for Deron to try and talk to me about the situation with Damian. Now that everyone knew I was a girl, most of the other guards treated me differently — they seemed to think that I was suddenly weaker than I used to be, even though *I* hadn't changed. I was still the same person — the same soldier — I'd always been. But no one else saw it that way, except for Rylan, who'd always known.

And Damian.

"You'd better not keep the runner waiting any longer," I said curtly, standing up taller, with a glare that I hoped clearly conveyed my desire to drop the subject.

He gave me a searching look but nodded. "All right. I'll see you tomorrow, then." He turned away again, and this time he didn't stop.

When he was out of sight, I had to fight the urge to sag against the wall; my legs felt strangely weak and my heart wouldn't stop racing. But instead, I stood up even straighter, throwing my shoulders back. I was a guard — this was my duty. I wouldn't be the one found relaxing on the job, allowing something, or someone, to get past me. My life was devoted to protecting my king.

But the expression on Damian's face wouldn't leave me, the pain he was so adept at hiding from everyone — everyone but me. I, who knew him best and had hurt him the worst.

What if the person he needed protection from the most was *me*?

⊰ TWO ⊱

THE AMBER LIGHT of sunrise began to filter through the windows at the end of the hallway just when I was afraid I wouldn't be able to keep my eyes open any longer. I'd long since given up pacing and instead stood stiffly in front of Damian's door, staring out at the jungle, which was slowly becoming visible beyond the palace walls.

I was exhausted — from lack of sleep, from standing for so long, from worry. From trying not to let myself think of the king. But try as I might, as the night wore on, I couldn't keep myself from remembering. The look on his face when he'd come to see me that first time after the battle, when Iker's unholy fire had destroyed half of my face before I'd finally been able to defeat him, kept replaying in my mind. When he'd told me that he needed me — that he loved me. When he'd pressed his lips to mine for the last time before I'd destroyed the hope in his eyes and replaced it with pain.

I shook my head violently, trying to force the images, the words, the memories away. That Damian was gone — at least to me. With others, he was friendly and solicitous. He was the man he'd always been but had been forced to hide for so many years. But when it came to me . . .

10

A door opened down the hallway, startling me out of my thoughts, and Rylan emerged, with Mateo on his heels. They shared a room, now that Jude was gone. A pang of guilt hit me deep in my gut, as it always did when I saw Rylan with Mateo. It was my fault Rylan's brother had died, that Jude was no longer the guard at his side. As I watched them approach, strapping on their scabbards and sheathing their swords, preparing for another day of guarding our new king, I forced the guilt away. Jude had chosen to sacrifice himself to help me save Antion. His death had given me the chance to reach Iker and to destroy him.

"Rough night?" Rylan asked when he got closer, his eyes sweeping over my face, only pausing for a split second on my scars.

"Yes." There was no point in lying. He knew me too well. "Deron will fill you in, I'm sure. I'm going to go catch a quick nap."

"Alexa, what happened?"

"Like I said, Deron will have to tell you. I'm too tired."

I turned away, striding quickly to my room, which was next to Damian's, as it always had been. I was the only one, besides Deron, who didn't have a roommate. Only now it was because everyone knew I was a girl. At least there was one benefit to everyone coddling me — privacy.

I could hear footsteps behind me, but I ignored them and pulled my door open. I made it into my room but didn't get the door shut before Rylan reached me, putting his hand out to stop the door.

"Alexa, please tell me what's wrong."

I looked up into his gentle brown eyes and saw nothing but concern. I sighed. "There's a Dansiian delegation on its way here and we don't know why," I finally responded.

11

Rylan's eyes widened. "How do we know they're coming?"

"A runner arrived in the middle of the night to announce them."

"Come on, Ry, let her sleep. She's been up all night," Mateo called from down the hall.

Rylan didn't move, continuing to study my face. "Is there anything else?"

"What do you mean?" I hedged. The way he stared at me made me want to squirm, to turn away. Instead, I forced myself to lift my chin and hold his gaze.

He started to raise one hand, but when I flinched, Rylan froze. Finally, after a pause, he let his hand drop. "Mateo's right. I should let you sleep." He took a step back.

I reached for the door, ready to shut it on him, but then he hesitated again and looked directly into my eyes. "If you ever want to talk about *any*thing . . . you know I'm here for you. Right?"

I nodded once, a quick jerk of my head. "I know."

Something flashed in his eyes, but before I could decipher what, he'd nodded and looked away. "All right. Rest well. I'm sure everything will be fine."

I watched him walk away silently for a moment. Now that I was truly alone, I let my exhaustion get the better of me. As I entered my room, I unhooked my scabbard and let it fall to the floor. Then, without even bothering to change out of my uniform, I curled into a ball on my bed, boots and all. I was drained, yet part of me was afraid to go to sleep. My nightmares were getting worse and worse. I never knew what horrible monster would come after me in my sleep anymore.

But, finally, I couldn't fight it any longer. My eyes shut and I was gone.

A pounding at my door jerked me awake; I sat straight up with a strangled gasp, clutching at my damp shirt right above my heart. Sweat coated my skin. My hands shook and my heart raced. Iker haunted me. His unholy fire chased me through my dreams, burning me over and over again. Whenever I thrust my sword through him, it came out charred instead of bloody. No matter how many times I struck him, he never died. Instead, his eyes glowed with the fires of the demons whose power he'd wielded, as he laughed and laughed at me. . . .

There was another loud pounding on my door, and I hurried to rise and strap my scabbard back on. "I'm coming!" I called out.

As I crossed the room, a whisper of pain streaked down my jaw and neck, an echo of the fire that had caused the scars. I paused before reaching for the doorknob, lifting my hand instead to touch the ruined skin of my face, a gesture that was quickly becoming a habit. My disfigurement was a constant reminder of my success — but also of my losses.

Deron was standing outside my door looking apologetic when I finally swung it open. "I'm sorry to wake you, but we need every available guard immediately. The delegation has already been spotted nearing Tubatse. They will be at the palace within the hour."

My heart lurched into my chest. They'd already reached the capital city, just below the palace? "It's fine. I wasn't sleeping well anyway." I closed the door behind me and followed my captain down the hallway. From the light streaming in through the window, it appeared to be mid-morning. I'd only slept a few hours, then. I could feel the lack of rest in the achiness of my body — an exhaustion that went beyond my head, deep into my muscles and bones. "Do we know how many there are? Or who is with them?"

Deron shot me a piercing glance. "If you're wondering about any sorcerers, King Damian has asked Eljin to scout them out and see if he can sense any before they arrive. But they're on horseback, so it will be difficult to get close enough to tell."

I nodded. Eljin had surprised us all by offering to stay after the coronation, rather than returning to Blevon with his father, General Tinso. He made most of the palace staff nervous, but I was greatly relieved to know he was here, as were Damian, Rylan, and all those who knew who he truly was — and what he could do. He and Tanoori, who had also stayed at the palace, had even become friends. Over the past month, I'd seen them walking and talking together quite a bit, but I hadn't had a chance to ask her about their friendship yet — she was busy with her assignment overseeing the displaced women from the breeding house and heading up Damian's initiative to reunite mothers with their babies whenever possible, and my days were filled with my duties.

"Where is the king?" I asked as we hurried down the stairs to the ground level of the palace.

"He's in the main throne room, awaiting the delegation. The runner from Dansii is there with him, as is the rest of the guard."

I wondered why the Dansiians were already here. The runner had said they were a day or two behind him. It made me nervous

14

that we hadn't had time to increase the number of guards before they arrived. Our only hope was that they didn't have a black sorcerer with them. I didn't think I could fight another one yet, especially after only a couple of hours of restless sleep in which I'd been unable to defeat Iker no matter how hard I tried.

Although we were walking quickly, it seemed to take too long to get to the king. I wasn't sure why, but something deep inside told me I had to be by his side when the delegation arrived. Standing next to Damian was one of the hardest places in the world for me to be, but it was where I belonged. It was where he needed me to be.

Finally, we reached the correct hallway, and I watched impatiently as Deron pushed open one of the heavy doors, and then I followed him into the massive room — the same one where Damian's coronation was staged a month ago.

The king of Antion sat on the throne, wearing his signet crown and collar of office, watching me as I strode down the length of the room to reach his side. His expression was inscrutable even though the room was full of golden sunshine, much like the day when he'd led his people to all bow to me. Our eyes met and held for a brief moment, and then he turned away to glance at an unfamiliar man in a long white tunic and plain brown pants that reached his ankles, standing below the throne to his left, who also watched my approach.

The stranger's expression was easily discernible: Disbelief curled his lip. He had red hair and a spattering of freckles across his nose, reminding me of Asher, but that's where the similarities ended. While Asher was tall and strong, and also quick to smile, this man was small and wiry, and his thin lips turned down at the corners. His hair was sparse on top of his head, and his eyes narrowed as he silently appraised me, his gaze first landing on my chest, then on my scars. I looked away, back to my king, as I came to a halt in front of the throne where he stood to greet us. A combination of indignation and shame twisted my stomach. I still struggled when people openly stared at my disfigurement.

"Sire," I said, pressing my fist to my shoulder and bowing deeply at the waist to Damian.

"You may rise," he said, his voice holding a note of tension. I straightened and ascended the stairs to take my place on his right side. Rylan moved over for me. Everyone knew that the king wished for me to be directly beside him whenever I was on duty. But very few knew *all* the reasons why.

Deron stayed at the base of the stairs, subtly moving closer to the runner from Dansii. The rest of the guard flanked the king, four to each side of the throne. Rylan and I and two of the new guards — Julian and Oliver — on the right. Asher, Mateo, Jerrod, and the other new guard, Leon, on the left. Looking at them reminded me that I wasn't the only guard who bore scars from King Hector's rule. Deron, Asher, Mateo, and Jerrod all bore matching red lines on their faces — their punishment for "letting" Eljin kidnap the prince, even though none of them had been on duty. But none was quite as disfigured as I was, after my battle with Iker. For some reason, people seemed to respect them more because of the marks on their faces. I was the only one who got the stares and whispers. I never knew if it was because of the striated, silvery scars covering my cheek, jaw, and neck on one half of my face, or the fact that I was a girl. Or both.

"I hope you were able to rest well," Damian finally spoke.

For a split second, I thought he was talking to me, but the runner from Dansii responded before I could embarrass myself by answering the king.

"The accommodations were quite suitable," the man said in our language, though his accent gave him away as being from Dansii. His was much stronger than Asher's, who had moved to Antion as a boy. "Though I hated to be woken quite so early after my long night of travel."

"I apologize for the inconvenience. We received word that the delegation was nearly here, however, and we assumed you would wish to be present at their surprisingly early arrival." Damian's voice was carefully neutral, but I could sense his unease in the stiffness of his posture as he sat on his throne, looking down at the man.

"They must have made better time than anticipated," he murmured. His gaze slid to me, for some reason, and then quickly back to the king. I didn't like the way he looked at me — the disbelief was gone, replaced by a calculating gleam in his eye that unsettled me.

"Indeed," Damian commented.

Silence weighed heavily for a long space of time, and then the runner finally spoke again. "The delegation traveled by horse, so I must have misjudged the amount of time it would take for them to reach the palace."

"I hope you found the roads to be in good condition." Damian sounded slightly bored now, but I was fairly certain it was an act.

"They were in tolerable condition — especially for a jungle

kingdom. They could do with some upkeep, but they were passable, so I suppose that is commendable. Although the same cannot be said for some of the villages we passed through."

Damian's fingers tightened on the armrests of his throne, but other than that, he gave no outside indication of his displeasure. "Well, as you say, we do a tolerable job. For a *jungle* kingdom." He paused, letting the sarcastic bite to his words sink in. "And especially considering the great toll the war took on our nation and people."

"Ah yes. The war that is now over. All thanks to you, if I've heard correctly." Again the runner's gaze flickered to me and then back to the king.

I glanced down at Damian out of the corner of my eye. Tension coiled around him, but he kept his expression slightly amused, as if this man were nothing more than a nuisance. "What did you say your name was again?"

"Felton, Your Majesty." He gave a tiny bow.

Before Damian could say whatever he'd been planning on next, the doors at the other end of the long hall opened. One of the sentinels entered. He saluted Damian and then loudly announced, "The delegation from Dansii has arrived and requests permission to come before Damian, king of Antion."

My hand immediately dropped to rest on the hilt of my sword. There was no word from Eljin yet, so until they got close enough for Damian to feel for himself, we wouldn't know if they had any sorcerers with them.

Damian moved as though he was about to stand but then apparently changed his mind and relaxed back into his throne.

"Let them enter," he said.

I felt Rylan stiffen next to me as we prepared for whoever — or whatever — was about to come through the doors.

And then the door closest to Damian flew open and Eljin burst in.

⇥ THREE ⇤

*E*LJIN RAN INTO the room without pausing to acknowledge anyone or even to bow before bounding up the steps and bending over to whisper in Damian's ear. I longed to know what he was saying, but I kept my eyes on the back of the room where the first four men from Dansii were walking in, dressed in matching outfits, the likes of which I'd never seen before. Dried mud splattered their boots and the loose black pants visible beneath their long white tunics, which extended to the middle of their calves. On top of the tunics, they wore matching sleeveless overcoats made of some sort of rough fabric, dyed a rich purple. Another length of cloth the color of sun-baked sand wound loosely around their necks and up over their heads. Wicked-looking curved swords hung at their sides. These were not outfits made for surviving the heat of the jungle — this was the garb of men from the deserts of Dansii, where the wind, sun, and bitter cold nights were the enemy, rather than storms, heat, and deadly predators.

My heart racing, I glanced down at Damian, trying to read his reaction. Eljin looked up at me quickly before turning to face the Dansiians. The look he gave me was one of warning, causing my stomach to drop. I tensed my muscles, preparing for whatever was coming.

The four men came into the room with matching strides, marching halfway toward the throne before halting and turning to face each other in twos. We watched in silence as another man came through the door. He wore no weapons and was dressed in what appeared to be religious robes of some sort. Did they worship sorcerers in Dansii? I had no idea. His black robe and white overvest reached the floor, and a red sash was tied at his waist. He walked slowly toward the four armed men, his face composed and his eyes on the king. Just before he reached them, he stopped.

"King Damian of Antion, I have the deep honor of presenting Lady Vera of Dansii. She comes to bear King Armando's condolences on your father's death, as well as congratulations on your ascension to the throne and the good wishes of the nation of Dansii for a continued alliance." The man's voice carried through the hall, and he bowed deeply to the king. I had to fight to keep my expression neutral, to keep my confusion from showing. A lady? All of this was to introduce a woman? I turned questioningly to Eljin, but he still stared forward, his face unreadable above his ever-present mask.

Felton fidgeted below me, and I glanced down to see him looking at the king in anticipation, a smirk on his face. What was going on? What was I missing?

Rylan suddenly inhaled sharply next to me, and my gaze snapped up to catch sight of the single most beautiful woman I'd ever seen gliding into the room. There was no other word for the way she moved. It certainly wasn't anything as mundane as *walking*. And it definitely wasn't marching or striding, the way I usually did. Damian straightened in his throne, giving up the pretense of uninterest. A sudden, sharp pain hit me in the chest, white hot and unwelcome.

Lady Vera wore a dress of deep blue that skimmed the floor as she moved toward us, and showcased her alabaster skin to great advantage. She was as pale as Asher and Felton, but she looked like a statue made of ivory — and every bit as perfect as a sculptor could only dream of creating. She continued past the man who'd announced her. He followed her toward the throne after she'd walked by. The four armed men fell into line behind her as well. She was significantly shorter than the men behind her, but her presence more than made up for her lack in height. Her eyes were on the king, and her mouth turned up in a hesitant smile when she noticed his rapt attention on her. As she drew closer, I could see that her hair was a rich mahogany red, and not a single freckle marred her nose or cheeks. Her eyes were such a strange, bright green that I could see the color of her irises from where I stood.

"Welcome to Antion, Lady Vera." Damian decided to stand after all when Lady Vera came to a graceful stop near Felton and Deron.

"Thank you, Your Majesty." She sank into a curtsy that made her skirt pool out around her and showed off her impressive cleavage — and the large ruby pendant that rested right above the deep V of her dress's neckline.

My heart thudded beneath my ribs. I glanced at Damian, hoping he wasn't so blinded by her beauty that he was forgetting to sense if she was a sorceress. I still didn't even know for sure how it worked — did he have to focus to find out? Or was it something he just felt, that he *knew*, even without trying? Or had Eljin been

22

able to get close enough to know already? Neither of them seemed concerned as King Damian inclined his head to her and gestured for her to stand. But I was far from reassured as she rose and smiled again, more boldly this time. King Armando was the one who had sent Iker to his brother. Why send Lady Vera now? What was he playing at?

"Do you bring word from my uncle?" Damian asked as he took his seat once again. I relaxed infinitesimally when he did. I'd been half afraid he was going to walk down and propose marriage to her right then and there. All the other guards were staring at her openly, some with their mouths literally gaping. I fought to suppress my irritation — and embarrassment. They were trained better than to be so easily disarmed by a pretty face. I stood up even taller, my hand tight on my sword handle. Just in case.

"I do. But I am tired from my journey. Would you mind very much if I requested a bath in my room to refresh myself before we converse at length? I do hope that Felton was able to give you enough notice of our coming for you to have rooms prepared." She said the words with a smile, but there was steel behind her voice. She wasn't about to take no for an answer.

I didn't think she deserved a bath and time to prepare for anything — even if she really did just bring word from the king and not a threat. We needed to know what the message was *now*. We needed to know why she was here.

"Of course," Damian said. "Take all the time you need." He made a signal to the sentries at the door nearest to him.

I had to clench my teeth to keep the shock from registering on my face. What was wrong with everyone? Damian, of all people, should know better than to trust someone from Dansii so

23

blindly — even if that person was seemingly nothing more than a harmless, beautiful woman.

"Sire, if I may —" I tried to protest, but Damian lifted a hand to silence me. Lady Vera's gaze turned to me for the first time and the look she gave me turned my blood to ice in my veins. The smile never left her face, but when her eyes met mine and then moved slightly to the left — to my scars — the smugness I saw there made my stomach fill with acid.

I refused to look away, glaring down at her coldly until she finally gave up and turned back to Damian. She might have woven some sort of spell around all the men, but I wasn't taken in. And I wasn't going to let her get within ten feet of Damian ever again — strictly because I was concerned about his safety, of course. It had nothing to do with the way he was still staring down at her when I glanced at him, his expression speculative. And appreciative.

The pain returned to my chest.

"I would like to know with whom I have the pleasure of speaking, however. What is your connection with my uncle?" Damian addressed Lady Vera.

"Of course, Sire. How silly of me not to announce myself more properly. I am Lady Vera Montklief. My father is the duke of Montklief and your uncle's most trusted advisor and friend." She curtsied again but kept her eyes on Damian. Was I the only one who caught the calculating gleam behind the flirtatious veneer?

"Interesting that he would send his daughter to bear a message from my uncle and not someone more . . ."

"Masculine?" Vera supplied, with an amused tilt to her lips. "My father and King Armando were concerned that you might not be as welcoming to a male guest from Dansii, after the unfortunate turn of events with Iker. We were all dismayed when we learned of the wicked deeds that Hector and Iker got themselves involved in. King Armando and my father had hoped that you would be more open to their message if it came from a less threatening source."

"Such as a beautiful young woman, like yourself," Damian said, nodding slightly.

Even though his words were true, it still stung to hear him call her beautiful.

Lady Vera inclined her head, a small smile playing on her lips. Her bright green eyes gleamed in the sunlight. "Indeed, Sire. And thank you."

I didn't believe her for one minute — I couldn't believe that Armando would have had no idea what Hector, his own brother, and Iker, the man Armando had sent to be his brother's closest advisor, had been up to for the last fifteen years or more. The two kingdoms had been allies ever since Hector and Armando had invaded Antion together and overthrown the previous monarchy, killing them all and placing Hector on the throne. And allies, not to mention brothers, were usually quite aware of the other's dealings.

But Damian was smiling at Vera, some of the tension leaving his body.

"Excuse me, Your Majesty," a servant spoke from the side of the room, near an open door, "if the lady will follow me, I will show her to her room."

The servant's head was bowed as she waited for Lady Vera to follow her.

"Thank you, Your Majesty. I will look forward to speaking with you as soon as I am refreshed from my journey." She looked up at the king through her eyelashes. "Perhaps at dinner?"

Damian descended the stairs and took her hand, lifting it. The pain flared again — a sharp, fiery stab in my gut — as he softly brushed his lips against the white skin of her fingers. Skin that hadn't been tanned and abused by sun, wind, rain, and sword fighting. "I would be happy to have you join me at dinner. I will send someone to show you where to go this evening."

"Thank you, Sire." She curtsied again and he let go of her hand.

As Lady Vera turned toward the servant waiting for her, the doors at the far end of the hall burst open yet again. A man dressed in uniform rushed into the room and hastily bowed to Damian.

"Your Majesty, a small squadron has arrived from Blevon, seeking audience with the king," he said as he rose to standing again. "My captain sent me to ask you if we should allow them in or detain them."

I couldn't see Damian's face to measure whether he was surprised or not, since he stood below me, facing Vera. No one had mentioned a possible visit from the Blevonese army to me. I wondered if General Tinso was with them. The thought brought a surprising amount of relief and excitement. Surely he would help Damian see that even though Lady Vera was a "beautiful young woman," she could still be a threat. I wasn't beautiful like she was, but I was a young woman, and if I were sent into the belly of King Armando's palace to deliver a message, he'd better believe I was the worst threat he'd ever come into contact with.

I could only hope Lady Vera wasn't as dangerous as I was.

26

"Yes, you can have your captain bring them in," Damian replied to the messenger. "I'll receive them here."

The soldier pressed his fist to his chest, bowed his head in acknowledgment, then turned and hurried back the way he'd come.

"You may go, Lady Vera," Damian said, turning to her. "I will see you at dinner tonight."

"Yes, Sire. I look forward to it." Lady Vera curtsied once more, and this time when she turned to leave, no one interrupted her. Her men fell into line behind her, including the one in the long robes and Felton, the runner. I hadn't failed to notice that she hadn't introduced the man in black. Was it on purpose? Who was he?

Only when they had all exited did Damian finally turn back to us. The coldness of his expression caught me off guard.

"Deron, I want Lady Vera watched at all times and her every word and movement reported back to me. Alexa, you and Rylan will stand guard beside me tonight at dinner."

Relief coursed through me as I realized he hadn't completely lost his head after all. He'd been playing yet another part. I should have known. Embarrassment that I had believed his charade as readily as Lady Vera wormed through my body. I knew Damian — I knew that beauty didn't blind him. He'd had his fair share of stunning women fighting to catch his eye for years, and he never once pursued any of them. Only a handful of weeks ago, he'd claimed to love *me*, one of the least beautiful women he knew.

He looked at me right then, almost as if he knew my thoughts — as if he knew what a struggle I'd been waging against myself from the moment Lady Vera had walked in. His eyes held mine for a long moment, and I nearly lost myself in their brilliant blue depths. That is, until the echo of the doors being thrown open and banging against the walls made me flinch.

"King Damian, I present the soldiers from Blevon." The same man bowed before the king again and then stepped aside as a line of Blevonese soldiers marched into the room. Damian strode back up the stairs to his throne while they entered. I watched eagerly, hoping to see General Tinso, but when the entire group had filed in, he was not among them.

There were ten of them, and as they marched toward the king, I studied their faces. Every single man stared straight ahead, face neutral, devoid of emotion. I glanced over at Eljin, to see if he was smiling in recognition or welcome. It was difficult to tell with his mask, but it seemed like he was frowning. His eyebrows were pulled down over his eyes as he watched them approach.

The ten men divided themselves into two rows of five and then halted. One tall man, with hair so long it was tied back at the nape of his neck, stepped forward.

"King Damian of Antion, we come bearing a message from Blevon." He spoke in our language, but his voice was heavily accented.

"You are most welcome here, and I will gladly hear your message," Damian responded from next to me, also in our language, though I knew he spoke Blevonese.

When the man looked up at our king, a shiver stole down my spine. His eyes looked strange — hollow. Something was very wrong here. I tensed, unsure of what to expect.

"You have brought peace between our two nations at great cost," the man said in that same voice, chillingly empty of emotion.

"The cost, though great, was worth the result, I hope," Damian said, sounding a bit more cautious.

I hazarded a glance at Eljin again to find him staring directly at me. He shook his head infinitesimally and widened his eyes. A warning.

"If you believe the result was peace, you are mistaken," the man responded, and my head snapped forward again.

The expressionless void was still in his eyes as he stared up at Damian, but he adjusted his stance, tensing slightly, and my blood ran cold. I began to pull out my sword but I was too late.

"There will never be peace for you or your kingdom." He whipped out his sword and lunged so fast that Deron, who had reached for his own sword a second too slow, was unable to deflect him. The blade sliced through Deron's bicep as he threw himself backward to avoid being run through. "The blood of your people will water the jungle floor!"

⊰ FOUR ⊱

ALL TEN BLEVONESE soldiers were suddenly running toward us, swords lifted. The shock of being attacked in Damian's throne room by our new allies quickly mutated into fury. I dimly heard Eljin shout at Damian to stay where he was as I vaulted over the railing in front of me, along with the rest of the guard, my sword raised. I slashed it down through the air as I landed. My blade bit through the shoulder of the soldier who had been below me, and his sword fell to the ground with a clatter from his suddenly useless hand. I left him behind now that he was no longer an immediate threat and rushed forward to the man who had sliced Deron's arm and was advancing on him again. The sounds of fighting echoed all around me as the rest of the guard and the sentinels from the doors fought to protect our king.

"Hey!" I shouted, making the Blevonese soldier stalking toward Deron pause and glance at me. That tiny moment of distraction was all I needed. I spun and brought my sword down hard. He barely got his own sword up in time to deflect my hit with a crash of our blades. Deron backed away, clutching his bleeding arm. His sword arm.

The man advanced on me now. Next to me, I could see Eljin fighting two men, but none of their blows got through; I could feel the pull of magic as Eljin summoned his sorcery to block their hits.

The soldier who had attacked Deron was strong but not as skilled as I expected. The only way he had managed to land a hit on Deron was with the element of surprise. The soldier lunged at me, and I easily spun away, avoiding his sword. He wasn't nearly fast enough, and he left his back unprotected just long enough for me to swing my arm around and embed my sword between his ribs, deep into his lungs.

"That's for Deron," I growled as I yanked my sword back out of his body. He dropped to his knees, looking up at me with those horrible blank eyes. But as I watched his life drain out of him, the strange emptiness vanished. He blinked, and when he looked at me again, his expression was one of fear and pain, and his eyes were full of tears. He said something in Blevonese — it almost sounded like a plea. But I couldn't understand him. He tried again, but his voice gurgled as blood filled his lungs and throat. My stomach twisted and I had to swallow hard.

Finally, his eyes rolled back into his head and he collapsed to the ground. Dead.

"Alexa!" Damian's cry made me start and turn in time to see a sword arcing toward me. I threw myself to the floor, barely avoiding the slice of the blade. The Blevonese soldier advanced, chopping down at me again. I flung myself to the side, rolling away, and the steel clanged on the stone floor of the throne room.

Gripping my sword, I rocked back onto my shoulder blades and then launched my body forward, landing nimbly on my feet, blade up and ready, but the soldier was standing still, his face purple. His sword lay on the ground, and he grabbed at the air around his throat, as though invisible hands were choking —

With a jolt of realization, I spun to face my king. Damian stood in front of his throne, his eyes flashing, his hand extended. It was all too easy to let myself forget just how *not* helpless our king truly was. He was not only an adept sword fighter but also a sorcerer.

There was a thud next to me, and I turned to see the man crumpled on the ground, unconscious or dead.

When I looked back at Damian, his chest rose and fell rapidly, his eyes on mine. He let his hand drop back to his side, but our gazes remained locked. When someone touched my arm, I jumped and spun to lift my blade, only to see Mateo next to me, his hands raised.

"Whoa. It's me." He stepped back. "Just wanted to make sure you were all right."

"I'm fine," I snapped. "I was just fine." I raised my voice, hoping Damian heard me. Though the end result had been the same, I hadn't needed his help. The kingdom was still unsure of how it felt about sorcerers, let alone the new king *being* one. I didn't like him demonstrating his skills unnecessarily. The people's trust in him was a tenuous, fragile thing, and I was afraid that one wrong act on his part would cause it to break.

"Sorry." Mateo held up his hands again and backed away. I glanced around to see all ten Blevonese men lying motionless on the floor. The members of the guard stood over the bodies, swords bloodied and chests heaving. Eljin was closest to me, staring at the man I'd killed before Damian's unnecessary "rescue."

"What did he say?" I asked urgently, remembering the way the man's eyes had cleared just before he had died, and the words he'd said. "Did you hear him — what did it mean?"

"He said, 'I didn't mean it. It wasn't me,'" Eljin explained quietly, lowering his own bloodied sword.

"Are they all dead?" Damian's voice directly behind me startled me. I spun around to see the king staring down at the man at my feet, his face a mask.

"Yes, Sire. All of them," Rylan answered from somewhere to my left.

My anger at Damian's intervention drained away as the reality of what had just happened sank in, leaving me shaken. "Why would they attack you?" I whispered. "We are supposed to be at peace with Blevon."

"Something wasn't right." Eljin also stared at the man I had struck down. "I couldn't sense any sorcery when they walked in, but that was no ordinary attack. As he was dying . . . that man almost seemed as if he . . . well, as if he *regretted* attacking us."

"Of course he regretted it — he was *dying*," Jerrod snapped from a few feet away, his face flushed and his sword bloody.

Damian was pale when he looked sharply at Eljin. "What are you suggesting?"

"I don't know, Sire." Eljin shook his head. "But I believe we just murdered innocent men."

33

"They tried to kill us!" Asher protested. "Look at Deron's arm — if he hadn't moved so fast, he'd be dead on the ground like the rest of them."

Eljin was silent.

"We defended ourselves and our king from a group of men who intended to kill us," Deron spoke up. "From now on, no one from Blevon is allowed into the palace unless they can prove they bear no harmful intentions to our people or our king."

"So much for the peace treaty," Leon, one of the newer guards, muttered.

"The peace treaty still stands. And we will not start turning away the people of Blevon because of this," Damian said at last, his voice harsh. "I don't know what happened here, but I agree with Eljin. Something was wrong with these men."

I agreed with Damian and Eljin, but I also agreed with Deron. We couldn't risk Damian being hurt — or killed — if anyone else from Blevon came supposedly bearing a message, then delivered it with a sword. Still, I couldn't get the image of the man staring up at me, the sudden change in his face — from blank to filled with emotion — out of my head. Fear. Desperation. Confusion. As blank as his eyes had been, as soulless as he'd seemed, in the moment before he died, he looked like an entirely different person. One who definitely had a soul — and who had claimed he didn't want to fight us.

So why had he come here and attacked?

"Someone ring for help. We need to get these bodies out of here and this mess cleaned up," Deron ordered.

"And you need to have your arm seen to," I interjected.

"Mateo, go find Lisbet and have her come at once. Asher, tear off a piece of your shirt. We've got to stop the bleeding."

Asher grumbled, "Why my shirt?"

"I'd do it, but I'd rather not expose myself," I pointed out with a glare. "Now shut your mouth and help him before he faints from blood loss."

Without another word, Asher quickly reached down and tore off a long strip of fabric.

"Your Majesty, perhaps you should return to your rooms and —" Whatever the rest of Rylan's suggestion had been was cut off when the doors opened yet again and General Ferraun, whom Damian had placed in charge of his entire army, strode into the room.

He froze, his eyes wide, when he saw the carnage and all of us standing in a sea of bodies and blood, including the king. "What *happened* here?"

Damian sighed. "I really don't know — yet."

General Ferraun's eyebrows lifted, but he remained silent.

"Was there something urgent, or can it wait, General?"

"I'm very sorry, Sire, but it can't wait."

The grim look on his face sent a shiver of fear down my spine. What now?

"A border village has been attacked."

"Attacked?" Damian repeated. "Where? How?"

General Ferraun gave the king an apologetic look. "It was on the northwest edge of Antion, on the Blevonese border. A black sorcerer killed the men and even some of the women."

"A black sorcerer?" Eljin cut in. "Are you certain?"

"He killed them with the unholy fire that Iker wielded," General Ferraun explained.

Damian stared at him in shock. "Where are the orphans? They must be brought here, for food and shelter."

"Sire, there's more." General Ferraun grimaced.

"More?"

"The sorcerer didn't act alone. He was leading a group of soldiers." The general paused. "Blevonese soldiers."

⊰ FIVE ⊱

*L*IKE I SAID, so much for the treaty," Leon said again.

"If you don't close your mouth, I will permanently close it for you," Asher threatened, taking me by surprise.

Damian hadn't spoken yet. The blood drained out of his face, and he seemed to age a year in a matter of moments before my eyes.

"Sire?" General Ferraun prompted him.

Damian shook his head slightly, as though trying to clear it. "We must convene a council immediately and discuss what we should do. I'll meet you in the library in thirty minutes, General. Please bring anyone who witnessed or brought word of this massacre."

General Ferraun saluted Damian sharply. "Yes, Your Majesty," he said and turned on his heel to march back out of the room.

"Asher, take Leon and Oliver and find help to clean up this room. Mateo, go get Lisbet and bring her here immediately to see to Deron's arm." Damian continued to issue orders in rapid fire. "Deron, go sit or lie down before you faint." Then he turned to Eljin, Rylan, and me. My sword still hung at my side, the blood of the man I'd killed drying on the blade. "You three, please accompany me to the library."

37

"To guard you or to offer counsel?" Eljin asked.

"Possibly both," Damian responded.

Rylan glanced at me, then back at the king. "Sire, I know you value Alexa's opinion and her expertise, but she was up all night and barely slept —"

Damian cut Rylan off. "Oh yes. I apologize for forgetting." He finally looked me directly in the eyes, his expression guarded. "I will take Rylan and Eljin with me, then, and you may go to your room to rest."

"I'm fine, Sire. I will accompany you."

Damian paused momentarily, as if considering, then shook his head. "No, you need to sleep. I still require your service tonight at dinner, though. I'll have someone fill you in on any new developments when you wake up."

"Sire, I —" I started to argue, but he silenced me with a cold glare.

"That is all, Alexa. You may go."

I swallowed my angry retort, all too aware of everyone's eyes on us. First, he intervened in a fight, making me look weak in front of the other guards. Now, he was actually sending me to my room. I lifted my bloody sword up in front of my face and bowed slightly in salute. "As you wish, Your Majesty," I said, teeth gritted, then stormed to the door, stepping carefully to avoid the bodies and pools of blood on the once spotless floor. I didn't need to *sleep*; I needed to help Damian — to keep him from further danger, to figure out what was going on.

I reached to yank open the door right as someone from the other side pushed it open, nearly hitting me in the face with it. I jumped back just in time. Tanoori started to rush into the room

38

but paused when she realized I was standing there. Lisbet was right behind her. She nodded at me and hurried past Tanoori. When Lisbet saw the bodies littering the ground, her steps faltered and I heard her gasp.

"Jax, you stay in the hallway," she called over her shoulder, and I looked past Tanoori to see the young boy — Damian's half brother — standing just outside the door. His eyes, the same startling blue as his brother's, were as round as the moon when it was full to bursting. His face had gone pale beneath the natural olive tones he'd inherited from Lisbet.

"What happened?" Tanoori breathed.

"We were attacked."

She looked past me, and when she saw Eljin, she rushed to his side without another word. I couldn't hear what she asked him; I could only see the grim shake of his head in response.

I made myself turn away and walk out of the room, shutting the door behind me to hide the carnage from Jax, who still stood there frozen. In shock, or fear, or fascination — I wasn't quite sure. Maybe all three.

"Come on, Jax. We've been sent away. Let's go." I sheathed my sword, even though I knew that meant I'd have to clean my scabbard later, but it freed up my hand so I could hold it out for him. Just in case.

He waited a moment, as though debating — probably wondering if it would be too babyish. But finally, he shrugged his shoulders and took my hand in a surprisingly strong grip.

"Why are they sending us away?"

"Because sometimes we are needed to stay, and sometimes it's better if we go somewhere else."

"Because I'm *too young*," he said in a singsongy voice that nearly made me burst out laughing — though there was very little humor in the current situation. "But why would they send *you* away?" he continued. "You're the best fighter Damian — I mean, the king — has!"

"Well, we can't all do the same job. And we have to follow orders when we're given them." I was leading him back to Lisbet's chambers, on the floor below Damian's, where she and Jax lived now. A vast improvement over the tiny, dark room in which they'd hidden for years in the old wing of the palace during Hector's — and Iker's — reign.

As we walked down the hallway to the stairs, a small group of girls turned a corner and headed toward us, dressed in the vibrant colors so popular in court. There were two taller girls, probably close to my age, and a younger one, holding herself up as high as she could, trying to look older than she was. The one in the lead pulled out her fan and opened it when she saw us, using it to cover her mouth and nose, and the others followed suit. The first one ignored me and Jax, lifting her chin as she paraded down the hall. But the other two looked straight at me. Their lips were covered, but I could still hear their words as they got closer.

The one who looked a bit younger than her companions whispered loudly, her eyes wide, "That's the girl who fought —"

"Ssh." The other one cut her off, her gaze fixed on my scars with a cold haughtiness. "Mother says it's vulgar for a girl to *speak* of such things, let alone *do* them. It's not proper for a girl to do a man's job."

"Oh. Right." The younger one's eyes were round with fascination.

40

I pulled my shoulders back, tightened my grip on Jax, and marched forward a little faster, making the boy practically jog to keep up as we passed by them.

Their giggles followed us as we hurried toward the stairs.

"What were those girls talking about? What does 'vulgar' mean?" Jax asked when we had turned the corner and left them behind us. "Were they talking about you?"

"Never mind them," I replied tightly. "They don't know what they're talking about."

Jax was quiet for a moment and then said, "Well, I think they're stupid for saying that. They should thank you for saving them."

I finally relaxed my grip on his hand, slowing down a bit. "Wouldn't that be nice?" I murmured with a shake of my head. He was right; I shouldn't spare them a second thought.

"So what did Dam — I mean, the king — order you to do?" Jax asked eagerly, already forgetting about the girls. "Are you going to go interrogate someone? Or spar out in the ring?" Jax loved coming to watch me spar. I'd promised to start teaching him to sword fight, but so far we'd only been able to sneak in two quick lessons.

"No, not today."

"Well, then . . . what?" he pressed.

I sighed as we climbed the stairs to the second floor, where Lisbet and Jax's rooms were. "I was ordered to take a nap."

Jax stopped in his tracks, nearly yanking my arm out of its socket. He stared up at me with his mouth partly open. "You were ordered to take a *nap?*" he repeated, and when I nodded, he burst out laughing.

"That's enough out of you." I pulled him forward again, up the rest of the stairs and down the hallway until we stopped in front of his door. "I'm sure your mother will be here soon. She just has to help Deron first."

"I know," Jax said as I opened his door and he slowly walked into his room. He sounded suddenly deflated.

"Hey, Jax," I called out to him. "Everything all right?"

"I guess," he muttered unconvincingly.

"You know you can always talk to me — about anything, right?"

He paused and turned around to face me again. "It's just that . . . Mama and Damian — I mean, the king —"

"Jax, I think it's all right if you call him Damian. He's your brother."

"Half brother."

I lifted an eyebrow at him.

"*Anyway*," he continued, "they are both sorcerers. They can both use magic and do so many wonderful things. I've been watching Damian practice sorcery with Eljin at night, and . . ."

"And?" I prompted when he trailed off.

"And, well, I can't do anything. I've tried. And nothing happens."

He looked so dejected that I couldn't brush off his concerns. Instead, I walked into the room and shut the door quietly behind me, then crossed to kneel down in front of him. "I'm not a sorcerer, but I think I can do some pretty amazing things, don't you?"

His eyes widened. "Yes. You're the best fighter I've ever seen. And you're a *girl*." This last was said as though he couldn't quite

42

believe that the two things were a possible combination of facts — a sentiment that many other people in the palace, and Antion, seemed to share. I wondered, if more people knew my father's nickname for me — *zhànshì nánwū*, which roughly meant "champion fighter" and "sorcerer" — would they be more or less enthusiastic about a girl guarding the king?

"Well," I continued, brushing off the thoughts, "if you keep training with me, I'll teach you how to be the best sword fighter you can be. So, while you might not be a sorcerer, that doesn't mean you don't have talents of your own. You can be amazing, too, in your own way."

Jax stared at me, total trust on his face. "You'll keep teaching me?"

"I've told you that I would."

"But you're so busy all the time."

I grimaced. "I know, and I'm sorry. But I'll tell you what. I'll try to do a better job of finding time to teach you, okay?"

"Promise?"

He stared at me with those blue, blue eyes — Damian's eyes — and something in my chest tightened. "I promise."

He nodded and then suddenly reached out and impulsively threw his arms around me. He let go before I even had a chance to return his hug. With a satisfied smile now on his face, he stepped back, puffing up his chest a bit. "You'd better go take that nap, so you don't get in trouble."

I shook my head at him with a roll of my eyes. "Thanks for the reminder."

When I shut his door behind me and headed for my own room, I had to fight a rush of emotions. To so many, I was a reminder of pain and loss, death and suffering. My scars frightened those who didn't know me — and some who did. But Jax didn't seem to care. To him, I was just the girl who had saved Antion, who had helped put his brother on the throne, and I was the best fighter he knew.

I was determined to keep my promise to him, even if it meant fewer king-mandated naps.

⇥ SIX ⇤

ALTHOUGH I'D BEEN ordered to rest, that didn't mean I could go to my room and pretend everything was fine. Damian was in danger. Antion was under attack — again. All signs pointed to Blevon, but that didn't make sense. Not after King Osgand and General Tinso worked so hard and risked so much to establish peace. Was it an offshoot of the Blevonese army acting independently of their king? But if so, why?

Though I was exhausted, my body burned with the need to do *something*. I curled up on my bed, but my mind ran in endless circles. After closing my eyes, I made myself breathe deeply and slowly. In and out. In and out.

When I opened them again, I was no longer in my room in the palace. Instead, I stood outside my old home, the jungle creating a thick, green wall around the small clearing where a tall man stood, holding a sword, his hazel eyes intent on mine. The instant I saw him, I knew I was dreaming.

"Again, Alexa. You need to use your agility to your advantage." My father's voice made my heart ache — even though some part of my mind recognized that this wasn't real. Nothing more than a memory poking through the uninhibited boundaries of sleep.

I was somehow simultaneously inside my body in the dream and yet still able to see myself as well. A younger me, maybe only seven or eight years old. My thick, dark hair hung straight down my back, and I blinked up at my father with wide, determined eyes. They were the same shade of hazel as his.

I could feel the weight of the sword I held — far too big for me — but I didn't let that slow me down; I grunted and swung it forward. I had always practiced longer than my twin brother, Marcel, determined to become a better fighter than he was. I had often stayed outside for hours by myself, even after our father called it quits for the day, trying to be faster, stronger — to be everything my father had believed I could be.

In the dream, he watched me, his eyes sharp. "No! Stop. You left yourself open on the left side." He strode toward me, and the sight of his quick, graceful movements as he demonstrated what I needed to do made me want to cry. Oh, how I missed him.

"When you fight the enemy, he may have many advantages over you. You have to be *quick* — like this." He lifted his sword and twisted, driving it through the air with a hiss, as though he moved so fast, he created his own wind. The younger Alexa in my dream imitated him, and soon they were swinging their swords in tandem, side by side.

"She'll never be as good as me." When I heard Marcel's voice, the pain in my chest grew, turning into a fiery stab of regret. He sauntered over, with as much swagger as an eight-year-old boy was capable of mustering. He smirked at me, so confident.

"Alexa, is that true?" Papa paused and looked at me.

"No. I'm going to beat you someday, and then you'll have to

do my chores for a week." I gripped the hilt of my sword harder as Marcel laughed and disappeared into the fog of memories again. I wanted to cry for him to come back, to let me see him, hear him. But he was gone. And Papa was fading now, too. Something was pulling me away, when all I wanted to do was stay here, to cling to the ghosts of my family.

"Alexa," my father said, reaching out for me. For some reason, his sword was gone. His gaze was intent on mine; he seemed so *real*. "You *will* beat him someday. You'll beat all of us. You will be faster than anyone else. But the enemy won't always attack with a sword. Be strong, my daughter. Use your strength, your mind, and your heart."

When I saw myself again, I looked as I did now — with a scarred face, wearing the uniform of the king's guard. I reached and reached, but I couldn't touch his outstretched fingers. He was disappearing into a whirl of mist that crept up his legs, covering his body bit by bit.

"I believe you have the strength to overcome *anything*, my beautiful girl." His voice was only a whisper when he looked straight into my eyes one last time. "My *zhànshì nánwū*."

And then he was gone and I was alone, standing in a sea of swirling gray fog, endless and terrifying.

I jerked awake with a gasp. My heart raced, and my cheeks were wet with tears. Deeply shaken by the dream, I threw my legs over the bed and stood up. No more sleeping for me; king's command or no, I was going down to the practice ring.

The palace was stifling with the humidity of an afternoon storm as I hurried through the corridors. I headed outside, heedless of the rain coming down in torrents.

I worked through my forms alone, fighting a horde of imaginary foes. I tried not to let myself think about the Blevonese soldier I'd killed earlier in the day. But my mind kept going back to the terrifying emptiness in that soldier's eyes until he'd been about to die. Was it some sort of spell? Eljin would have known about it if it were, and he seemed as baffled as the rest of us.

Jabbing, swiping, spinning in a fury of movement, I forced myself to think of something else. Anything else. But the alternative wasn't much better — the memory of Vera smiling up at Damian through her eyelashes surged back up. Anger clutched my heart again, but this time, it was from a different source. I wasn't the bearer of lily-white hands, but my hands — rough and reddened as they might be — were also the hands that had saved countless lives. Not only from the soldiers today, but from Iker. The scars I bore were proof of the battle I'd fought — and won. For once, as the rain cascaded over me, I didn't let myself think of the lives I *hadn't* been able to save. I'd saved Damian. I'd saved us all.

And though I didn't understand where the newest threat was coming from or why, I was determined to save Damian again. As many times as I had to, to keep him safe. I thought of my father's words from my dream — that the enemy won't always attack with a sword — and the unease in my gut grew stronger.

When I was finished, my muscles burned and my hands ached from clenching the wet hilt of the practice sword, but my head felt much clearer. The heavy clouds above the jungle began to break apart. The rain had diminished to a misty drizzle, coating my skin with moisture but no longer drenching me.

My boots squelched through the mud on my way back to the palace. I was still unused to seeing the open space where the breeding house had once stood, before Damian had demolished it shortly after taking the throne. Now all that remained was a pile of rubble that was slowly being removed. The process would have been much faster if the army wasn't so short staffed. And with a new threat looming, it didn't look like it would get finished anytime soon.

I hurried to my room to change into something dry before going to the council; I didn't want them to realize I'd been out sparring by myself in the rain instead of sleeping.

Once I'd changed into a clean, dry uniform and scraped my wet hair back into a short braid, I strapped on my sword and headed to the library. I figured the wet hair could be attributed easily enough to a bath.

I reached up to knock on the door to the library just as it swung open and Eljin strode out. The door slammed shut behind him.

"Alexa." Eljin's eyes widened in surprise above his ever-present mask when he saw me standing there. "I was just coming to wake you."

"Has something else happened?"

"No, thankfully." He gestured for me to follow him a little ways down the hall. When we were a good twenty feet away from the door, he stopped and faced me. "I understand that you need your rest, but we need you in there." He paused, as though gathering his thoughts. "I know my country and I know our army — we don't have any black sorcerers. The one orchestrating these attacks is not of Blevonese descent. I can guarantee that. And if a rogue sorcerer showed up, he would definitely not be given a position of power or control."

"But how certain can you be? A black sorcerer killed my parents with the Blevonese army. There were many attacks from black sorcerers during the war."

"Which is exactly why I wanted to come find you. I remember you said that when we were at my father's castle, and it struck my father and me as being impossible." Eljin's eyes were intent on mine.

"Are you saying that I lied about it? Or that I don't understand what really happened?"

"No — of course not. Based on what I know of their deaths, I completely agree that your parents were killed by a black sorcerer. I have no doubt about the veracity of your claim. However, I know for a fact that no Blevonese general or captain would allow a black sorcerer to work with him or remain under his command."

"Then how do you explain these attacks? And how can you be so sure? Fighting with a black sorcerer on your side virtually guarantees a victory in battle. Who could resist that, if one offered to help? How can you prove that it's impossible?"

"I can't guarantee that it's *impossible* — I suppose anything is possible. But you must trust me. I *can* promise you that not one general or captain would accept their offer. Not in Blevon."

"If it comes down to the possibility of another war with your kingdom, you will have to find a way to prove your claim. Otherwise, the people of Antion aren't going to accept that what you're saying is true — not when they're dying at the hands of a black sorcerer who's leading some part of the Blevonese army."

Eljin stared at me for a long moment. "Then I will have to find proof. But I am not at liberty to tell you why I am so certain. I'm sorry."

I considered this silently. What secret could he possibly be keeping — and why would he refuse to share it if the alternative was war? "Why do you want to ask me about it, then?"

"I want to know the details of what happened, though I understand that it might be quite difficult for you to talk about. But it's vital that you think of every last detail you can remember of what happened that day. What you saw, what you heard, what you smelled and felt — all of it."

My stomach turned over as my mind unwillingly dredged up the images of my parents lying broken and burned on the ground in front of me all those years ago. "I remember the horn being blown from the watchtower, warning us that the enemy had been sighted nearby," I began.

"Not here." Eljin stopped me. "Everyone needs to hear what you have to say."

"Do you think the two attacks are connected?"

Eljin peered at me, then turned on his heel without answering and walked back toward the door. I sighed and followed him. Just before reaching for the handle, he paused and said in a low voice, "I believe so. But there are still so many unanswered questions. . . ." He trailed off and then shook his head.

Oh, how I hated unanswered questions.

Without another word, he opened the door and announced,

"I believe Alexa might be able to help us shed some light on this situation."

The conversation that had clearly been underway — and appeared to be heated — immediately stopped, and all heads turned toward us. Or toward me, rather.

I took a deep breath and walked into the council.

⊰ SEVEN ⊱

I THOUGHT I ORDERED you to go rest," Damian said sharply as I strode into the room with Eljin close behind me.

"We need her opinion, Sire," Eljin said.

"I couldn't sleep anyway." I decided to answer honestly.

The library had a massive desk where Damian sat with two rows of chairs set up in a semicircle in front of him. The walls were made up of shelves filled with books of every size and subject known to our people. It had been a dusty room during King Hector's rule, hardly ever used. But Damian had it cleaned shortly after his coronation and spent a great deal of time here ever since, turning it into a makeshift office.

There were no empty chairs, so I walked to the side of his desk and stood, half turned to the king and half to the rest of those gathered. General Ferraun was there, as well as a few men I didn't recognize but who were dressed in the uniforms of the Antionese army. Another woman, who appeared to have been crying, sat next to one of the men. Rylan and those from the guard who were in the room sat behind them, and Eljin moved to stand just behind Damian's left shoulder.

"I think it's important that Alexa tells us what happened to her own parents in an attack very similar to this," Eljin said. "It will help shed light on the similarities between the attacks — to see if they might be connected."

"But that was years ago, during the war," Rylan pointed out from his seat.

"If my theory is correct, these attacks were not related to the war — at least not directly. Or, Blevon was not responsible for them, I should say." Eljin folded his arms across his chest.

"What do you mean? What theory?" Damian turned to look at Eljin.

Eljin ignored Damian. "Alexa, go ahead."

Damian nodded curtly, and I started describing the horror we'd felt when we'd heard the horn warning us of the enemy's approach. The memories of that day threatened to overwhelm me as I dredged up the details I'd spent years suppressing. The fear on Mama's face as she'd begged Marcel and me to hide in the protective cover of the jungle that cradled our house, the sternness in Papa's voice when he'd forced us to promise not to come out and fight. We'd obeyed, but we'd watched what happened through the massive leaves we crouched behind. The determination in Papa's stance as he'd fought the Blevonese soldiers. He'd been unstoppable, almost single-handedly keeping the army from advancing into our village — until the sorcerer had ridden up and coolly dismounted from his dark horse. He didn't even pull out his sword; he just lifted his hand, and I'd watched in horror as first my father and then my mother were devoured by his unholy fire and left on the ground like nothing more than dross. Charred. Dead.

Eljin was sympathetic, but determined, as he questioned me for details. What did the army wear? Were their uniforms new or tattered? What did they all look like? I didn't remember clearly —

it had been too traumatic. But I easily recalled the sorcerer: He'd been tall, pale, and terrifying.

"So he was pale skinned, not olive toned like us?" Eljin pressed, gesturing at me, Damian, and himself — all of Blevonese descent.

I thought of the sorcerer standing over my parents' bodies, his cloak billowing, and shuddered. "He didn't look like us; he was very pale. His hair had a lot of gray in it, but it looked like it had been light brown." As I forced myself to think of the man I'd spent years trying to forget, something dawned on me. "Actually, he looked a lot like Iker."

Damian's expression was grave as he listened. I knew that of anyone in the room, he understood how hard this was for me. But he wouldn't look in my eyes, staring instead at his desk, or my shoulder, or Eljin.

"He was not Blevonese, then," Eljin said. "Perhaps he was also from Dansii?"

"He was definitely not Blevonese," I agreed.

"Which doesn't matter, as Blevon could have hired a black sorcerer from another nation, if they had wanted to," General Ferraun pointed out. "This is all very interesting, but I'm not sure what you're trying to prove."

"An army from Blevon — a *true* army from Blevon — would never hire a black sorcerer," Eljin said.

"What are you getting at?" The general sounded impatient. "Spit it out already."

Eljin leveled a piercing glare at him. "I don't believe these attacks are coming from Blevon."

There was a pause of surprised silence, and then the general began to laugh. "Oh, you don't, do you? Even though the attack on the village *and* the one on the king were done by the Blevonese army? That's really ripe, especially coming from a Blevonese sorcerer. Of course you want to protect your nation, but that doesn't mean —"

"How dare you accuse me of such a thing," Eljin bit out coldly, cutting him off. I wondered what General Ferraun was thinking, baiting a sorcerer. "I'm not protecting my nation — I'm stating fact."

"What proof do we have of your loyalty to us, other than King Damian's belief in you? You abducted him and killed two of his best men to do it!" General Ferraun was on his feet now.

"And why should we trust *you*? You've been fighting out on the borders of the war for years — the borders where many black sorcerer attacks happened that were falsely blamed on Blevon!" Eljin shot back.

"I have risked my life and the lives of my men for years to protect this kingdom, you arrogant, little —"

"Both of you, stop immediately!" Damian jumped up, throwing out his arm to keep Eljin from storming forward. "General, that is enough. Eljin did not kill those men — my father did. And Eljin abducted me *at my request* as part of my plan to overthrow my father. You know that."

General Ferraun seemed about to say something else but snapped his mouth shut instead.

"And, Eljin, I trust the general, and that's all you need to know about that. Now, I need you to explain yourself. Share with us the reason why you can guarantee that Blevonese armies would never hire a black sorcerer."

Eljin's eyes, above his mask, were unwavering on Damian's. "I cannot in present company."

"You know I trust you, Eljin. But you may not have a choice, if you wish to help me avoid another war with your kingdom," Damian said.

They locked glares, caught in some sort of silent battle.

"What secret is Blevon keeping from us? Whatever it is, it doesn't make me inclined to trust you or your people," General Ferraun interrupted.

"I do not believe Blevon is behind these attacks — during the war or after." Eljin finally turned away to face the room again.

"If not Blevon, then who?" the woman suddenly cried out, pointing a shaking finger at Eljin. "Who killed my husband? I saw them — I saw your army marching in behind that sorcerer."

"The men you saw — did they look like me or your king?" Eljin leaned forward, putting his hands on the edge of Damian's desk.

"They looked like murderers, is what they looked like! All of them! Come to kill us all under the pretense of a truce!" She began to wail, her words turning incomprehensible.

"Was there anyone else there who could describe the men?" Eljin ignored her outburst.

There was a knock at the door, and a servant entered and bowed to the king.

"Yes, what is it?" Damian asked, his voice curt.

"Sire, dinner will be served shortly. I was sent to let you know that Lady Vera requests that her taster be allowed in the kitchen to sample her dishes before being served, merely as a precaution."

Damian pinched the bridge of his nose, his eyes shutting briefly. "Yes, of course. That is fine. Show him where to go." He waved his hand, and the servant backed out of the room, bowing once again. "It appears that our meeting must draw to a close for now. General Ferraun, please see if you can bring us any other witnesses from this village. And see to it that the orphans and widows are taken care of, please."

"Yes, Your Majesty." General Ferraun stood and bowed to the king.

"I also would like to know anything that can be learned about the Blevonese soldiers who came here today. What direction did they come from? Did they talk to anyone else and what was said? Anything. It's rather suspicious that the attack came shortly after the Dansiians arrived at the palace."

"Of course, Your Majesty. I've already assigned some of my top men to do exactly that."

"Very good. Bring me a report tonight, if you discover anything of note."

"Do you still desire my presence at dinner tonight?"

"Yes, thank you, General."

The general bowed again and turned to leave, his men and the woman trailing after him. She glanced back at Eljin one last time, disgust evident on her face. If the people of Antion felt the same way as this woman, it didn't bode well for our peace treaty — or our alliance.

"Eljin" — Damian turned to his friend — "you'd better find a way to back up your claims. I can't believe Blevon is behind the attack here today, or on the village, but the evidence is pretty damning, even with it coming on the heels of the Dansiians' arrival. I need to know who my true enemy is — and soon."

His words made me wonder if his suspicions, like mine, were on Dansii and Lady Vera, who had supposedly come to bring a peaceful message from his uncle. The same one who had sent us Iker.

"I will do everything I can to discover the truth. I know my nation is blameless. We sacrificed much to ensure this peace between us. No one would be foolish enough to bring more death and suffering needlessly on our people."

Damian studied him silently. "I hope you are right."

Eljin lifted his chin. "I am."

⇥ EIGHT ⇤

WHEN I RUSHED into the room where dinner was being served, Vera hadn't arrived yet. Damian lifted one eyebrow at my own late arrival but didn't comment as I strode across the room to where he sat at the head of the table. I took my place a few feet behind him. My heart beat an uncertain cadence in my chest as I let my hand drop to the hilt of my sword and silently waited for our guest to arrive.

Rylan stood on the other side of Damian. When I glanced over, he was watching me, his expression questioning.

Everything all right? he mouthed.

I shrugged and turned to the table. How could everything be all right? A border village had been targeted by a black sorcerer again, the king had been attacked in his own palace, I'd just been forced to recount one of the most horrible days of my life after barely sleeping in the last forty-eight hours . . . the list kept going. A sharp pain began to throb beneath my skull with each beat of my heart.

The reason I'd been late to the dinner was because I'd made a quick stop in the kitchen to meet this "taster." I didn't like the fact that Lady Vera had supposedly traveled all this way with a taster. It seemed like a rather wasteful person to drag along on a jungle trek.

Unless she was expecting to be poisoned. Or wanted to place someone in a prime position to poison one of us — including the king.

I don't know what I expected when I walked into the kitchen — to see a stranger huddled over the soup, perhaps — but I couldn't even find him at first. The chef had to point this taster out to me. The man was of average height, his shoulders slumped, his eyes on the ground. His hair and beard were the same remarkable shade as Vera's, dark mahogany, but I couldn't see the details of his face, since he cowered in a darkened corner of the massive kitchen as though he were afraid of his own shadow.

"You there," I'd called out, and he'd flinched, not looking up at me. "Are you Vera's taster?"

He'd nodded, swallowing so hard his Adam's apple shot down his throat, then back up again. He lifted his head a little bit, but his eyes stopped when he saw my sword.

"Why are you hiding in the corner?"

"Sorry, miss. Just trying to stay out of the way." He'd spoken softly, his accent thick.

"Do you have a name?"

"Rafe, miss," he'd responded, his gaze dropping back to the floor again, and I'd finally given up. He wasn't armed; he looked completely harmless. Looks could be deceiving, which I knew better than anyone, but as he bowed to me and scuttled back against the wall when a servant rushed in between us, carrying a board laden with four steaming loaves of bread, I sighed and turned away. "Keep an eye on him," I muttered to one of the sentinels at the door, jerking my head toward the taster.

My attention was drawn back to the dining room when Damian shifted in his chair, impatience evident in the taut lines of his body. There were a number of people at dinner tonight. Damian usually preferred to dine alone, or with his closest advisors — which was a very small group. But he'd apparently decided to increase his circle tonight. I had to wonder if it was for Vera's benefit or his own.

Four other men and five women sat at the table. General Ferraun was one; he had entered shortly after I did. And I knew two of the other men were part of the royal court — Duke Tussieux and Baron Durand. But the last man I knew only by face.

Duke Tussieux's wife sat next to him, as did Baron Durand's. I recognized two of the girls from the hallway earlier, when Jax and I had been walking together. My fingers tightened on the hilt of my sword, but otherwise, I gave no indication of my unhappiness that they were included in the dinner.

The three unmarried daughters of the royal court glanced at Damian coyly while waiting to be served. They were obviously thrilled to have been invited to eat with the king, a rare honor, and one that I was pretty certain he'd never given any females from court since his ascension to the throne. Again, I wondered what he was hoping to accomplish. At least half of the court had left the palace after his coronation, choosing to return to their homes and lands now that Hector was gone. Damian's father had forced the nobility to reside at the palace, prey to his every whim and desire for a party or lavish dinner, but Damian had given them the option to stay or return home. It hadn't escaped my notice that most of those who had chosen to remain had unmarried daughters.

My stomach twisted unhappily as I forced myself to look away from the table and stare instead at the door, waiting for Vera to arrive.

If I'd admitted to Damian that I still loved him that first time he'd come to see me after I'd been burned, if I'd ignored my conscience and followed my heart, how different would this dinner be? Would I be seated at his side, dressed in something finer than anything Vera owned, with a ring on my finger proclaiming me the king's betrothed?

A giggle from the table caught my attention, and I glanced down to see two of the young women whispering to each other. The one who had shushed her younger sister earlier looked up at me — or at my scars, to be more accurate — and then quickly away when she realized I was watching them. I clenched my jaw, forcing myself to keep my expression impassive. It was amazing how quickly the gratitude of the court had changed; the first few days after the coronation, I'd been nearly overwhelmed with expressions of appreciation. But all too soon, many stopped looking me in the eye, stopped saying thank you, their gazes lingering elsewhere as they whispered behind their hands.

I watched the third girl glance at me as well, but her eyes were on my pants while she whispered to her friend.

This was exactly why my fantasy was nothing more than that — a useless dream. I would never be seated next to the king, not as his betrothed, never as his queen, not even as his friend. I was his scarred guard, and this was what I would remain.

Damian suddenly stood, his chair scraping back, and I snapped to attention as Vera finally swept into the room, accompanied by two of her guards and the man in the black and white robes. If it was possible, she looked even more stunning than the first time I'd seen her. She'd changed into an ivory dress with deep blue embroidery lining the sleeves and hem. Her hair was a mass of rich auburn curls, pinned up so that the graceful slope of her shoulders and neck was enhanced to prime effect. I felt my own unsightliness acutely in comparison, particularly after having just let myself daydream for even a moment about what might have been between me and Damian.

"Lady Vera," Damian said, his deep voice traveling across the room. "I hope that you were able to rest and recover from your journey."

"The room you gave me is very lovely indeed," she said as she glided toward the only empty chair, across the long table from Damian. It was a place of honor, but it also put her as far away from the king as possible. She lifted an eyebrow but didn't comment as one of her guards pulled out the chair for her. The other man lifted her napkin and laid it across her lap after she sat down. Once she was settled, Damian reseated himself as well.

The servants immediately brought out the first course, a fruit salad tossed with lime and honey. Damian leaned back in his chair, his posture one of nonchalance. But I could feel tension rolling off him in waves as he began to eat.

Vera glanced up at the man in the black and white robes. Some sort of silent communication seemed to pass between them, and after he gave a slight nod, she finally lifted her fork and took a hesitant bite of the fruit.

"I wasn't expecting such a large gathering," she said after her second bite. She looked up at Damian and gave him a brilliant smile. Then her gaze slid past Damian, to Rylan just for a brief moment. Without moving my head, I glanced at him and noticed his stance relax and his lips turn up slightly as though he was holding back a smile. When Vera turned back to Damian, his shoulders relaxed slightly as well, and I wondered what expression was on *his* face. I couldn't see it from behind him. Her beauty seemed to have quite the effect on the men, and I had to suppress another surge of frustration.

"The palace is abuzz with your arrival," Damian finally responded. "I had so many requests from the members of court to dine with you tonight, I was forced to turn the majority of them away. These are a few of my closest advisors and their guests from the royal court. They wanted to see if you are as beautiful in person as it had been rumored from those who saw your arrival."

"And? Do you find me to be as beautiful as you were told?" Her question should have been addressed to the rest of those seated at the table, but her eyes didn't leave Damian's.

Damian sat up taller in his chair and leaned toward Vera. "Though I saw you earlier, I had convinced myself that you couldn't truly be as beautiful as I remembered. But seeing you now proves me wrong. You are even lovelier than my memory served." He took his wine goblet and lifted it to her in a salute.

Vera's smile was radiant as she took her own goblet and lifted it back. The others at the table hastily grabbed their glasses and joined in the impromptu toast. The young women who had been whispering about me weren't giggling anymore as they took sips with everyone else in tribute to Vera's beauty.

"I heard that there was an . . . *unfortunate* event following my arrival earlier today." Lady Vera's voice was the perfect tone of innocence, but I stiffened, wondering how she'd heard about the attack — unless she'd had something to do with it. True, the entire palace was probably buzzing about it, but I'd hoped the servants and staff would have known better than to gossip about it with anyone from Dansii.

"Nothing you need worry about. It was a minor disturbance and was quickly dispelled." Damian waved his hand. "As are all threats to me or my nation."

"It must be so comforting to have such confidence in your safety and that of your people." Again, Lady Vera's voice was perfectly innocent, but I shivered inwardly at what I perceived to be a hidden threat in her words.

Damian didn't respond right away, choosing instead to take a bite of fruit. When he'd finished chewing, he changed the subject. "Would you care to share the message you brought now?"

"Let's enjoy this lovely meal with our eager audience first. Pleasure before business, as they say." Lady Vera smiled coyly at the king.

"All right, let's eat first," Damian agreed.

I had to force myself to stare at the wall instead of glaring at Vera.

After the first plates were cleared away, the servants brought out the main course. It appeared to be some sort of fish with a mango puree artfully drizzled on the top and a garnish of fresh herbs. The smell was tantalizing, but I had no appetite as I listened to Damian flatter Lady Vera, complimenting her on her dress. Her eyes flickered to mine as she used her fork to cut herself a bite of fish, the smug expression on her face making me want to grab her plate and dump it in her lap.

When the door burst open and a servant ran into the room, everyone paused, including Lady Vera with her fish halfway to her mouth.

"Stop!" he shouted. "Don't eat it! *Poison!* It's poisoned!"

⊰ NINE ⊱

SOMEONE GASPED AND one of the younger women spit out her food. But my gaze immediately dropped to Damian, who had already brought his fork to his mouth. Before I could even think through what I was doing, I dove for him. I grabbed his wrist and knocked the fork out of his hand, splattering Duke Tussieux's wife with flaky bits of fish and bright orange mango. She screamed and jerked back, but I didn't care. My only thought was to see whether he'd already eaten any or not.

Damian stared at me with wide eyes, his hand now empty, hanging in the air, with my fingers still encircling his wrist. Our faces were only a foot apart. My chest heaved with fear — and a sudden awareness of how close we were.

"No, not the king's," the servant said, and I jerked back, letting go of his wrist. "It was *Lady Vera's* taster. The poison was delayed — he just collapsed."

I spun around to see Lady Vera drop her fork, her skin even more pale than normal. "Mine? Someone poisoned *my* food?"

"Did you eat any?" I asked as her guard leaned forward to shove the offending plate of fish away from her.

"No," she said, pressing one trembling hand to her bosom. "No, not yet." Her voice quavered. "Is . . . is he dead?" She looked up at the servant who had brought the warning, and he shook his head. I thought of the poor man in the kitchen. Apparently, Rafe had reason to be afraid after all — though I couldn't quite believe it.

"I don't know, my lady. I was sent to warn you the moment he collapsed. He'd tasted the fish at least ten minutes ago, so it was deemed safe."

"Rylan, fetch Lisbet and ask her to tend to the taster immediately." Damian stood up next to me. "I expect the palace to be searched and the kitchen staff questioned. It is unacceptable for an esteemed guest to have come so close to tragedy." His voice was sharp as he barked out orders. "Lady Vera, I apologize most profusely for this shocking turn of events."

"I hadn't thought my presence so unwelcome." Her voice still trembled, but as Damian continued to issue orders, I noticed a fleeting glance between her and the man in the black and white robes. It was so quick that I almost missed it. For that brief instant, the horrified expression on her face slipped. But when she turned back to Damian, the fear in her eyes and the way her hands shook seemed genuine enough. Was I so jealous of her that I was imagining things — or was something going on that we were missing?

"If I may retire to my room, Your Majesty. This has been most upsetting. Perhaps it would be better for me to deliver my message to you in private at a more convenient time." Lady Vera stood as Damian nodded.

"Yes, of course. Again, I apologize. My guards will not rest until we've found the culprit." Damian inclined his head to Lady Vera, who dropped into a deep curtsy.

"Thank you, Your Majesty. After all, I'd hate to think that you had anything to do with it, King Damian." Lady Vera's words were honeyed, but I noticed the thread of steel in her voice.

Damian stiffened next to me. "My lady, I can assure you that *I* had nothing to do with this." His voice was cold. "I hope that you might rest well this night, and I will send for you in the morning so that you can deliver your message. I'll also have the chef prepare a new dinner for you that he will personally deliver to your rooms, to ensure the safety of the food. Our healer will send word as soon as we know the fate of your taster."

Lady Vera stood tall again and smiled sadly at Damian. "Thank you for your concern. I had grown fond of him over the last couple weeks of travel. The poor man." With a shake of her head, Lady Vera signaled her guards. "Until the morning, then." With a sweep of her voluminous skirts, she turned and exited the room. As soon as she was gone, I noticed Damian's shoulders sag slightly.

"I apologize for cutting this dinner short, but I need to ask the rest of you to return to your rooms." Damian glanced around the table at the rest of his guests, who had watched the entire exchange with frozen expressions varying from shock on the older guests' faces to curiosity on two of the younger girls' faces. The third looked so pale I was afraid she was going to pass out. Everyone hurried to rise at Damian's dismissal and bowed and curtsied as decorum dictated, then left. Duke Tussieux's wife took her napkin with her and was still trying to wipe the mango stain off her dress as she trailed behind her husband.

"General Ferraun, a word before you go," Damian asked as the general also stood to leave.

"Of course, Your Majesty." He was a tall, broad man, with graying hair and steely gray eyes. General Ferraun had been stationed at the front of the war, along the border between Antion and Blevon, for the last few years, but Damian had sent word for him to return to the palace soon after being crowned king. He'd only arrived recently, and I still didn't know very much about the general, other than what I'd seen and heard from him today after the attack. But Damian clearly trusted him.

"There's no need to stand on such pretense when we're alone," Damian said, sitting back down in his chair heavily. "Not from the man who taught me how to wield a sword when I was barely even able to lift it with two hands."

I looked at the general with new interest. So he was the one who taught Damian how to fight?

"You are the king now, Sire. And I will address you as such — whether in front of the people of Antion or alone in your quarters. The mantle of a king never leaves his shoulders." General Ferraun's expression was an interesting mix of concern and sternness.

Damian sighed, and I couldn't keep from glancing over at him. His face was drawn and he appeared to be exhausted.

"And we are *not* actually alone," the general continued.

I looked back up to see him watching me.

Damian also looked up, glancing around the now empty room until his gaze landed on me, still standing at attention a few feet away from him. Our eyes met for a brief moment before he turned back to the general. "Oh, you mean Alexa. You may speak freely in her presence. There is no one in the palace whom I trust more than her."

My heart skipped a beat at Damian's words. Despite his recent coldness to me — despite my own harsh words to him — he still felt that way?

General Ferraun's expression was inscrutable as he gazed at me in the light of the hundreds of flickering candles that had been lit for the now ruined dinner. "I see" was all he said.

I wondered what, exactly, it was that General Ferraun saw. His pointed scrutiny cut through me. Before, his attention had been focused mostly on Eljin, but now that it was aimed at me, I had to consciously square my shoulders, rather than cower before him. Damian had chosen an appropriately intimidating man to lead his armies.

"I have no idea who would have attempted to poison Lady Vera," Damian said, bringing my attention back to the immediate problem at hand. "And I've never heard of a poison that has a delay like this one supposedly did. Will you personally look into the matter and report back to me?"

"Of course, Sire. I will bring you word as soon as I discover anything. And I hope that we might be able to meet tomorrow to continue our earlier discussion."

Damian nodded. "Yes, of course. I believe I have time immediately following breakfast. Assuming no one else is poisoned before then."

General Ferraun nodded grimly, then saluted Damian and turned on his heel to march away but paused to give me one last hooded look before going.

When the general was gone and the door shut behind him, Damian dropped his head into his hands. I stared down at his dark hair, acutely aware of the fact that we were completely alone. It was the first time since he'd come to see me as I recovered from my wounds. When he'd told me he loved me.

For the next couple of weeks after his coronation, he had treated me with kindness — he'd sought me out, tried to speak with me alone. But I'd rebuffed him again and again, even though it hurt me as much, if not more than him. Until, finally, over the last few weeks, he'd backed off. Grown cold again. I still wasn't sure which was worse — having to reject him over and over or having him treat me with icy indifference.

I stood at attention, forcing my hands to stay motionless, even though I wanted to reach out to him — to brush the hair back from his forehead. To cup his face and stare into his eyes until everything else faded away. The hopeless dreams and wishes that I could usually force into the dark recesses of my mind, except in the stillness of the night, surged up, washing over me in a wave of longing.

"She's very beautiful, isn't she?" His quiet question broke into my thoughts.

Heat suffused my face. Here I was dreaming about touching him, and *he* was thinking about Lady Vera.

"Yes, Your Majesty." My voice was practically strangled as I forced out the words. Embarrassed, I cleared my throat, hoping he'd think I'd just had something stuck that made me sound so odd.

Damian looked up at me sharply. "Do you suppose her purpose in coming is to engage my interest?"

The intensity of his vibrant eyes was almost more than I could bear. Why was he asking me this? He lifted one eyebrow when I didn't respond right away. "I couldn't say what her purpose is,

Sire," I responded quietly. Once, he and I had shared our darkest secrets with each other. Now there was a void between us that made me afraid to even tell him the truth about my concerns. A void of my own making. "Not yet. But that does appear to be at least one of her goals."

"Yes . . . it does, doesn't it? And how would you feel about having a Dansiian noblewoman as your queen? It would strengthen the alliance between our two kingdoms quite strategically, would it not?" His gaze never wavered from mine; his expression was almost fierce as he stared into my eyes. His questions hit as though he were stabbing me; I could hardly tell where the pain his words caused me originated from — my heart, my belly, my head? All of me hurt at the thought of him marrying another — especially Lady Vera. But it was I who had told him that he must do exactly that.

Willing my voice to be steady, I responded, "I would respect your decision and know that you had chosen what was best for yourself and the nation of Antion, Your Majesty."

"Alex, don't *you* dare do that to me." Damian stood up to face me, shoving his chair back so forcefully it crashed to the ground. I flinched but didn't move. His expression was thunderous as he stalked forward, closing the gap between us, so that only a foot separated our bodies. Half of me yearned to throw myself into his arms, and the other half screamed to back away, to put distance between us. Instead, I held my ground. My heart beat painfully beneath my ribs, slamming against my lungs and making it hard to breathe normally.

"Did you not want me to agree with you, Sire?"

"*Enough*, Alex! Stop using my titles. Stop acting like you are nothing more than my guard." His eyes flashed with anger, and his hands clenched at his sides.

"But . . . I *am* nothing more than your guard."

"You and I both know that is a lie."

Despite how weak my legs felt and the way my body trembled, I stood tall. "No, it's not," I said, and I couldn't keep the sadness from my voice. "You just asked me if I thought Lady Vera was beautiful, and I won't lie to you. She is absolutely breathtaking. But be careful. I don't believe we should trust her . . . yet," I added, just in case he ever did decide to marry her. The thought of standing guard over him, knowing he would be going to her at night, was more than I could bear. If he chose Vera for his wife, I would resign my post — promise or no promise. But he didn't need to know that.

A muscle in Damian's jaw stood out and he closed his eyes, as though he were fighting an internal battle. "The first time we've been alone in . . . too long . . . and I'm wasting it by fighting with you." He opened his eyes and the anger was gone, replaced by such a deep pain and longing that my heart lurched, and it was all I could do to stay still, to keep my hands motionless at my side. Everything in me cried out to reach for him, and it took every ounce of willpower I had to resist.

"I could have died today, if you hadn't reacted so quickly." He took that last step and closed the gap between us so that our bodies nearly touched.

"It wasn't just me," I said, my voice slightly breathless, much to my chagrin. I knew I should step back. I should put space between us. *Do it now*, I told myself. *Now.*

But I didn't — couldn't — move.

Slowly . . . hesitantly . . . he reached up, pausing just before his fingers would have brushed my cheek. His hand hung in the air, shaking ever so slightly. My eyes burned and I squeezed them shut to keep him from seeing the truth of my feelings. There was a charged moment of silence, of nothing — no words, no sound, no touch . . .

And then his fingers finally brushed my skin, so softly it made me shiver. My breath caught in my lungs. The heat of a need I'd been denying for a month raced over my skin and made my entire body tremble. I wanted nothing more than to turn my face into his hand, to have him take me in his arms and —

With a strangled gasp, I took two hasty steps backward. I tripped over the leg of another chair behind me and nearly fell. Damian lurched forward, reaching out to help steady me, but I yanked my arm out of his grasp and stumbled even farther away.

"I can't," I said, my voice strained. "Damian, please . . ."

He froze when I said his name, his hand still outstretched.

I stared at him, breathing hard.

"Do you have any idea what it does to me?" he asked, his voice low. "To have you stand by me all day, outside my room all night, and to have to treat you like everyone else on the guard? To pretend to be your king and nothing more?" Damian wore the crown and robes of the king, but all I could see was the unmasked pain on his face when he looked at me.

"Yes," I whispered. "I know what it's like to pretend. I know what it does to *me* to . . . to . . . But it doesn't matter," I finished more forcefully. "A few more dinners with Lady Vera, and her beauty will sweep away any feelings you might think you still have for me."

"Alex, you can't possibly —"

The door behind us flew open, cutting off whatever Damian had been about to say, and I spun around to see Rylan coming in, followed closely by Eljin.

"Your Majesty," Rylan said, his eyebrows lifting slightly when he glanced at me, then back at the king, "Lisbet has asked you to come immediately."

"Is it about the taster?" Damian's voice was completely calm; he slid back into the persona of the king without missing a single beat. My pulse still raced, and I could only hope I didn't look half as alarmed and unsettled as I felt.

"Yes," Eljin answered, stepping around Rylan to come forward. "Well, partially."

"The taster died," Rylan said. "He was dead before he hit the floor."

Damian scowled at the news, his expression darkened. "Why does Lisbet wish to see me, then?"

"Because she left the room where they had brought him to find out what Lady Vera would like done with his body," Eljin said, "and when she came back, the body was gone."

"Gone?" I asked, drawing the attention of all three men to me. "How could a dead body just disappear?"

"That's only the beginning." Rylan's expression was grim. "Not only did the taster's body disappear, but so did Jax."

"Jax?" Damian repeated in disbelief. "I'm sure he's just off somewhere in the palace, doing who knows what. Causing mischief, no doubt."

Eljin shook his head. "He was in the room with Lisbet when they brought the taster's body to her. She asked him to wait in the hallway, but when she came out, he was gone. She didn't think much of it, until the body went missing as well. We've searched everywhere, but no one can find him."

The blood drained from Damian's face. "Maybe he's hiding." He looked to me, and I knew we were both thinking the same thing — the secret passageways that so few knew about. The ones that Jax had used to deliver Damian a "letter" all those months ago when he was testing my loyalty.

"We've looked *everywhere*," Eljin said, and I remembered that he, too, knew about the secret passageways. "I'm sorry, but we can't find the body or Jax."

⤜ TEN ⤛

THE PALACE WAS in upheaval as every able person searched for the missing boy. Damian was more concerned about his half brother than he was about the missing body, but Lady Vera had sent a message that she was extremely dismayed to hear that the taster's body was gone and felt that it was further evidence of a plot against her. She believed the perpetrator did it so that we couldn't discover what type of poison was used. She demanded that her guards be allowed to help search as well.

Deron, whose arm was now healed thanks to Lisbet, had argued with Damian for a good ten minutes but finally agreed to let the Dansiian guards search outside the palace, where it would be easier to keep an eye on them. He didn't seem to trust them any more than I did.

I combed through the older wings of the palace, and even the courtyard, desperately hoping Jax was hiding somewhere or playing some sort of game. But as the hours bled past midnight and crept toward morning, it became increasingly evident that he was not in the palace or on the grounds. Exhaustion pressed down on me like a physical weight, but I forced myself to keep looking, hoping, praying that he was curled up asleep in a dark corner somewhere, blissfully unaware of the turmoil he'd caused.

Thunder growled in the distance as a storm headed toward the palace. A full moon hung just above the shadowed canopy of the jungle, enormous and pale. I retraced my steps through the older wings, holding a torch in one hand to banish the darkness the moonlight couldn't reach and my sword in the other — just in case — as I opened door after door and searched empty room after empty room.

I was crouched over, looking under a bed, when the door behind me creaked open. I jerked up, lifting my sword in front of me. But when I saw who it was, I lowered it again.

"Sorry, I didn't mean to scare you," Rylan said, stepping into the room, holding his own torch, with his empty hand raised. "Eljin sent me to find you."

"Why? What's going on?" I took a deep breath, preparing myself for the worst.

"A ransom note arrived for Jax. The king has called off the search inside the palace — Jax isn't here. He's been taken."

My legs buckled and I half sat, half collapsed onto the bed I'd been searching under for the boy. I had just been with him this afternoon — had just promised to teach him to fight. If only I'd done it sooner, if he'd only known how to protect himself better. Would he still have been captured, or could he have fought back and saved himself?

"We need to go after them — they can't be far," I burst out desperately. "If we split up the guard into patrols —"

"No." Rylan cut me off. "He was taken hours ago, and it's the middle of the night. Damian sent a few members of the guard to search outside the palace and in Tubatse, but the rest of us will have to wait for daylight if they aren't successful. Then we can look for clues when it's not dark." Rylan strode over to my side and gently took the lit torch out of my hand and set it in a bracket on the wall across from me, then placed his own torch in a second bracket.

"But if it rains, the clues will be washed away." I couldn't believe Jax had been taken from the palace, right beneath our noses. "I need to go after him. I'm the best Damian has. I can't believe he didn't send me."

Rylan came back and pried the sword from my hands. "You're beyond exhausted, Alexa. You need to rest." He set the sword down on the floor and then sat beside me. His weight made the mattress dip me toward him, but I didn't have the strength to pull away. Through the last month, he'd always been there, quietly supportive, never again mentioning the feelings he'd expressed before the coronation.

"How could we let this happen? How did no one notice him being taken?" My voice was strained, on the verge of hysterical, and tears burned infuriatingly close to the surface.

Rylan put his arm around me and urged my head to his shoulder. The dam of emotions I'd been forcing down all day broke loose, and I couldn't contain my sobs. He held me tightly as I cried. "I can't lose him. I can't let another person I love die."

Rylan stiffened at my words but didn't comment. He just held me as the sobs tore through me. Exhaustion, fear, confusion, desperation — I couldn't even name everything I felt after all that had happened in the last twenty-four hours.

When my tears finally slowed and I was able to regain control of myself, I pulled away and Rylan immediately let me go. I reached up and wiped my face, sweeping the wetness from my cheeks.

"There's nothing more you can do tonight," Rylan said gently. "You're going to be completely useless if you don't get some sleep soon."

"I couldn't go to bed until we found him."

He nodded sadly, his expression grim. "I know." Rylan stood up and reached for my hand. "Let me help you to your room, and then I promise we'll start the search again at first light if the other guards already out there don't find him first." I put my hand in his and let him pull me to stand next to him. Then he bent down and picked up my sword and sheathed it for me.

"I'm not a child, you know," I said.

"Trust me, I know. But you *are* about to tip over from exhaustion, and the last thing we need is for you to fall on your sword." Rylan steered me toward the door with one hand on the small of my back. Normally, I would have moved away or told him to stop it, but I was just too tired. And as much as I hated to admit it, he wasn't entirely wrong — I did feel like I might collapse at any moment. Sitting down and crying like that had made my head swim now that I was walking again.

He led me to the newer wing of the palace and the staircase that would take us up to our rooms. After walking in silence for a while, I finally asked, "What did the note say?"

"It was written in Blevonese."

"*Blevonese?* Are you sure?"

"Yes." Rylan took my arm as we began to climb the stairs. It was beginning to irritate me, having him treat me like I was helpless, but I swallowed my annoyance and allowed him to continue to assist me. "King Damian didn't read it out loud. All he said was

82

that it was a ransom note and to call off the search in the palace so we could refocus our efforts outside of it."

"I don't believe it. Why would someone from Blevon do such a thing, just when Damian has reestablished peace?"

"Maybe not everyone in Blevon is as happy about the peace treaty as *King* Damian and the rest of us are."

"But it doesn't make sense" — I ignored his jab about not using Damian's title — "Jax is half Blevonese. He's not their enemy."

"The king is half Blevonese as well, and it would appear that they don't care about that." He paused. "Look, I don't want to believe it, either. But what other explanation is there? All the evidence points to them."

"It could be Dansii. They could be framing Blevon."

"Dansii? But why? They're supposedly our allies, too, don't forget."

I shook my head. But before I could respond, the toe of my boot caught on the top stair and I stumbled forward. Rylan's hand tightened around my arm, but I'd already regained my balance and straightened back up.

"Are you —"

"I'm fine." Unable to stand feeling so helpless any longer, I pulled my arm free of his grip. Anger coursed through me — anger and horrible, crippling regret. That I wasn't there, that I didn't protect Jax. I reached up and pressed the heels of my hands to my temples, trying to force the building pressure behind my skull to recede.

But if I'd been with Jax, the king would have been unprotected. And after the attack today, he needed me by his side more than ever.

"Promise me you're going to go to bed," Rylan said, taking a step back, his expression guarded in the flickering light of his torch. "There's nothing more you can do tonight."

I clenched my teeth, tempted to say something less than kind, but I knew Rylan didn't deserve my anger. He was only trying to help because he was concerned about me.

"Alexa, please, don't do anything else until you get some rest. There are guards out there looking for him. And if they aren't successful, I'll come get you first thing in the morning. We'll figure out what happened and we'll get him back." Rylan's gaze was unwavering, his eyes imploring. "I promise."

As much as I wanted to rush out into the darkness to help search for Jax, I knew Rylan was right. With a sigh of frustration, I relented and nodded. "Fine. As soon as the sun is up. Right?"

"I promise," he repeated.

When I made it to my door and opened it, Rylan was still behind me, watching. I paused before going in and looked back over my shoulder. He stood a few feet away. He couldn't hide the expression on his face fast enough, and the troubled look in his eyes struck me deep in the gut.

"Thank you for letting me know about Jax," I said.

Rylan lifted his chin in acknowledgment. "Of course."

We looked at each other silently for a moment. The concern on his face changed, becoming something darker — something more powerful. A sudden, strange tension surged up in the gaping space between us and made my heart constrict in my chest. I was reminded yet again of how different life would have been had I never discovered Damian's true nature — if I'd never fallen for the man who was now our king. Rylan took a hesitant half step toward me.

84

"Good night, Rylan," I said quietly, and he froze.

He swallowed once, hard. His hand flexed and unflexed at his side. "Good night, Alexa," he finally responded.

Without waiting to see what he did next, I shut the door and leaned my forehead against it. The pressure behind my skull had turned into a sharp, stabbing pain. I'd be lying if I didn't admit that part of me was still attracted to Rylan. But I could never go down that path — could I? Not when he knew my true feelings. He'd know that he would always come in second to the only man who had ever truly captured my heart.

Though I was as tired as I'd ever been in my life, my mind still whirled relentlessly. I straightened up and turned to face my empty room. I had to cut off thoughts of Damian and Rylan. There was no time to worry about either of them — not like that. I had to focus on the immediate problems at hand.

So many pieces didn't make sense. The attacks from Blevon, Lady Vera, her taster's death, the body's disappearance, and now Jax being taken. I hated unanswered questions, and in this case, I wasn't even sure I was asking the *right* questions. I thought about the suggestion I'd made to Rylan — that maybe Dansii was framing Blevon. It was possible, wasn't it? We knew they had black sorcerers, since it was King Armando who sent Iker. And Eljin was adamant that Blevon didn't have any. But why would they do it? Why would Dansii want us to go to war with Blevon again?

I stumbled toward my bed. Maybe if I slept, I could make sense of it all in the morning. I had to be missing something. I couldn't keep my eyes open as I laid my head on my pillow. I didn't realize I hadn't unstrapped my sword until the hard scabbard bit into my hip when I rolled onto my side. But I didn't bother trying to remove it. The exhaustion weighed me down so heavily I felt as though I were being pressed into my bed by some unseen force. I couldn't have moved if I'd wanted to. Sleep had already begun to claim me.

And then the wall opened and Damian walked into my room in his breeches and a partially unlaced tunic and nothing else.

I squeezed my eyes shut and then reopened them, not entirely sure I was awake. And if I *was* awake, I was pretty sure Damian standing in my room was a hallucination. Until he started to talk and the tightness in his voice made me realize he was very real and this was no dream. If I'd been dreaming, he wouldn't have said the words that came out of his mouth:

"I'm sorry to disturb you when I know you need your sleep, but we need to talk." He stepped toward me. "I think someone is trying to frame Blevon for kidnapping Jax."

⊰ ELEVEN ⊱

Somehow, I forced myself to sit up in bed, even though my body practically groaned in protest. "You think Blevon is being—"

"Are you sleeping on your sword?" Damian cut me off, his eyes widening when he saw my scabbard underneath me.

"Did you just use a secret passage that I didn't know about to sneak into my *room*?" I shot back.

A brief, awkward silence fell, and then I said, "I was too tired to take it off—"

"I didn't want you to think I'd ever use it to spy on you—"

We both spoke and cut ourselves off at the same time. Another awkward silence fell.

"*Have* you ever used it to spy on me?" I finally asked, not able to meet his eyes. This was the same room Marcel and I had shared before his death. Damian had decided to keep his old quarters, even after being crowned king. Had he ever come during the night to watch me? I couldn't imagine him doing that, but —

"Never." His voice was vehement. "I promise, Alex. I'll show you how it works, if you'd like. You can use it anytime — day or night — if you ever need me."

"Need you? For what?" The question was out before I realized how it could be taken.

Damian lifted one eyebrow, his eyes inscrutable in the darkness. "To speak in private, for one. As is the case tonight, for me. But if you can think of any other reasons . . ."

My cheeks were hot, and my nerves were on high alert with Damian standing only a few feet away, barefoot, his well-muscled chest exposed by the open V in his tunic, his dark hair mussed. The exhaustion still bore down on me as well, making my body feel like a strange battleground. When I finally looked up at him, the room spun around me . . . or possibly *I* was the one lurching to the side, even though I was still sitting down, because suddenly Damian rushed across the space between us and grabbed my shoulders. The spinning stopped as I stared into his blue, blue eyes.

Oh, how I loved his eyes.

"How long have you been awake?" His fingers flexed against my shoulders, and it took every ounce of will I had to keep from letting my head fall forward and rest against his chest.

"If you don't count my nap . . . a while. Two days? Maybe three?"

He smelled just how I remembered. The subtle aroma of his soap and the even more subtle scent of his skin — the smell that was uniquely him, that was *Damian*. I wanted to rest in his arms and turn my face to his neck and breathe him in.

The light of the moon was blotted out by the clouds from the storm that finally arrived with a torrent of rain pelting my window and the palace walls. Damian's eyes were shadowed in the darkness; his face was so close to mine. Too close. I jerked back suddenly.

"Why are you here?"

He released my shoulders and straightened. "I couldn't sleep. Don't worry, you have made your feelings for me very clear, but I . . . I needed to talk to you about my suspicions. About the ransom note for Jax and the attack earlier today. All of it. I . . . I just wanted to talk to you." He paused and my heart lurched. "It would seem that now is not the best time, however."

I hoped he couldn't read the emotions on my face. I made my voice stay firm and detached when I responded, "Well, it *is* the middle of the night. . . . Although that does seem to be a favorite time of yours to speak with me." I regretted bringing up the past the moment the words were out of my mouth.

"Yes, I suppose so," he said, his voice tight. Controlled. "You obviously need to rest. We can speak in the morning."

"Why didn't you just wait until morning to begin with? You kept this particular passage a secret for this long." I widened my eyes to force them to stay open. It was a testament to the sheer exhaustion I was battling that I had to fight so hard to stay awake when Damian was standing so close to me. In my bedroom. Alone. "Why reveal it now?"

"I'm concerned about this delegation from Dansii. I don't think they are all that they appear to be. Sometimes —" He shook his head, cutting himself off. After a pause, he continued, "I don't know who I can trust right now. But despite everything, I still trust *you*. I needed to talk to someone, and I didn't want to be overheard." Damian crossed his arms in front of his body as he stared down at me, with a look of concern on his face very similar to the one Rylan had worn earlier. "But it'll have to wait. You need to sleep. We can talk tomorrow."

"We can talk now. I'm fine. See?" I swung my legs over the edge of the bed and stood up. The blood rushed up through my body or down or somewhere *wrong*, and everything went momentarily black.

Damian's hands closed over my upper arms, holding me up. Did I need to be held up? I was pretty sure I'd been standing. Although my legs did feel strange and the room seemed to be swaying beneath me. Stars popped as my vision slowly returned to see him staring down at me. The heat of his fingers burned through my tunic, and the warmth of his body, only inches from mine, was a tantalizing invitation. His eyebrows pulled low over his eyes as I stood motionless beneath his hands.

My gaze dropped to his lips, and my heart began to thud in my chest. The pain in my head, the exhaustion, the worries and fears all faded away as I stared at his mouth. Without letting myself think or question what I was doing, I lifted my face to his. This was what I wanted — *he* was what I wanted. Who I *needed*. I'd been a fool to reject him. *He*'d been a fool to believe me. Did he truly think I could stop loving him so easily? When he looked at me as he was now, with a hunger and need to match mine so evident on his beautiful face and in his eyes, I knew he didn't see my scars — inside or out. He only saw *me*. Alexa.

"You need to go to sleep," he said suddenly, his voice gruff, pushing me away gently but firmly so that the backs of my knees hit the edge of my bed. My legs gave out, making me sit down hard on the mattress. "But this time, take your sword off first."

"Damian . . . did I . . . was I wrong to . . ." I couldn't seem to make the right words come out as my body flamed with embarrassment. I'd lifted my mouth to his, asking to be kissed. And he'd *rejected* me?

"You're not feeling well. I don't want you to regret anything in the morning, especially since I know how you truly feel when you're not delirious from exhaustion. Go to sleep, Alexa. I'll find a way to speak with you alone tomorrow." Damian looked at me for a moment longer, his expression indecipherable in the darkness. Then he turned away. I watched him with my heart in my throat as he felt along my wall until he found some sort of latch or lever and it popped open again. In the blink of an eye, he slipped through the opening and was gone.

I woke the next morning stiff, my head still aching. The weak gray light of predawn fought to break through the lingering cloud cover. The events of the night before seemed like a combination of a dream and a nightmare. When I looked at the floor, I saw my sword still in the scabbard, which I'd finally taken off and tossed next to my bed before curling into a ball on top of my blankets and falling almost immediately into a nightmare-ridden sleep.

This time, it wasn't Iker who haunted me. Instead, Damian stood far above me, at the top of a massive marble staircase, staring down at me with hatred in his eyes. His voice thundered, making the ground beneath me shake, but I couldn't understand what he said. I kept trying to hurry up to him, but no matter how many stairs I climbed, he never got any closer. Suddenly, Vera stood beside me, and when he extended his arm out to her, she glided up the stairs without touching them until she stood by his side. When they grasped hands, a physical pain tore through my body.

Suddenly, the stairs began to split apart, dividing down the middle and then crumbling into pieces. And still, Damian and Vera towered above me, held up by an unseen power that filled the air with darkness. I tried to grab on to something, anything, but my fingers slipped and I fell, tumbling, head over feet until I landed flat on my back on a ground scorched black by fire, barren of life.

Rylan stood beside me, but rather than reaching down to my broken body, he stared up at Damian and Vera, his gaze adoring. I tried to reach for him but was unable to move. This time, Vera spoke, and at her command, fire flared up all around us, rushing to devour Rylan and me. And yet, he still watched her, motionless, his eyes shining with blissful unawareness. I screamed and screamed as the flames closed in, and then I jerked awake in my bed inside my own room.

As I hurried to wash and dress in a clean uniform, the lingering terror of my nightmare wouldn't go away. *It's a dream and nothing more*, I tried to tell myself. But I was determined to find out the truth about why Vera was here as soon as possible. After I found Jax and returned him to safety — he was the priority. My heart lurched as I thought of the poor little boy, alone and terrified. I wanted to rush out to begin searching for him immediately, but first I had to find out what Damian knew — what the ransom note said, if it gave us any clues.

My headache had already returned by the time I strapped on my scabbard and opened my door. I thought about trying to find the secret passageway for a moment but quickly decided against it. Jax needed me, and figuring out how to travel secretly to the king's rooms didn't help him.

When I walked out, Asher stood outside Damian's door, looking half asleep.

"Who's supposed to relieve you?" I asked.

"Leon," he replied, snapping back to alertness. "He'll be here any minute, I'm sure." Asher paused. "Shouldn't you still be sleeping? I heard —"

"I'm fine." I cut him off. "I slept for a few hours, and that's enough for now."

He shrugged. "Whatever you say."

"Any word on Jax?"

"No one's been up yet. So I guess not."

I sighed. "If Leon doesn't show up in the next few minutes, go wake him up. I'm going to speak with the king."

Asher gave me a mocking salute. "Yes, ma'am. *Private* matters to discuss?"

"I might be tired, but I could still knock you flat on your back without even trying, Asher. Don't test my patience." I turned and swung open the door to Damian's outer chamber.

"I wouldn't dream of it," Asher said behind me. "Alex*a*."

I ignored him as the door shut.

After taking a deep breath, I walked into the room where I had slept on a cot all those months ago, when I had first learned that Damian wasn't who I thought — that he'd been hiding who he really was for years. Just like me.

When I knocked at his door, there was no response. I pushed it open slowly, and peeked in to see Damian standing by his window, his arms folded across his chest.

"Your Majesty —" I started to say, but stopped when he startled and whirled to face me.

"Alex," he breathed in relief. "What are you doing — do you need something?"

"I knocked, Sire," I said lamely, gesturing to his door.

"I was lost in thought. I'm sorry, I didn't hear you." Damian took a few steps toward me, close enough that I could see circles the color of bruises beneath his eyes. "And please, at least when we're alone . . . can you just use my name? I miss hearing it. Especially from you."

His words wrapped around me, as warm as a caress. "Didn't you sleep at all?" I asked abruptly.

"Do I look that bad?" He lifted one eyebrow.

I opened my mouth and then closed it, not sure what to say. Even with the dark circles, he certainly didn't look *bad*. He was as handsome as ever, so much so that it actually hurt to look at him, a sharp barb somewhere between my chest and my stomach.

"I can't stop thinking about Jax out there . . . somewhere. And the ransom note," he continued, reaching up to shove a hand through his hair. He seemed to be trying to fix it, but instead, he only made it messier. "Why did you come?"

I forced my eyes away from his hair and focused on his chin instead. A chin was harmless. I didn't want to run my hands through his chin. "I came to see what you wanted to talk to me about . . . last night."

"Ah yes. What was so urgent that I risked your wrath by showing up alone in your chamber?" Damian went over to his massive desk and picked up a scroll of parchment. "I wanted to talk to you about this, for one." He held it out toward me.

I had to cross his room to take the parchment from his hands. Memories of the week I had spent in the bed — his bed — as I recovered from the battle with Iker flooded back. This was the room where I'd first seen my newly disfigured face, and it was also where Damian had looked at me and told me for the first time that he loved me, in spite of my scars.

I cleared my throat, forcing the memories away, and looked down at the missive. The handwriting was tight, and it looked as though it had been written in a rush. "I don't read Blevonese."

"I don't think the person who wrote this is a native of Blevon, either. While the language is technically correct, some of the grammatical choices he made are odd — basically old-fashioned. As though he'd learned the language from a book or someone very elderly." Damian took the letter back and stared down at it, as though it could somehow impart answers to him.

"How do you know it's a 'he'?" I asked, thoughts of Vera on my mind. "A woman could be behind it."

"Of course. I just figured the handwriting looked masculine." He glanced up at me and then quickly away, out the window.

Silence weighed heavily over us for a long moment. My instinct was to go to him, to take him in my arms, to comfort him. Instead, I stood stiffly, battling myself and the feelings I knew I needed to crush once and for all.

"I wish I could go after him," Damian said softly. "I feel so trapped here, in my palace. On my throne. I am a king, and yet I've never felt more powerless to *do* something."

Despite my best intentions, I took a couple of steps closer to him and hesitantly reached out to rest my hand on his arm. "You're far from powerless. You have the entire army of Antion to do your bidding. As well as your guard and all those who care about you and Jax."

"An army that is already stretched too thin, without the threat of a new war." Damian put his hand over mine, gripping me tightly. He stared down at our interlaced fingers, his face filled with unmasked pain and desperation. "I'm supposed to fix Antion, to heal her . . . and instead, I feel as though she's being torn apart at the seams. I haven't been king more than a month." He laughed once, a mirthless, bitter sound.

"You are doing the best you can, Damian. Antion *is* healing because of you. And I promise that I will do everything in my power to bring Jax safely back home."

Damian looked up; our eyes met and locked. I knew I should back away. I *knew* it — just as I'd known it last night. But something in me was coming unraveled. The strength I'd clung to for the last month was leaving me, and I couldn't bring myself to do it. When he bent forward slightly, hesitantly, I stood unmoving, my heart slamming into the cage of my ribs.

He paused a hairsbreadth away from kissing me. "Alexa," he murmured, his lips brushing mine with the sound of my name. "I — I need —"

And then he could say no more because I couldn't hold back any longer. I lifted my face so that our mouths met. He let go of my hand to wrap his arm around me, pulling me against his chest. My heart jolted within me, shocked into stillness for the space of a breath before restarting with a frantic lurch. I pressed into him, molding myself to his body, as his lips moved on mine, hard, desperate, full of the need we'd both been denying for weeks and weeks. Every day, I'd stood by him and forced myself to suppress my feelings, but now . . . *now* I was finally whole again — in his arms, with his mouth on mine. My heart beat without pain for the first time since before my battle with Iker.

He reached up to thread his fingers through my hair, tilting my head slightly. His lips parted, and when his tongue brushed my mouth, all the strength left me. My fingers curled around his tunic and I clutched at his back, gasping for air.

But in the small corner of my mind that was still functioning, reality pulsed — demanding my attention. I'd told him no once before, and it had nearly destroyed me.

Now, because of my weakness, I had to do it again. I couldn't delude myself into thinking anything had changed. I was still not suitable to be his queen. And there was still no future for us. No matter how right this felt. I needed to leave, right now, before I couldn't. I had to go find Jax.

"Stop," I gasped, pushing at his shoulders. Damian froze but didn't let go of me yet. Until I pushed again, harder. "Stop," I repeated, louder. "We can't do this."

He let his arms drop and took two quick steps back. His eyes were darkened, and his chest rose and fell with his labored breathing. "Why? Why *must* we stop?"

"Nothing has changed," I said. My mouth burned from his early-morning stubble, and my blood still raced through my veins.

"What do you mean?" he asked quietly, carefully.

"What I told you before is still true."

"Which part — when you told me I was a good king? Or are you referring to the day I told you I loved you, and you told me you could never trust me and didn't want me?"

I jerked back as though I'd been slapped. Any warmth that had been in his eyes was gone, replaced by a cold anger. I had to clench my jaw to hold back the tears that threatened to surface. I couldn't let him see me cry. I couldn't let him know just how badly it hurt me to do this — to him . . . to me . . . to *us*. If only he knew it was because I loved him *so* much that I wanted what was best for him and Antion.

"As I see it, both statements can't be true. You can't possibly think me a good king if you still find me untrustworthy. Can you?"

I blinked hard, once. "I believe that we have many threats to deal with right now, and I shouldn't have distracted you from that."

"*Distracted* me?" Damian laughed again, harshly. "Is that what this was — a distraction?"

"Sire." I had to look down, away from him. "If you truly believe Blevon is somehow being framed, then we must ascertain the true threat before anyone else suffers . . . or is killed."

There was a long pause, and then, "Yes, you are right. Of course."

I glanced up to see that the bitter anger on his face had drained away at my words — at the reminder of Jax's danger — leaving his expression grim and resigned. He turned away from me, his shoulders thrown back stiffly. "No more *distractions*." He bit the word out. "From now on, we will only focus on the problems at hand."

I stood there, helplessly watching him close off from me, yet again. *It's for the best*, I chanted silently to myself. But my mantra felt hollow next to the blinding pain beating through my body once more.

"We must go after Jax, as soon as possible, if the trail hasn't already been washed away," I said, desperate to escape now that I'd been so foolish as to let the unthinkable happen. I'd kissed him. I'd led him to believe I'd changed my mind, and now I'd hurt him again, when so many things were already going wrong. Shame heated my neck.

"They're going to bring him here — if we give in to their demands." Damian still didn't turn to face me.

"They are?"

"The ransom dictates that they'll bring the boy back if their demands are met in the next three days."

When he didn't continue, I haltingly asked, "What do they want?"

Damian finally turned to look at me, his face carefully empty. But pain still lurked in his eyes when they met mine. "They want you."

⊰ TWELVE ⊱

THE JUNGLE SEETHED with life all around us as Rylan and I walked outside the palace wall. The morning sun was already hot on my face, and sweat trickled down my spine from the pressing humidity. Insects buzzed, and I swatted at the air around me as I searched the ground.

"Keep your eyes down and look for any sign of his abduction," I instructed.

"I know how to track someone," Rylan said, lifting an eyebrow at me. "*If* there's anything left to track, after that storm last night."

I sighed, refusing to lose hope. I had to find Jax and get him back, otherwise Damian would be forced to choose between his half brother and me. I had three days. Three days until I'd have to give myself up, or else Jax would die.

"Why don't you head that way, and I'll go this way." I forced away the terrifying worries. I couldn't afford to let them eat away at me and distract me. I had to focus. I had to find him.

"I don't know if it's a good idea to split up," Rylan disagreed. "Let's stay together for now."

I shrugged, but secretly I was glad. I hated being alone in the jungle. Even if it would have been more efficient to split up, I felt better with him by my side.

The awkwardness from last night still lingered as we walked silently around the perimeter of the palace, searching for any sign of Jax's abduction. I studied every leaf, twig, and rock for a hint of a track. The encounter with Damian was still fresh on my mind, and it took all of my control to force away the memory of his mouth on mine. General Ferraun had come in right after Damian told me the terms of the ransom letter, to discuss the attack on the villages and the missing taster, and I had excused myself, needing to get away — to *do* something.

Rylan was in the hall waiting for me. He'd been looking for me to keep his promise to go searching first thing in the morning. He didn't comment on the fact that I'd been in Damian's quarters alone; he merely asked if I was ready to look for Jax, and we'd set off.

We made it around the first half of the wall with no success, but then I skidded to a halt.

"What is it? Did you find something?" Rylan hurried back to my side, and I pointed.

"There, do you see it?"

He squinted through the blinding sunshine. "The broken branch?" He sounded cautiously excited as he spotted what I'd noticed. A few feet into the jungle, there was a thin branch that had been mostly broken but not completely torn off, hanging at just about the height of a man's arm. I carefully stepped toward it, searching the ground.

"These plants look as though they've been pressed down, even though I can't find any boot marks." I pointed down, below the branch, where the ground cover did look slightly trampled, as though multiple people had walked over it, pushing it down so hard into the soil it was impossible for it to bounce back up.

"Let's follow it for a bit, see if we can find something else."

"We're supposed to report back to Dam — I mean, the king — if we find anything," Rylan reminded me.

"Once we make sure we've actually found something, we can report back. I'm not convinced yet." I carefully pushed my way forward into the jungle, moving painfully slowly, scanning the soil and trees, the bushes, plants, and flowers for any other signs of intrusion or struggle.

I made it about fifteen feet when I caught sight of a partial boot print, nearly washed away. But there was no mistaking the tread mark, deeply pressed into the mud. The plant cover was thick here, thick enough that it had kept the rain from completely erasing the print.

"There," I said, pointing. "It has to be one of the abductors'. Who else would be traipsing through the jungle by the palace?"

"And look — a smaller print, right there." Rylan moved past the partial boot print, and I followed him to see a smaller footmark in the rich, moist soil. Just the right size for a young boy's foot to make.

"We're lucking out. They were careless to leave prints behind." I straightened up, my stomach twisted with worry for Damian's brother.

"It was dark and they were in a hurry. Maybe they figured the rain would take care of them." Rylan glanced up at the thick tree cover, which blocked out the sunlight, casting him into shadow.

"They didn't take into account that the trees might block the worst of the rain and leave evidence behind."

"Or else they don't care if they are followed."

Rylan looked at me silently, his eyes unreadable in the shade.

"Let's go give our report to the king." I turned around and headed back the way we'd come, my heart racing.

"And then what?" Rylan asked from behind me.

"Then we go after them and get Jax back."

Rylan and I walked back into the palace and headed toward Damian's office in his mother's library, where he'd been meeting with General Ferraun and some of the other high-ranking officials from the army when we left.

"What are we planning on doing if we do find Jax's abductors?" Rylan asked as we strode down the hallway. Sunlight streamed in through the windows, creating squares of light every few feet, illuminating the pale stones beneath our boots and making them practically glow. The heat was almost unbearable, even inside, and I could feel the hair around my temples and at the nape of my neck growing moist and curling.

"We'll scout them out, see what we're dealing with, and then decide. But I'm not going to make Damian choose."

"What do you mean — what choice does he have?"

I didn't answer, and Rylan grabbed my arm, forcing me to stop.

"Alex, what choice are you talking about?"

I looked into his warm brown eyes, so full of concern, and pursed my lips. "It doesn't matter. We're not going to let them dictate to us. That's why we have to find Jax — so we can regain control and stop them."

"What don't you want to tell me? What is it that they want?" Rylan's grip on my arm tightened. "Alexa, tell me!"

"It's *me*, all right?" I yanked my arm free. "They want Damian to give me to them in exchange for Jax."

Shock made Rylan's eyes widen. "*You?* Just you?"

I nodded.

"But . . . why?"

"They didn't say." I turned and continued down the hallway, striding through the swirling motes of dust visible in the rays of sunshine.

"Is he going to do it?" Rylan's voice followed me.

I paused and then kept going. "I don't know what he's going to do," I said so quietly I wasn't sure Rylan could even hear me. This morning, when Damian had told me, I'd had the same question, but he hadn't answered. He'd just stared at me wordlessly, his face a mask. And then the general had come in.

When we reached the library, the door was shut. I knocked once, firmly, but no one responded. After waiting a moment, I knocked again. When there was still no response, I cautiously cracked the door open. The curtains were drawn; the room was dark and empty.

"He's not here." I shut the door and turned to face Rylan. He stared down at me, his expression troubled. I sighed and crossed my arms over my chest. "What? I know you want to say something, so spit it out."

Rylan shifted his weight and glanced away from me. "Just . . . don't be a martyr, okay?"

"What are you talking about?"

"The reason you want to find these people — it's not so you can turn yourself in, is it?" Rylan barreled on without letting me answer, speaking in a rush. "Because I know you still care about him, even if you try to pretend you don't. And maybe you think that would be the noble thing to do — to help him get his brother back. But he needs you, too. If these people want you gone, it's because they want to make the king vulnerable."

When Rylan stopped, his chest rising and falling rapidly, I just stood there, not knowing how to respond. Finally, I shook my head. "I'm not going to turn myself in" was all I said.

The rest of his words hung between us, but after a pause, he nodded. "Good."

"But we need to find Dam — the king — so we can get permission to go after Jax and get him back, so it doesn't come down to making him choose. All right?"

Rylan nodded again. "All right."

We went back the way we came and headed up the stairs to search for Damian in his quarters. The palace was immense, and the king could be in any number of places, but I hoped since it was close to lunchtime that he might be back in his rooms, seeking time alone, as he often did before meals.

When we were halfway up the stairs, Deron rounded the corner and began making his way down.

"Oh, there you two are. Any luck?" The captain of the king's guard quickly descended to where we were and glanced between us.

"Yes, actually," I said. "We need to find the king and request permission to continue following what we think are tracks left by the abductors."

"What direction were they headed?" Deron asked.

"North," Rylan replied without hesitation.

"Toward Dansii?" Deron's eyes narrowed.

"If they continued north, then, yes, toward Dansii."

I was sure I wasn't the only one thinking about the ransom note that had come — the one written in Blevonese. "Do you know where King Damian is?" I asked. "We need to follow after them as soon as possible. They already have too big of a head start on us, and I don't want to lose the trail."

"Lady Vera asked for a tour of the palace grounds, so they could speak without an audience." Deron sounded slightly miffed.

"You sent some of the guard with him, right?" I asked, a sudden knot of unease tightening in my gut.

"No, she told the king that they needed to be alone. We were ordered to keep our distance."

My heart pounding in alarm, I turned on my heel and ran back down the stairs, without even asking my captain for permission or waiting to hear another word.

I rushed through the palace and out the first door I could find. Bursting into the sunlight, I had to stop until my eyes adjusted to the glare. I lifted a hand and quickly scanned the grounds. I heard Rylan behind me but ignored him, continuing to search for Damian and Lady Vera. I didn't know what she was trying to do, but I didn't trust her. No one asked to see the king alone and was granted their request, particularly someone from a kingdom that was most likely our enemy. Why did Damian agree to *her* request?

"Any sign of him?" Rylan caught up to me.

"No." I could hear the desperation in my own voice. "You go that way and I'll go this way, all right?" I pointed to my left, and he nodded. This time, we had to split up. We couldn't waste time sticking together. How long had they been alone? I thought of the brief, calculating look she'd shared with the man in the black and white robes at dinner the night before, and acid filled my stomach, burning as it churned.

I took off at a jog, the relentless sun bearing down on me, oppressively hot. I ran past the empty training ring toward the newly demolished breeding house and the tent city, where women, the former prisoners of the breeding house, milled around — some doing laundry in large buckets and others preparing food over a fire. A couple of women stood together, cradling babies in the protective curves of their arms, smiling at one another as they talked. Black smoke curled up lazily toward the sky. One of the women lifted an arm at me, and I paused, squinting. She handed the baby she held to a younger girl standing next to her, then started toward me. As she drew closer, I recognized Tanoori. She looked healthier, her bones no longer stood out so prominently, and her face had filled in slightly as well. In her clean dress and with her hair pulled back into a simple chignon at the nape of her neck, she looked quite pretty. It was hard to believe she was the same woman who had attacked Damian so many months ago — or the girl I'd once known in our village years before that.

"Alex, what's wrong?" Tanoori's glance strayed to my scars but quickly darted back to my eyes.

"Have you seen the king?"

Tanoori nodded. "He walked by here about ten minutes ago, heading toward the old gardens." She pointed past me, around the ruins of the breeding house to the older section of the palace where there had once been a massive garden with winding paths surrounded by large bushes. As long as I'd been at the palace, it had never been anything but a mess of weeds, unkempt bushes larger than most men, and half-strangled flowers, but I had heard stories about how gorgeous it once was — when Damian's mother was alive.

I turned to go, but Tanoori touched my arm softly. "Have you seen Eljin?" she asked me.

"No, not since last night. Why?" I didn't have time to waste talking to her, but I didn't want to brush her off rudely, either.

"He was supposed to meet me for lunch — he was going to bring a picnic. But he never came. It's not like him to forget." She glanced away, a blush staining her cheeks.

If I'd had time, I would have questioned her about her involvement with Eljin, but I had to find the king before it was too late. "I'm sorry, I haven't seen him. But if I do, I'll remind him to come find you."

Tanoori nodded and stepped back. "Sorry to keep you," she said, and I waved at her as I turned and ran toward the dilapidated gardens. When she'd asked if she could stay at the palace, Damian had given her a position as overseer for the displaced women and babies. She was in charge of keeping them fed, clothed, and taken care of, and she was surprisingly good at it.

"Good luck!" Her voice followed after me as I ran around the rubble toward the overgrown gardens. What interest could Lady Vera have in any of this? The palace grounds weren't beautiful, rather they were mostly barren, cleared to be used for functionality — for the small army barracks kept at the palace in case of a threat, for the women and babies now, for the practice rings and stables and other small utility buildings. I ran along the overgrown paths, glancing left and right, painfully aware of how easy it would be to miss them if she didn't want to be found. If she'd done something to my king —

And then I heard her voice, a soft laugh. A sound of enticement. I paused, straining to decipher what direction it had come from. The stone paths were choked with weeds, and massive, untrimmed bushes rose on either side of me. Flowers still blossomed, a riot of crimsons, deep purples, shocking pinks, vivid oranges, and more; but vines and weeds wound around the plants, smothering them. There were no extra hands to tend the garden and bring it back to its former glory, and despite the walls, the jungle was trying to reclaim it.

When I heard the laugh again, a velvet, throaty sound to my left, I spun and swiftly moved in that direction, while trying to keep my steps quiet. The paths wound and crossed, almost like a maze. The bushes grew even higher the farther in I went. Sweat dripped between my breasts and down my spine as I hurried toward my king.

When I rounded a corner and saw them standing together not more than ten feet away, I ground to a halt. Damian had his arms around Vera, and he was kissing her neck. She had her head flung back, giving him full access to her alabaster skin. I covered my mouth with my hand to smother my cry of shock. Had it just been this morning that he'd kissed me — that he'd held me so tightly in his arms and asked me why we had to stop?

My heart pounded; I could barely breathe. I had to get out of there — immediately.

I knew in that moment that I couldn't do it. If he married another, I was going to have to resign and leave. The reality of seeing him holding someone else — kissing someone else — was too much. A sharp pain stabbed through my skull; the sunlight was too bright. I stumbled back, and in my carelessness, my boot crunched on a half-broken stone.

Damian lifted his head, turning to look directly at me. Our eyes met and I froze. Lady Vera spun to look at me as well, and the triumph in her gaze was almost more than I could stand. I'd been envisioning all manner of horrible situations, but it had never occurred to me that she wanted him alone to seduce him — or that he would be so easily seduced.

"Alexa," Damian said, his voice so calm it made my head spin, "did you need something?"

Jax. You have to hold it together for Jax, I told myself, even though each breath ripped through me, and my heart felt as though it were being shredded in my chest. "I apologize for interrupting you." I made myself look to the side of them, at a particularly tall bush with large magenta flowers blooming near Damian's head. "If I might have a word with you, Your Majesty. It'll only take a moment."

"Vera, would you excuse me for just a minute?"

"Of course, if you must. But hurry back." Her voice was mellifluous, but her words felt like a command.

I turned my back on them and strode away, around the corner so she was out of sight. I kept going until we were far enough away to be out of her hearing and then stopped to wait for Damian. I squeezed my eyes shut, desperately trying to force back my emotions.

"What do you need?" His voice behind me startled me, and I hurriedly composed my face into a mask before turning to face

110

my king. The man I loved. The man who had just torn apart my heart.

He stood there in the sunlight, so tall and achingly beautiful, and seemingly unconcerned. His eyes met mine, and I couldn't see a trace of remorse or guilt in them. In fact, his face was devoid of all emotion, except, perhaps, for impatience.

"I found some tracks, Sire, and I am requesting permission to follow them." I forced myself to glance away from him. I couldn't bear to look at his eyes or his mouth and think of him holding her, staring into her eyes . . . *kissing* her. Only hours after what had happened between us in his room at dawn. This time, I had obviously hurt him too much — he'd finally decided to move on. To make me regret my decision to reject him.

It worked. The pain was nearly blinding.

"You think you've found a trail? You think you can find Jax?"

When he reached out and touched my arm, I jerked away, taking a step back. "Yes, Your Majesty."

"Alex . . . what's wrong?"

I couldn't keep myself from turning to stare up at him in open amazement — and anger. "What's *wrong*? Are you seriously asking me *what's wrong*?"

I couldn't decipher his sudden change of expression; he almost looked . . . bemused by my reaction. Did he honestly think I'd be *happy* for him to move on this quickly? Had I been that convincing in my rejection? He reached up to press his fingers to his temple, like he had a headache. I wanted to tell him that it might be his conscience pounding on his thick skull, but I snapped my mouth shut and refrained. I knew what an impressive actor he was, when he wanted to be. He was probably just trying to play on

111

my sympathy. Two could play this game, if that was what he wanted.

"Do I have permission or not, Sire?"

Damian stared at me, one eyebrow lifted over his stunning eyes. Eyes that still made my belly tighten when he looked into mine, even after my having just seen him with another woman. With that viper, Lady Vera. Anger boiled up as I thought of her entrapping him in her coils. It pulsed hot in my blood, barely under control.

"Yes, of course," Damian said. "But only if you promise to return by nightfall to give me a full report of what you find."

"As you command, Sire," I responded curtly. "I apologize again for interrupting you."

"Yes. I have to get back to her." Damian's eyes narrowed, all emotion wiped clean from his face once more. "Isn't that right, Alexa?"

I clenched my jaw, trying to keep my own riotous emotions under control. "Yes. You've made your feelings very clear. Lady Vera is waiting for you, *Your Majesty*." I spun on my heel and strode away, refusing to let him know how deeply he'd hurt me.

He called after me, but I ignored him. As soon as I knew I was out of his sight, I broke into a run, desperate to get away. To leave him and Lady Vera behind. Tears blinded me as I tripped over roots and weeds. My toe caught on a broken stone and I nearly fell. I stumbled to a halt, gasping for air past the horrible, burning pain that clawed at my chest. I was nearly out of the gardens, and I couldn't allow anyone to see me like this.

With a deep, shuddering breath, I straightened my spine and wiped at my face. I had asked for this — I'd told him no, more than once. But I supposed, in some deep corner of my heart, I'd always hoped that somehow, some way, he would know the truth of my feelings and find a way for us to be together.

Pulling back my shoulders, I stepped out of the gardens to see Rylan hurrying toward me from the other direction.

"Did you find him?" he asked, his expression panicked.

"Yes." My voice broke, and I cleared my throat and repeated myself, louder. "Yes, I found him."

"Where is he? What happened?" Rylan ground to a halt in front of me. "Have you been crying? Alexa — what's wrong?"

"No, I wasn't watching where I was going, and I got hit in the eye by a branch," I lied. "The king is fine. He gave us permission to go, but we have to be back tonight to report." I strode away from him, toward the closest gate that would release us from the palace grounds and out into the untamed jungle of Antion.

"Alexa, are you sure —"

"I'm fine!" I practically shouted. "Let's go before we waste any more time. Jax needs us, all right?"

I didn't look back to see if Rylan followed me as I left the gardens — and my shattered heart — behind us.

⊰ THIRTEEN ⊱

HOUGH THE TRACKS were few and far between, we managed to continue to find traces of the abductors' passing, along with one or two smaller prints that I was now absolutely certain belonged to Jax. The kidnappers seemed to be avoiding civilization — staying far away from the small towns and roads that had been painstakingly carved out of the underbrush, vines, and trees, keeping to the deep, lush jungle instead. As we made our slow progress through the tangled vegetation, I tried to force my mind to stay focused on tracking Jax. But over and over, the scene of Damian holding Lady Vera in his arms, his head bent forward, his lips on her skin, replayed. Despite the oppressive heat, a cold chill had taken hold of my heart, sending icy regret deep into my body. Maybe I'd been wrong to think I wasn't worthy of being his queen — surely I was a better option than Vera.

"Alexa, look," Rylan called out, startling me. We'd been trekking through the jungle for more than an hour already.

I stopped and turned to look back at him. Even in the shade of the canopy overhead, perspiration coated my skin and made my hairline damp. Rylan's tunic was dark with sweat along the collar, in between his shoulder blades and underneath the leather straps that crossed over his chest and fastened a quiver of arrows to his back. He gestured for me to look at a tree a few feet away from him. A tiny scrap of fabric hung from a branch. I stepped forward, careful to avoid a hole in the ground that was probably some creature's home, and pulled the fabric free.

It was the same material and color as one of Damian's tunics — definitely something from the palace.

"Do you think it's Jax's?"

I nodded. "It has to be. It's too big to just be an accidental snag. Maybe he tore off a piece and tossed it when they weren't paying attention, to give us a clue of where to go." *Smart boy*, I thought.

"Well, at least we know we're on the right track."

I replaced the fabric, just in case we needed help finding our way back to the palace.

For the next hour, the signs grew fewer and farther apart. The random boot prints all but disappeared, and there were no more pieces of fabric to guide us. The canopy overhead wasn't as thick here, which made it possible for the rain to have washed away all traces of their passing. I was continuing forward on instinct more than anything, and a determination not to go back to the palace without Jax. The poor boy was probably terrified. And I knew Damian was frantic with worry for his brother.

Unless Vera was doing too good a job *distracting* him.

"Alex, maybe you should slow down. We might miss something," Rylan said from behind me, but I ignored him and kept pressing forward. My stomach was churning and my eyes burned. I was glad Rylan was behind me, where he couldn't see my struggle.

I just didn't understand how Damian could do this. Why now? Why *her*? Women had thrown themselves at him for years, and he'd

115

never reciprocated. He'd claimed the reason was because of me — because he'd known my secret from the beginning and had fallen for me. But it seemed foolish of me to have believed him. If he truly loved me —

"Alex!" Rylan cried out from behind me, and before I even knew what was happening, he'd grabbed my arm and pulled me backward just as a massive snake dropped from a branch above where I'd been standing only a split second earlier. I screamed and jumped even farther back as Rylan drew his sword, ready to slice the snake open. The snake coiled its body, its head lifted, flicking its tongue out and back, over and over again. As I slowly stepped away, it lifted its head higher, preparing to strike.

"Rylan, back away," I whispered, and he inched backward along with me. I reached for the bow that was slung across my chest, pulled it over my head along with an arrow, swiftly nocked the arrow, and then let it fly. The arrow struck the snake through the mouth and out the back of its skull. It flung its head back with a horrible, strangled, hissing sound. Rylan leaped forward and finished the job with his sword, chopping the head clean off the body, and the snake fell into a lifeless heap on the ground.

My heart racing, I lowered my bow and glanced at Rylan.

"Are you all right?" My voice came out shaky. My last encounter with a snake in the jungle rose up unbidden. That time I hadn't been so lucky; the snake had taken me unaware and wrapped around my body before I'd had a chance to react. Marcel had been the one to save me then, rushing up and cutting the snake off me before it could squeeze me to death.

"I'm fine." Rylan stepped toward me, resheathing his sword. "Are you?"

I shook my head, and he reached out to take my shoulders in his hands. The tears I'd been fighting abruptly broke free, spilling over onto my cheeks. Rylan put his arms around me and held me as I cried. And I let him. I hadn't felt this weak in a long time, but I couldn't hold back the sobs.

I was so alone. My entire family was gone, and right then I missed them so much it was a physical pain, lodged in my chest. Rylan held me tightly as I cried out my hurt, my frustration, my loneliness. He ran his hand over my hair, cupping my head and holding it to his chest. The feel of his arms around me was comforting, but nothing more. I wanted to be held by Damian. I wanted him to look at me the way he had this morning before I'd told him to stop — again.

But I'd made my choice. And now he'd moved on from me.

"Alexa." Rylan's voice was quiet and low.

I lifted my head to look up at him. The gold flecks in his earnest brown eyes were more prominent today for some reason. Or maybe it was because I was standing so close to him, with our bodies touching and his arms around me, that I could see them so well.

"Thank you," I said quietly.

"Just keeping my promise."

Yet another reminder of my brother — Rylan's promise to Marcel to watch out for me and to protect me. I smiled sadly. The sudden grief on his face echoed my own. We'd both lost our brothers. We were both completely alone in this world.

Unless . . . I gave in to what he wanted and let him into my heart. We could have each other — if I let it happen. I knew how Rylan felt. As he stared down into my eyes, I could see the need that he struggled to hide from me. He wanted to kiss me — I could feel it. I *knew* it, even without looking at him.

But I couldn't do it.

Despite what I'd seen today, my heart was Damian's. Kissing Rylan would be a lie. It would only hurt him in the end. Unless there came a day when I no longer loved the king we served, nothing could happen between us. Rylan was my only true friend, and I couldn't let anything ruin that.

I gently pulled away from him, and he let go without a word.

"We'd better keep going" was all I said.

Rylan nodded, his expression guarded, but I could see the resignation in his eyes before I turned away.

We walked carefully around the dead snake, and I suppressed a shudder. Rylan stayed closer behind me now, and I didn't complain.

At least half an hour passed before I found another boot print. Reassured that my instincts were correct — that we were on the right path — we kept pressing forward. And then finally, *finally*, we heard it: the sound of voices ahead of us.

⊰ FOURTEEN ⊱

I GESTURED SILENTLY AT Rylan to flank me on the left, and we crept forward slowly, eyes and ears alert for any sign of an outer watchman who would warn the abductors of our presence. But as we made our way closer to what seemed to be a hastily set up camp, there was no sign of anyone keeping guard. They were a cocky group, if they assumed no one could track them through the jungle.

We crouched behind a large bush in the shadow of a copse of trees and peered into the camp from our hidden vantage point.

They'd found a clearing of sorts and had haphazardly set up a smattering of small tents and one larger one. In the middle of the clearing was a makeshift fire pit. Several men sat on the ground around it, talking and laughing. They wore clothing common to Antionese villagers, but I didn't recognize any of them — or their language. Though I didn't speak Blevonese, I knew what it sounded like, and these men were not speaking the language in which the ransom note had been written.

Damian was right. The kidnappers weren't Blevonese — it was a setup.

They had to be from Dansii, then. But why? What did King Armando have to gain by causing another war with Blevon? He obviously didn't want the alliance, for which Damian had sacrificed so much, to last. But to what end?

Rylan grabbed my arm and pointed silently. I followed his finger and stiffened. Jax was sitting on the ground in the shade of a tent, tied up with rope. One of the men tossed something at him, and he stared down at the ground with dismay on his familiar face. It looked like food, but he couldn't reach it with his hands tied behind his back. Anger pulsed hot through my blood as I watched Jax try to bend his body forward and eat the food off the ground like an animal. The men watching laughed and mocked him. When he finally bit into whatever it was, the closest man reached out and swiped the food from his mouth so that it rolled through the dirt and out of his reach. Jax sat back up, his shoulders sagging in defeat. Even from here, I could see how he clenched his jaw, but his thin body trembled as though he was trying to hold in sobs.

Fury strangled me, but when Rylan moved like he was about to jump up and charge into the clearing, I grabbed him and yanked him back down. He glanced at me, his eyes wide in surprise, but I shook my head and gestured for him to follow me back, away from the camp. We melted into the depths of the jungle, away from the clearing and Jax.

We had to think clearly. There were eight men visible and probably more in the tents. We were both talented fighters, but those were not the best odds, even for us. My bigger fear, though, was that Jax was in the middle of them — they could easily hurt or kill him if we tried to attack, using him as leverage to make us stop, and then they'd have captured us as well.

When we were quite a distance from the camp and well out of earshot, I whispered, "We need backup. There are too many of them to get to Jax."

"We can fight them — it's too big of a risk to leave him. They could keep going, and then we wouldn't find them again in time," Rylan argued.

"That isn't a makeshift camp for a short break. They aren't going anywhere until their demands are met — or their threat fulfilled. We have two more days. And yes, we could fight them, but what if they hurt Jax? What if they threaten him to make us stop? What then?"

Rylan stared at me in frustrated silence. "You're right. We have to get back to the palace and report to Damian," he said.

"You go."

Rylan turned to me. "By myself? And what exactly are you planning on doing?"

"I'm going to watch over Jax." I wasn't thrilled about the idea of staying in the jungle alone, but I couldn't leave the boy at the kidnappers' mercy, completely without help or hope. If something happened to him now, I could never forgive myself.

Rylan looked like he wanted to argue with me, but he clenched his jaw instead and just looked at me wordlessly for a long moment.

A bird cried in the distance, a haunting sound that echoed across the thick foliage, and I shivered. But as I thought of Jax sitting on the hard, moist ground, his arms bound behind him, being forced to eat like a dog, my fear turned to resolve. "Tell Damian that we found him but we need help — enough men to surround them and get them to surrender without a fight. Bring them back to me by morning, and I'll make sure Jax stays safe until you get back."

Rylan shook his head. "I can't let you stay here alone. It's too dangerous."

"We don't have a choice! We're outnumbered, and we're running out of time before they follow through on their threats. We *have* to split up. It's the only way to save him."

"And you," Rylan added.

We were silent for a long moment, looking at each other. Fear beat in time with my heart, but also determination. This would work — it had to. Rylan would bring help, and we would save Jax. Damian would do what it took to save his brother. And this way, I didn't have to go back to the palace yet. I didn't have to see him and face the reality of his apparent infatuation with Vera.

"Be safe," Rylan finally said, his voice so soft I could barely hear it.

"I'll be fine, Ry," I said, lifting my chin, hoping I looked braver than I felt. I couldn't let myself think about what had happened the last time I'd been alone in the jungle. My shoulder suddenly ached, a reminder of the jaguar attack that should have killed me.

Rylan blinked at his nickname — which I hadn't used in a long time — and then nodded. He reached up and let the back of his fingers trace down my cheek to my jaw. I didn't speak or move.

"All right," he said at last, letting his hand drop. "I'll bring all the help I can at first light."

"You be careful, too."

He smiled wistfully at me. "I will be."

Rylan turned and walked away from me, toward the palace. I

watched him for a long moment and then squared my shoulders and plunged back into the jungle toward the camp — and Jax.

I moved as quickly as possible, leery of the unseen dangers of the jungle. No one was here this time to save me if a predator decided to make me its next meal. Suddenly, I heard a noise behind me and spun around, expecting death to be on my heels. Instead, I got smacked in the face with a low-hanging branch. There was a chattering in a tree a few feet back, drawing my attention upward, where I saw a small black-and-white monkey clinging to a branch, watching me with enormous eyes.

Heart still pounding, I turned my back on the monkey and continued on my way. I kept hearing sounds and glanced over my shoulder to see the monkey following me, swinging from tree to tree in my wake. When I looked at it, the creature would freeze and wait for me to keep going. I tried to ignore it, hoping it would lose interest soon, but as I got closer and closer to the camp, the monkey stayed on my trail, chattering and calling after me. Unless I turned around, in which case it would stop and watch me silently.

As the sun sank lower in the sky and the jungle began to settle into the indistinct shadow of twilight, I decided I was grateful for my unlikely companion. As long as the monkey was interested in following me, it was probably safe to assume no predators were nearby.

When I was close enough to the camp to hear the men's voices, I slowed to a crawl, pulling out my sword — just in case — and melted from tree to tree, my eyes and ears tuned for any sign of a lookout. But just like last time, there was no one outside the camp keeping watch. I drew close enough to spy Jax still sitting on the ground, his head lolling to the side. The poor boy had fallen asleep sitting up. His dark hair was plastered to his forehead, damp with sweat, even though the temperature was finally cooling off with the lowering sun. The black-and-white monkey swung itself up higher into a tree near the camp, staring down at the men without a sound, his tiny face cocked to one side.

"Sure, now you're quiet," I muttered under my breath as I searched for a good spot to spend the night — somewhere safe, where I could keep an eye on Jax. I finally decided I would be safest in a tree as well, one with large branches and thick leaves, where I could sit down, hide, and maintain a good view of the camp. And as luck would have it, the best tree available was the one my furry companion had chosen. I silently sheathed my sword and crept over to the base. It was massive, with a thick trunk, branches wide enough for me to sit on, and large leaves and vines twining through it. It would be a little bit harder to see the camp through all the greenery, but it would also protect me from being spotted.

The bark scraped my hands as I grabbed the lowest limb and soundlessly pulled myself up. When I was a good twelve feet above the ground, I found a nice wide branch and decided to stop. I twisted my scabbard so that my sword hung next to me, and slung my bow across my chest, beside my quiver of arrows. I settled back against the trunk of the tree, extending my legs out in front of me. The monkey chittered softly at me from its perch a few branches up and then turned its attention back to the camp.

I did the same, searching for Jax. He was still sleeping, his chin against his chest now. A few men stood by him. I watched as they gestured to one another and at Jax, seemingly arguing about something. I could hear their voices but didn't understand their language. One of the men threw his hands up in the air and then bent down and smacked Jax across the cheek. I stifled a gasp of outrage as the boy startled awake, his eyes wide with fear and pain.

"What? What do you want?" he asked, his voice shaking with terror.

"No sleep," the man said brokenly in our language, his accent so thick he was barely understandable. "Rafe." He pointed behind himself at the biggest tent.

I started at the name — I'd heard it before. But I couldn't remember where.

After a moment, a man strode out of the tent into the dimming light. He looked vaguely familiar for some reason, but I couldn't place him. He was of medium height and build, dressed in a very fine tunic and breeches, with tall boots.

When he turned to face Jax and I got a good look at his face, I sucked in a sharp breath. He looked almost exactly like Vera — only a male version. The same shade of hair, the same mouth, even the same fluid way of moving. I wasn't close enough to see, but I guessed his eyes were the same as well. Only his nose was noticeably different, a bit more angular than hers. Her brother, then — he had to be. Possibly even her twin. My heart leaped into my throat and adrenaline coursed through my body, demanding that I *do* something. But I was trapped, unable to do anything other than watch in helpless fury and confusion as this man — Rafe — sauntered over to where Jax sat.

"No, please, not again," Jax said when Rafe crouched down so his face was level with Jax's. The boy squeezed his eyes shut and turned his face away.

Rafe grabbed Jax by the chin and yanked his face back. "Look at me, boy," he said in perfect Antionese, his voice as cloying as

Vera's but with that same thread of command underlying the soft tones. "I'm not going to hurt you. I just want to talk."

"I'm not talking to you!" Jax shouted, still keeping his eyes tightly shut. My heart pounded in my chest as I bent forward. Why was Jax afraid to look at him?

"If you don't look at me, I might have to make one of my men cut your eyelids off. Then you'll have no choice but to look into my eyes."

Jax's eyes flew open, his body trembling, and Rafe laughed.

"Much better," Vera's brother said. "Now tell me, young Jax. Who is this sorcerer that the king has working for him?"

"I . . . I don't want to —"

"Tell me," Rafe repeated, more forcefully.

"Eljin," Jax said, the fight going out of him. "His name is Eljin."

"And he's from Blevon?"

"Yes."

"Is he a black sorcerer?"

"No. They don't have any black sorcerers in Blevon."

"Ah yes," Rafe said, nodding. "Their ridiculous beliefs. I always forget about those quaint superstitions. Well, that only makes my job that much easier."

Jax tried to turn his head, but Rafe's grip on his chin tightened, keeping the boy's eyes trained on him.

"And Alexa? Is she a sorceress?"

"No," Jax said.

"What is she — how is she such a masterful fighter? How was she able to kill a black sorcerer?"

Jax tried to pull away again, but Rafe shouted, "Tell me!" and the fight went out of him again.

"Mama believes that her father was a sorcerer and that she inherited her skills from him. But mostly she just trains really hard."

I could hear the hero worship in his voice, even now, and it made something deep in my chest clench. I knew he was scared, but I wished he wouldn't answer Rafe's questions quite so readily. What else had Vera's brother gotten out of the boy?

One of the other men walked over to them, speaking rapidly in their language, and Rafe stood up with a look of irritation on his handsome face. They spoke back and forth heatedly for a moment, and then Rafe turned back to Jax.

"We'll have to continue this delightful discussion a little bit later. Someone give him some water; we can't have him dying before it's time." When no one else moved, he threw his hands up in the air and said something in their language, his irritation obvious.

One of the men ran off and brought back a small cup of water for Jax, lifting it to his lips. After Jax took a long drink, the man pulled the cup away and dumped the rest over the boy's head, drenching his hair. Indignation burned through me. I wanted so badly to go down there, to cut my way through them all and save Jax before they could hurt or humiliate him any further.

But instead, I sat stiffly on my branch, my hands balled into fists. I hoped Rylan had made it back to the palace and gotten the help we needed. "Hurry, Rylan," I whispered under my breath, as though he could somehow hear my plea from across the space between us. "Please, hurry."

I'd forgotten about the monkey until it suddenly swung down in front of me. I jumped back in shock, scaring it in the process, causing it to nearly lose its grip on the branch. The monkey clung on at the last second, but it broke a smaller shoot with its foot, causing a loud *crack*.

The activity below paused at the sound, and all eyes suddenly turned in my direction.

⤐ FIFTEEN ⤏

I FROZE, MY BLOOD pumping through my veins. The humidity and my own sharp fear made my hands slick as I clung to the bark, my heart crashing against my lungs, stealing my breath.

Rafe said something in their language, pointing at my tree, and a few of the men pulled out swords and began to stalk forward. It was dark enough that they probably couldn't see me hiding on my branch — yet. But I wasn't dressed to blend in at night; I still wore the uniform of the king's guard: a white tunic, my dark vest, breeches, and boots.

I stiffened, preparing to fight. This was it — they were going to find me, and I'd have no choice but to try and cut my way through them and get to Jax before they could do something to him. I was good, but the odds were not in my favor.

Then the monkey shocked me by dropping down another two branches and chattering loudly at the men.

They paused and started to laugh, their attention on the monkey. One of them called something over his shoulder, and Rafe shook his head, turning away with a look of disgust on his face. The soldiers resheathed their swords and walked back to camp, leaving me trembling on my branch.

The monkey swung back up toward me, pausing for a moment to look at me and then moving on, continuing to climb higher into the tree.

"Thank you," I whispered to my little friend. That monkey had probably just saved my life — and Jax's.

Rafe sat down near the fire, watching his men rush around as they prepared a late dinner. He'd occasionally say something to them, and they'd hurry to do his bidding. I wished I understood Dansiian, because I had no idea what was being said. Jax also watched them work with longing on his face as the scent of roasted meat wafted through the heavy air of night. I glanced up at the darkening sky to see clouds tumbling across the navy expanse, just as I'd predicted. To the west, there were still streaks of crimson and burnt orange, dying flames of light before the sun relinquished her throne to the lesser reign of the moon.

A commotion below me drew my attention back to the camp to see a familiar man striding toward Rafe. I squinted through the darkness, trying to figure out who he was. When he stopped in front of Rafe, the firelight danced across his face, and I realized it was Felton, Lady Vera's "runner" — who had come ahead of her to announce her arrival to King Damian. What was *he* doing here?

He said something in Dansiian as well, but Rafe replied in Antionese. "Don't speak our language. I don't need these imbeciles listening to what you have to say."

"What about the boy?" Felton switched languages, nodding at Jax.

"There's no need to worry about him." Rafe walked over to

Jax, who scrambled back and tried to turn his head away again. But just as before, Rafe grabbed his face and forced him to turn toward him. "You won't tell anyone what you hear tonight," he said forcefully. "Right, you little half blood?"

"No, I won't," Jax repeated, his voice toneless and his shoulders sagging.

Rafe gripped his face for a moment longer and then pushed him away with a grunt of disgust, sending Jax sprawling on the ground. "See? No need for concern."

Felton nodded, eyeing Jax warily as the boy struggled to right himself without the use of his hands. Outrage burned through my gut, but I forced myself to remain still, my fingers digging into the branch until I felt one of my fingernails tear on the bark.

Rafe gestured for Felton to follow him a little way out of the camp, closer to me. I stiffened, holding myself perfectly still on my branch, hoping they wouldn't look up — praying my monkey friend stayed silent.

"What news from the palace?" Rafe asked, continuing to speak in Antionese.

"The deception went off without a hitch. The palace is completely out of sorts, trying to figure out who to blame for the poisoning, while still dealing with the attacks on the outer villages. Everyone believes our taster's body has disappeared, just as you said they would."

"Of course they did. I told you the potion would work. Someday you might learn to believe me."

"Of course, my lord, of course," Felton said quickly, bowing low, almost as if he was groveling before Vera's brother. And it suddenly dawned on me: If he truly was her brother, this meant Rafe might be next in line to become the duke of Montklief, who apparently held a position of extreme power in the kingdom of Dansii. The thought sent a chill down my spine.

"You should have seen the look on the boy's face when I opened my eyes and stood up." Rafe laughed, a cruel sound, full of malice. "He's obviously never seen someone come back from the dead before."

Felton joined in with his laughter. Dismay spiraled into horror, turning my stomach sour as it all clicked into place. *Rafe* had been the taster. That's why I recognized the name but couldn't place it. He'd told me his name was Rafe, but since I'd thought him dead, I hadn't bothered to remember it. I dredged up the memory of the cowering waif of a man in the kitchen, trying to reconcile it with the person standing below me. He'd had a beard and he'd slumped his shoulders. Even his voice had been soft, subservient. Rafe was apparently as good an actor as Damian. And he'd refused to look up at me — probably because he knew I'd recognize his eyes, even if he'd disguised his face with the beard.

How did he pull it off and why? Why fake his own death? I couldn't imagine how terrified Jax must have been when Rafe had "woken up" and grabbed the boy, fleeing the palace amidst the chaos into the jungle under the cover of night. Had the kidnapping been part of the plan all along?

The memory of Damian kissing Vera made me even sicker now. Would he still hold her, gaze at her with such passion in his eyes, if he knew her brother was the one who had kidnapped Jax?

"And the king? What progress there?"

"Things started off a bit rocky, but with Alexa gone all day, Vera has been *very* successful in engaging the king's affections."

Felton sounded pleased to report this, but it made my heart turn to lead.

"*Gone?*" Rafe repeated sharply. "What do you mean, *gone?* Where is she?"

Felton backed away hastily. "I d-don't know. We assumed she was sent out on duty or searching for the boy." His voice trembled, and he stumbled back again when Rafe advanced on him.

"You *assumed?* You never assume anything!" Rafe reached out and snatched Felton's tunic, yanking him closer. "Our entire plan hinges on her."

"Yes, milord, I know. I — I will find her as soon as I return. I p-promise. Please don't punish me." Felton's begging was almost too pitiful to watch; he looked like he was at least twice Rafe's age. "She won't leave the king for long."

"You're certain of that?" Rafe still gripped Felton's tunic, making the other man tremble with fear. Why was everyone so afraid of him? He wasn't large, and he didn't seem particularly frightening. But Felton was cowering before him and stuttering like he was completely terrified.

"Y-yes, milord. It's common knowledge throughout the palace that she has feelings for the king. She rarely leaves his side."

"Until today," Rafe pointed out angrily. "And you didn't think to find out why?"

"I — I was trying to —"

"That is enough," Rafe said, his voice quiet all of a sudden, and Felton immediately fell silent. "I must know where Alexa is at all times — I can't risk losing her. In penance for your mistake . . ." Rafe trailed off for a moment, as though considering. Then, with a cruel laugh, he continued, "Ah yes, I know."

Felton shook his head violently, his eyes widening in terror, but he didn't protest.

"You will go to the fire and put your left hand in it. Leave it there until the pain is unbearable. You may then pull it back out."

Felton made a small sound of dismay, but I watched in horrified fascination as he nodded and turned toward the fire. He was actually going to *do* it? It had to be some sort of test. To see how obedient he really was.

Rafe trailed behind him, his arms crossed, watching the older man make his way to where the fire burned, red hot, the deadly flames a glowing beacon in the darkness. I bent forward on my branch, straining to see through the black night.

Felton stopped before the fire and knelt down. I watched his shoulders rise and fall once, as though he'd taken a deep breath. And then he shoved his left hand forward, straight into the flames.

I clapped my fingers over my mouth to keep from crying out in shock. Felton stiffened at first, and then his body began to shake, and still he kept his hand in the fire. After a few moments, his head flung back and he began to scream, howling in agony, and *still* he kept his hand shoved into the flames.

"Stop it!" Jax shrieked hoarsely. "Make him stop!"

But Rafe just laughed. He watched Felton's suffering and he *laughed*.

Just when his screams of agony had grown so horrible that I was considering shooting him through the head to put him out of his misery, Felton yanked his hand out of the fire and collapsed on the ground, his body convulsing. Hot acid rose in my throat as the scent of burned flesh drifted to where I balanced, staring at the scene in shocked horror. In the darkness, and from my vantage point, it was hard to see the damage, but his hand appeared black and red, probably oozing blood.

Rafe continued to laugh and then shouted something in Dansiian. The other men, who had all watched the event with rounded eyes, stiffened to alertness. One of them came forward and bent to help Felton stand. Rafe continued to speak in Dansiian as the man helped Felton into a tent. The others stared at him with terror written on their faces and then jumped into activity when he finished speaking and sat down, completely at ease.

One of them brought Rafe a plate with some sort of meat and fruit on it, which he immediately began to eat, as though nothing had happened. Another man took a tiny portion of food to Jax.

Jax was huddled into himself, tears running down his face, his shoulders trembling. When the man put the plate down in front of him, Jax turned away, ignoring it. I didn't blame him; I was so revolted after witnessing whatever it was that had just taken place, there was no way I would have been able to eat, either.

It was impossible for Felton to have done that out of blind obedience. His instinct for survival, for relief, would have overcome any desire to obey Rafe. He'd somehow been *forced* to do what Rafe told him to do.

My mind whirled, trying to piece together the puzzle. Was Rafe some sort of sorcerer? Was there a type of magic that made a person able to control others with just his words? But neither Damian nor Eljin had sensed a sorcerer in the convoy — and Rafe had been in the palace. At least in the beginning.

There had to be something else, something we were missing. He could control people somehow. That was the only answer — the only way I could explain what I'd just witnessed.

Then I remembered Jax refusing to look into his eyes, trying to turn his head away. Maybe it was a combination — his words and his eyes — that forced others to do whatever he wanted. Maybe that was why he was so sure Jax wouldn't tell anyone what he heard, because he'd commanded him not to.

Then a new thought occurred to me, one that made my blood turn to ice in my veins and my heart drop as though it had turned to stone beneath the trappings of skin and bone.

If Rafe could control someone to the degree I had just witnessed by looking into his eyes and saying a few words — what could his sister do?

The scene from the garden this morning took on new meaning to me, and sudden panic nearly overwhelmed me.

Damian. That's why he'd seemingly fallen for her so quickly.

Vera was controlling the king.

⤐ SIXTEEN ⤏

I SAT TREMBLING ON the branch for a long time after watching Felton destroy his own hand, my body thrumming with shock. That had to be the answer — the reason why she'd wanted to see him alone, so there were no witnesses when she commanded him to kiss her. Was it possible to command someone to fall in love with you? To forget your feelings for someone else?

My stomach burned from the bitterness churning in it. I had to get back to Damian. I had to warn him — to stop Vera. But how? How did I break her control over him? I didn't know if it was even possible. And that would also mean leaving Jax here, completely alone with a madman.

Everything inside of me felt clenched, seeking rebellion against my helplessness. Suddenly, I remembered the soldiers who had shown up at the palace and attacked Damian. The strange emptiness in their eyes and how confused the man had been just before he died.

It was beginning to make sense now — though I still didn't understand what they were hoping to accomplish. That had to have been Rafe's work — he'd sent them and forced them to attack us, and they hadn't been able to stop, or even realize what they were doing, until they were dying. He was definitely framing Blevon. But the biggest question was *why*.

If I left Jax to try and save Damian, would they keep him safe? Or would Rafe turn his malice on the boy?

Damian still had until sunrise a day from now to turn me in and get Jax back. They couldn't kill him before then, I reasoned. But with a sickening twist in my gut, I realized that alive didn't necessarily mean unharmed. Rafe had laughed at Felton's agony. He'd found amusement — even satisfaction — in making his own man suffer. What if he turned that malevolence on Jax?

Impossible choices. Rush through the jungle in the dead of night and try to save my king — the man I loved — or stay here to watch over and protect his brother?

Below me, the camp slowly fell into silence. A while later, Felton reemerged from the tent with his hand bandaged, his face pale and a sheen of perspiration on his skin. Rafe walked up to him and said something too quiet for me to hear. Felton nodded and bowed, keeping his eyes lowered. And then he turned and walked away from the camp, into the darkness, back toward the palace.

My heart thudded in my chest, pushing my blood in galloping leaps through my body. Feeling as though I were being torn apart inside, I finally made my choice and sat up tall on the branch. When Felton had passed my hiding spot and disappeared into the dark depths of the jungle, I silently swung down from my perch, descending as quickly as possible.

I'd almost made it to the ground when I miscalculated where the last branch was and slipped. I tried to grab something — anything — to stop my fall, but my hands scraped along the bark without gaining purchase, and I hit the ground with a thud.

I sat there frozen for a split second, hoping no one had heard the noise of my fall.

Someone shouted in Dansiian from behind me, and I leaped to my feet, ignoring the pain in my body to rush away from the camp into the darkness without looking back. My monkey friend chattered loudly from the tree at my pursuers, and I silently said good-bye to the creature as I plunged into the inky depths of the jungle.

Just then the clouds that had been converging above me decided to unleash a deluge of water. Rain pounded down on the thick foliage, drenching me in a matter of seconds as I stumbled over roots and rocks in my desperation to catch Felton — and to escape Rafe's men. I could hear Felton ahead of me, but I could also hear men from behind, coming for me.

Shouts reverberated through the torrent of water, the sound muted by the noise of the driving rain. Lightning lanced above the canopy, illuminating the jungle in a blinding burst of light, and then thunder tore apart the earth, so close it trembled through my body, filling my ears and head so that in the seconds following the boom, I couldn't hear a thing except deafened silence.

My hearing returned seconds before I realized someone was directly behind me. I yanked out my sword and spun around just in time to parry a blow aimed at my shoulder. My sword collided with another in a resounding crash. I caught a small glimpse of my attacker before I twisted away and swung my sword in an arc, so fast he couldn't block me in time, and I sliced it cleanly through his side, sending him toppling to the wet ground.

I gripped the hilt tightly, my hands made slick by the rain, and squinted into the darkness to see another man headed right for me, with three more on his tail. Lightning flashed again, not as close this time, as I charged forward, my sword an extension of my fury and desperation. I was outnumbered, but I didn't care. I wouldn't let them stop me. I had too many people counting on me — too many I had to save — to let these nameless soldiers strike me down and leave me for dead in the middle of the jungle.

As I moved and moved again, turning and spinning, my blade colliding and striking, a surge of something filled my body. Strength — awareness — *power.* I spun and twisted, lunged and blocked and parried in a blur of motion. Over and over, the sound of sword hitting sword echoed through the jungle, and then sword on flesh. Again. And again. My blood surged through my body, hot with fear, with anger. I wouldn't let them stop me — I *couldn't.* I needed to get to Damian. I had to save him, before it was too late.

When the next bolt of lightning struck, it illuminated five bodies on the ground and no one else coming for me. I stood there, my sword lifted, my chest heaving, the rain pouring down my hair and face, waiting. Waiting. There were more men than this in that camp. Had Rafe remained behind with them? Was anyone else coming?

And then I heard slow clapping coming from the depths of the jungle, over the dull roar of the rain.

"I have to admit, that was even more impressive than expected, Alexa," a voice sounded from nearby, concealed in the darkness. "I know it is you."

"And I've seen what you can do," I shouted back.

Rafe's laughter turned my blood cold. "Then you will make the right decision, I hope, and turn yourself in to me before anyone else gets hurt."

My sword shook in my trembling hands as I spun to face the direction of his voice, but he remained hidden. The rain continued to fall, rushing over my eyes and obscuring my vision, but I didn't dare lift a hand to wipe my face.

"I will do it — I will turn myself in to you. But not yet."

"Would you have me kill the boy now, then? I can make it very . . . interesting."

His threat hit home — I knew he meant it. But somehow I had to figure out a way to get back to Damian first and then save Jax. If I went with Rafe now, there would be no hope for any of us. I remembered Damian asking me if it was better for one man to die than to let an entire kingdom perish. He'd been thinking of me then — I wondered what his answer would be if he knew the life in the balance was his brother's.

"You gave Damian until dawn, a day from now, to give me up in exchange for Jax's life."

"I see no need to wait when you so obligingly came to me early." His voice was closer now, and I gripped my sword more tightly, lifting it up higher in preparation for another attack.

"I didn't come here alone," I replied, thinking quickly. "I sent the other guard back to the palace to report on you. He'll return here with a battalion of the army to annihilate you and bring Jax back alive to Damian."

"How kind of you to warn me. I'll be sure to vacate the area immediately."

"There is nowhere you can hide that's close enough to make the exchange where they won't be able to find you. And then your plan will fail. You don't know the jungle like we do," I continued, squinting through the darkness and rain. "You will never capture me right now, and you can't get close enough to play your mind games on me. You'd be dead before you tried."

"I have eight more men waiting for my signal to attack," Rafe said, amused.

"And I will kill them all. You saw what I did to the five who were unwise enough to challenge me." I gestured to the bodies littering the ground. "I may not understand the power you wield entirely, but I can guarantee that you can't comprehend the power *I* wield. Do not underestimate me. You will never succeed in taking me by force."

There was silence for a long moment as he considered my words. My bluff. I prayed he wouldn't hear the lie in my voice.

"What is it that you propose, then, my dear? You seem to care for this boy; as I said, I could just kill him if you don't turn yourself in to me right now."

"Let me go — for now. Save your men's lives, rather than wasting them on an ill-fated attempt to bring me in by force, and I promise to turn myself in to you by dawn a day from now in exchange for Jax's life."

His laughter sounded again, making me shiver. "Do you think me stupid? Let you go, so that you can be at the head of the battalion you've already admitted is coming for me and my men? I think not."

My mind churned, seeking a solution — an escape. Then an idea — a horrible, desperate idea — occurred to me. "Your ability,

142

the way you can command others and tell them what to do . . . can anyone resist it?"

"No." His answer was quick and firm.

"But if your demands are met, is the person free from your command?"

A pause, then musingly, "Yes. Depending on how I phrase the command."

I stared into the jungle, where he stood somewhere, watching me. I was bargaining with a demon, and my entire body shook with fear from the offer I was about to make. But it was my only hope to save both Jax and Damian. "Use your power, then, and command Jax to die if I haven't turned myself in by dawn a day from now — command his heart to stop if I break my oath. I love him as if he were my own brother. I won't let him die. You'll have your guarantee that I'll return. And then he will be free to go — and free of your control."

Silence again and then: "I like the way your mind works, but that's unfortunately the one command no one can follow. I can't command someone's heart to just stop. I could kill him myself, but that's so *boring*. Plus I already threatened that." He paused. "I'll tell you what. You want me to let you walk away right now? Here's *my* offer."

The rain poured over me, rushing down my face like tears as I held my breath.

"In exchange for letting you walk away, I'm going to go back to camp right now and command *Jax* to kill *himself* if you don't give yourself up to us."

I gasped, horror coursing through me, but he wasn't done.

"And, I'm going to make it even more interesting. I will also tell him to kill himself if I'm captured or harmed in any way when you return. And the same goes for if you harm or kill my sister, Vera. So you might want to rethink your little plan of rushing back there to stop her and bringing an entire battalion back with you. There's nothing you can do to protect your king now, but by all means, if you agree to my offer, you're welcome to try." His voice was mocking, hinging on laughter as he finished. "My guess is that he'll be the one to bring you to me, with Vera at his side."

My blood ran cold, pulsing through my limbs, my torso, my heart, turning me to ice. It was one thing to let him take Jax's life — but to force the boy to do it to *himself*? What had I done?

"Answer me or my offer is rescinded. Do we have a deal?"

I stared blindly into the night. Terror, as sharp and hopeless as my future, stabbed through me. But I'd left myself no choice.

"Deal," I said, so softly my voice was barely above a whisper.

"Then you are free to go, but you'd better hurry back or else Jax will only be the first to die."

The rain blinded me as I turned and fled, diving into the protection of the jungle. Desperation burned in my chest as I pushed bushes and trees and vines out of my way, cutting my face, my arms, and my hands. It didn't matter. None of it mattered. My life was forfeit — I was now Rafe's.

My only hope was that I could save Damian first, before I had to turn myself in to save his brother.

⊰ SEVENTEEN ⊱

I CAUGHT UP TO Felton shortly after leaving Rafe and my ill-fated promise behind. Rather than confronting him as I'd originally planned on doing, I stayed far enough behind to keep him from realizing I was following him back to the palace. I let him guide me through the dark, wet jungle. My emotions were a tangled mess. I'd bluffed my way out of immediate capture — I'd led Rafe to believe I wielded power that I didn't. And now I had to return to him and turn myself in, or else Jax would die an even more horrible death. I'd bought myself time, and I could only hope it was enough to save Damian from Vera's grasp.

The storm finally blew itself out just before the looming palace wall came into view. The tumultuous clouds slowly broke apart to reveal the pale light of the moon as I waited to see how Felton would reenter the palace.

He walked up to one of the smaller doors in the wall and tapped lightly on it three times with his good hand — one long, then two short beats. It took a moment, and then the door cracked open. I couldn't hear what was said, but before I knew it, Felton was admitted back into the palace grounds, and the door was shut and locked again. I hadn't gotten a good look, but I was pretty sure the man who had let him in was wearing the uniform of an

Antionese soldier. Not one of Vera's men, then. Did that mean she had control of the entire perimeter guard already? Or just one key person? Would she have told them to not let me in, or would I be able to reenter the palace unharmed?

My head ached as I crouched in my hiding spot, trying to piece together what I knew so far of Rafe and his sister, how to get to the king in time, and how to go about breaking Vera's control over Damian. From what I'd seen, the only way to put a stop to one of their commands was to kill the person under their spell, or to fulfill the demands. But there wouldn't be a demand in Damian's case — not that I could think of. And there was no way I could kill him to break her control. And now I couldn't hurt or kill her, either, without causing Jax to die as well. What was I going to do?

The memory of him holding her, kissing her, in the garden sprang back up, stabbing through my heart. Even though I was sure now that he'd been forced, it still hurt to think of Damian holding another woman — to imagine him kissing her, telling her he loved *her*, not me.

I stood up suddenly, forcing my fears away. I didn't have time to waste, sitting here wallowing in self-pity. I had to go find him and do the best I could to break the spell she had cast over him, if that's what it even was. Maybe Eljin could help us. I'd find him next, if I couldn't figure out how to help Damian on my own.

I finally decided the only way to get to him was to take my chances with the perimeter guard. Hopefully, they hadn't been commanded to keep anyone loyal to Antion out.

I walked up to the gate and pounded on the door and then waited for the perimeter guard to open it and peer out at me.

"What are you waiting for?" I asked when he didn't immediately pull the door open, my stomach sinking. "Let me in!"

"No one comes or goes in the night unless you know the phrase," the perimeter guard said gruffly. He looked about twice my age, but not particularly large. Only an inch or two taller than me.

"I'm a member of King Damian's personal guard, and I order you to open this gate right now," I said, reaching for my sword.

The man stiffened, and I noticed him make a small gesture behind his back. When he looked back into my eyes, the expression on his face had turned into that awful blankness that made my blood run cold. Apparently, I'd given him the wrong answer. He'd been fine — normal — until then.

"By commission of King Damian, I place you under arrest and command you to surrender your weapons at once," the man said, pulling out his sword and lifting it up, prepared to fight me.

My heart beat harder in my chest as I pulled out my own sword. I didn't want to fight my own men. Vera had done this — she'd somehow put this man under her spell. How much of the palace and army was already in her power? Fear for Rylan twisted my gut, but I couldn't let myself wonder if he was all right or what might have happened to him and the other guards if Vera had control of the palace.

"You don't want to do this," I warned the man.

"If you resist arrest, I have been authorized to bring you to the prison by force."

There was no way I was ever going back there, but I didn't want to kill this man, either. He opened the door wider and charged at me, lifting his sword. I easily deflected him but was

147

momentarily distracted by the sight of four more men standing inside the palace wall, swords raised, apparently ready to fight me if I got past the first one.

I felt him coming up on my left and spun around to parry another blow. He wasn't aiming to kill me — yet. With a sigh, I fought back, careful not to hurt him while still trying to protect myself. Finally, I saw my opening and was able to hit him in the side of the head with the butt of my sword, knocking him out.

Once he'd collapsed, I turned to see the other four men rushing at me.

"Remember to keep her alive!" one of them shouted, just before they reached me.

One on four, when I was trying very hard not to severely injure or kill any of them, was much more difficult than one on five when I was willing to do whatever it took to save myself. I spun and twisted, trying to deflect their hits, while refusing to cut them back, but there were too many. If I wanted to avoid injury or capture, I had to fight better than this. I had to be willing to hurt them, or else they were going to succeed in taking me to the dungeons, leaving Damian and the entire palace to Vera's control.

With a silent apology to these men, who were not in their right minds, I tightened my grip on my sword and began to attack. I was careful to land my blows on nonvital parts of their bodies, but I was a sudden flurry of flashing blade and barely controlled fury. The men were shocked and unprepared for my ability, as if Vera's mind control had somehow made them forget who I was and what I was capable of.

I disabled two of them in moments, slicing through their sword arms, just enough to make them unable to continue fighting me, but not so deeply that they wouldn't heal. But as I turned to the third, angling my sword to cut through his thigh and temporarily cripple him, I momentarily lost track of the fourth man. Just as I deflected the third man's jab and twisted my blade so that it bit into his leg, fire exploded along my back. Instinctively, I rolled away from the blow, inadvertently driving my sword deeper into the third man's leg so that it severed his artery. He dropped to the ground with a scream, clutching his thigh, which was now bleeding uncontrollably.

I spun to face the fourth man, whose blade glistened with my blood.

"Surrender now or face the penalty," he said, staring at me with empty eyes.

"I can't," I replied. "I'm sorry."

Ignoring the pain in my back, I lifted my sword one last time. I'd noticed that he favored his right side, and I lunged at him, making him think his weakness was my target. He raised his sword to deflect me, but at the last second I twisted and caught him unprepared on the left side. I barely nicked his arm, but he reacted to the pain as I expected he would, by recoiling, and I took my opening to then knock his sword free from his right hand and hit him in the temple with the butt of my sword, knocking him out as well.

The throbbing in my back nearly took my breath away, making me wonder just how deeply he'd cut me. Then I surveyed the men on the ground: two knocked out; two wounded, their arms useless, and avoiding my eyes, probably hoping I didn't do anything else to them; and one pale from blood loss, nearly dead already.

I reached around to touch my back hesitantly and felt a deep gouge in the middle of my rib cage. It went down to my spine but luckily hadn't gone through my nerves and bone. I could still walk and move and breathe, even if it hurt so much that I was shaking. My hand came away coated in the warmth of my own blood.

The man on the ground clutching his leg looked up at me, his eyes clear now that death was upon him. "Stop her," he whispered, his voice unsteady. "Alexa . . . you . . . you have to . . ." A shudder overtook him, and his voice dropped off. His grip on his leg relaxed as his eyes closed. He took one last gasping breath and then succumbed to the blood loss. My eyes burned as I stared down at his unmoving body.

I'd killed one of my own men.

Because of Vera. She'd *forced* this upon us. Upon me.

I turned away with a gasp, fighting the urge to fall to my knees and vomit.

Pain shot through my body with each step I took away from the perimeter guards, past the palace wall, and onto the grounds. I had to get to Damian, but now I was afraid of what else I'd find — or who else would try to stop me. Ignoring the throbbing in my back, I clutched my sword and stuck to the shadows, slipping silently forward. Two men were jogging toward the gate where I'd come in, probably drawn to the sounds of fighting. But they were too late; I'd already made it in.

I had to hurry, though, if I didn't want to fight them, too. Soon enough, the call would be sounded, and every guard and soldier on duty would be looking for me. How many of them were under Vera's control? Was it the entire palace already?

Rather than going toward the main entrance to the palace, I slipped toward the tent city of displaced women and children, where Tanoori was. I was beginning to feel light-headed but fought the spiraling weakness as I inched my way to the tents, hoping, praying that these women had escaped Vera's notice. Somewhere past me, there was a whimper, and I heard the low tones of a woman soothing a child. Just when I reached the tent, a shout came from the wall behind me. I parted the flaps of the tent closest to me and slipped into the darkness.

"Who's there?" a woman asked softly, her voice trembling with fear.

"It's Alexa," I said, risking honesty to try and appease her fear. I'm sure I made quite a sight, showing up in the middle of the night, in my bloody uniform, holding a stained sword. "The king's guard."

"Alexa," someone else breathed. "Oh, thank the heavens above. Go, fetch Tanoori, quickly."

The first woman hurried to stand up and slipped past me, out into the dark night, like a ghost in her white nightgown.

I could hear more shouts in the distance. In moments, the palace grounds would be crawling with men searching for me.

"I'm hurt," I said softly. "But I have to get to the king."

The second woman had stood up, and she gently took my arm and led me deeper into the tent. "Here, sit."

As my eyes adjusted to the darkness, I was able to see the long braid of her hair and the pale cast to her skin. She reached for my arm and assisted me to the ground.

"Let me wrap this for you," she murmured quietly, not quite meeting my eyes. For some reason, she seemed familiar to me. She lifted the hem of her nightgown, and without a second thought, tore it into a long strip. "It's hard to tell in the dark, but this wound looks fairly deep. You're going to need to see the healer."

"Is she still here?" My question had a double meaning — was Lisbet still at the palace and was she still in her own mind, or under Vera's control?

"Tanoori will be able to answer your question better than I. We only hear whispers out here, but she still goes to the palace daily."

She had me lift my arm slightly so she could bind my back. I had to grit my teeth against the pull of my own flesh and the searing pain that shot through my body. Air hissed between my teeth as she quickly wound the material tightly around my torso. Once she'd bound my wound, she tied the bandage off and rocked back on her heels to finally look me in the face.

When her eyes met mine, that's when I knew — when I remembered. I inhaled sharply, which pulled at my new binding and sent a jab of pain through me. Breathing more shallowly, I searched for the words, for anything I could say to right the wrong I'd caused her. My mouth opened and then closed silently.

Her expression softened, as if she knew my thoughts, and she reached out to gently touch my knee. "It's all right. I know you didn't have a choice."

I shook my head. She was one of the girls Iker had made Marcel and me lead into the breeding house all those months ago — the one who'd tried to lie about her monthly courses and avoid the horrific fate awaiting her there. "It doesn't matter; I shouldn't have done it. I should have done whatever it took to save you. All of you."

"You did," she said, her voice quiet and full of an infinite sadness I could probably never fully understand. "You did save us, Alexa. I admit that I hated you. I hated *everyone* that was a part of that night. But once we found out the truth — that you were a woman in hiding — I realized there was nothing different you could have done then, except reveal yourself and get thrown in there with us. But what you *did* do freed us all in the end." Her hand tightened on my leg and her eyes shone with withheld tears. "We are all indebted to you."

"Which is why we will do whatever it takes to help you," a different woman said from the opening in the tent, her voice just above a whisper.

I looked up to see another rail-thin girl, who couldn't have been older than sixteen, entering with Tanoori right behind her. They hurried to close the tent flaps and then sat down next to us on the ground.

"The perimeter guards are calling together a full-scale search," Tanoori reported quietly, looking directly at me, her sharp gaze questioning. "What happened?"

I sighed. "I'm sure you're aware of the delegation from Dansii that arrived at the palace this week." I kept my voice to a whisper but spoke quickly. Time was short; I had to somehow make it to the palace and to Damian before Vera was alerted to my presence — if she hadn't already heard. "The woman who came must be some sort of sorceress that we haven't encountered before. She can control others by looking into their eyes and telling them what to do. She's turned the guard against me — they tried to arrest me, and when I refused to come willingly, they attacked me."

153

Tanoori blanched in the darkness of the tent. "We knew something was wrong but weren't sure what yet. She can't be a sorceress, though — Eljin would have known, and he hasn't sensed any magic in her blood."

"I don't know what she is, but she has power. That's all I know. And I have to try to stop her. I only have one day."

"Why?" Tanoori asked.

I couldn't bring myself to answer her. Instead, I slowly climbed back to my feet. The other girls quickly did the same. "I have to get into the palace right away."

"But how? The grounds are crawling with men by now, and if Vera's control has reached the perimeter guard, she probably has most of the palace under her control as well," Tanoori whispered.

My mind whirled, scrambling for an answer. And then it hit me — the old gardens, where Vera and Damian had been kissing yesterday. "The queen's old gardens are near the oldest section of the palace, right?"

"Yes," Tanoori said, her face suddenly lighting up. "And that's where Lisbet is hiding."

"She's hiding?"

"I told you we all knew something was wrong — we just weren't sure what. After Jax was taken, she and Eljin went into hiding. I can show you where they are. And if we can make it to the gardens without being seen, we should be able to get into the palace without a problem."

I nodded. This could work. It had to. And if I could make it to them, Lisbet could show me where the secret passage was that Jax used all those months ago when he delivered Damian's fake message to himself, when he was testing my loyalty. It would take me into the outer chamber of his rooms. My heart beat faster as I headed for the flap.

"Wait, you can't go out there like that." Tanoori grabbed my arm, stopping me. "Anyone who sees you will immediately know who you are."

"What do you suggest?" I whispered back impatiently. Every minute wasted was one minute closer to Vera discovering I was back and heading for the king.

"Here, put this on." The girl who had bound my back — the one who had torn her nightgown to help me — now lifted her nightgown over her head, leaving her in only a thin shift. "Put this on. Then if anyone sees you, they'll think you're one of us."

"Thank you . . ." I trailed off as I took the gown from her outstretched hands, grimacing when I realized I didn't even know her name.

"Lenora." She smiled at me. "My name is Lenora."

"Thank you, Lenora."

"Here, let's hurry and get this on you." Tanoori helped me pull the nightgown over my uniform; there wasn't time to completely change, and my back prevented me from doing it by myself. As it was, I had to clamp my teeth when I lifted my arms to let her guide the sleeves over my hands. "You need to take off your sword. It shows beneath this."

"I can't leave it here — I'll be completely unarmed," I protested. "We'll just have to hope no one comes close enough to notice."

Tanoori looked like she wanted to argue with me, but instead she closed her mouth and shook her head as she finished pulling the skirt of the nightgown over my scabbard and sword.

"Here, maybe this will help." I twisted the scabbard so that my sword lay in front of my body, instead of to the side. It would make it harder to draw if I needed to fight, but considering it was under a nightgown, I would have a hard time getting it out no matter where it was hanging.

"That'll have to do." Tanoori reached up to my hair and undid the braid, running her fingers through it until it fell in messy waves around my face. "All right, let's go. And if anyone approaches us, let me do the talking, all right?"

With my heart in my throat, I agreed and followed her out of the relative safety of the tent and into the dark night once more.

⇥ EIGHTEEN ⇤

ANOORI MOVED SWIFTLY and silently through the tents. I hurried after her, until the tangled, unkempt gardens rose into view before us. I kept glancing over my shoulder but hadn't seen anyone else yet.

"Stop doing that," Tanoori hissed under her breath. "You look guilty, like you expect someone to be coming for you."

"I *do* expect someone to be coming for me," I responded in a whisper.

"Not if you are just a displaced woman on an errand to the palace."

She paused, giving me a sharp look, and I nodded. She had a point. I was sufficiently chastened to realize my friend, who had no training whatsoever, was thinking more clearly than I was at the moment. It was the blood loss, I reasoned.

When we reached the end of the tents, Tanoori and I both paused, glancing surreptitiously toward the palace.

A shout from behind us made me jump.

"Everyone up! If you're indecent, cover up quickly. This is a mandatory search!"

Tanoori and I stared at each other for a moment of frozen panic. She turned and began to run toward the gardens. *So much for being secretive*, I thought, and then dashed after her. A baby began to cry somewhere nearby, in one of the tents, and I hoped the sound would mask any noise we were making.

We were at the far end of the tents, and there were so many of them, the guards hadn't noticed us — yet. We ran as fast we could, but as the pain in my back escalated, making me short of breath, Tanoori began to outdistance me. I tried to ignore it and push on, but I could feel myself slowing, falling behind. The gardens were close, so close. If I could just get within their darkened wings before the guards noticed two women in white nightgowns fleeing in the middle of the night, we'd be safe. I knew it.

Tanoori made it before me, her ghostly figure disappearing into the depths of the overgrown foliage, hiding her from sight. My sword clanged against my legs, threatening to trip me, as I ran as hard as I could.

"You there! Halt!"

The shout came from much too close behind me, making my blood run cold. I didn't even pause to look back. The gardens were so close. I was almost there. Almost to safety.

But if he followed me . . . what then?

"I said halt!" The soldier shouted even louder this time.

Almost there, almost there, I chanted, and then, finally, I reached the border of massive, untrimmed bushes that lined the outer edge of the gardens. I ran past them, hoping I'd disappear as completely as Tanoori had to me. I didn't stop, even when I noticed her standing a few feet in, waiting for me.

"He was yelling at you," she said as she grabbed my arm and began to run alongside me, deeper into the winding, twisting paths of the garden. In the nighttime, the bushes, trees, and overgrown flowers turned into ominous masses, crouching low or hanging overhead, closing in on us. Touching, grabbing, hindering, with leafy hands and thorny nails. I ran forward blindly, hardly knowing where I was going, except away from the man who would keep me from reaching Damian.

"Alexa, stop!" Tanoori yanked on my arm at last and forced me to grind to a halt.

I stared at her with wide, panicked eyes, gasping for air. Perspiration coated my face and neck, partially from the hot night and partially from the pain that pulsed an agonizing beat with each pump of my heart.

"You have to go that way — it'll take you to an entrance to the old section of the palace." Tanoori pointed down a path that I'd run right past. "Lisbet is hiding in a room on the main floor." Above the foliage loomed the most ancient wing of the palace, hulking and dark. Abandoned — I hoped.

"Aren't you coming with me?"

"They only saw one girl run into the gardens, right?"

"Yes."

Tanoori set her jaw. I shook my head when I realized what she meant to do, but she barreled on before I could protest.

"I'll go back and tell them I was frightened. That I'm scared of men because of what I've been through and so I fled."

"Tanoori, no. I can't let you risk yourself like this."

Her grip on my arm tightened, and I saw a steely resolve in her eyes. "Alexa, I'll be fine. They don't have orders to arrest a helpless survivor from the breeding house."

"But you're not a helpless survivor —"

"There's a lot you don't know about me, Alexa." She cut me

off. "You weren't the only orphan in that village after the sorcerer came."

I stared into her eyes — her beautiful, haunted eyes, at the well of pain and hurt that I'd noticed before but never understood until now, in a sharp, horrifying moment of clarity. "No," I whispered. "You were with the Insurgi. You . . . you were . . ."

"I was barren. I couldn't breed for his army, so after three years, they threw me out to die. But Borracio found me first."

"*No*," I breathed. "Tanoori, I didn't —"

"I know," she interrupted, her voice urgent.

In the distance, the sound of the man's shout echoed through the gardens. He was coming for us. For me.

"Go, Alexa. I'll be fine. You have to stop her. Save the king, and stop being so stubborn already."

"What do you —"

"GO!" She pushed me away, and I turned to flee down the path, my heart in my throat, and my stomach full of lead.

Tanoori had been a prisoner in the breeding house. All those years that I'd trained and perfected my fighting and earned my spot on the prince's guard, she'd been there. Until they threw her out to die, like a useless animal.

As I ran through the gardens, her anger at the king and the prince, her bitterness, how starved she'd looked when I'd first seen her again, and the alternating defeat and wildness about her suddenly all made sense. And her hatred for me. I'd escaped her fate and didn't even realize it.

And now she was risking herself to help me — again.

I burst out of the garden and found myself directly in front of the palace. I immediately froze, looking for more guards. There

160

was no one there, at least that I could see. I was still careful to slip from shadow to shadow, until I reached the door Tanoori had said would be there.

It opened silently, as though the hinges had recently been oiled, and I hurried into the pitch-dark palace, shutting the door behind me.

My heart pounded a drumbeat as I stood, leaning against the surprisingly cool stone of the wall, trying to catch my breath. My entire torso was a mass of pain, fire, and agony, pulsing along with my blood. I was pretty sure my binding had soaked through, and I was probably now bleeding onto the rest of Lenora's nightgown.

Slowly, my eyes adjusted to the dark, and I felt my way forward. I wondered if Lisbet was in the same room as before, when Damian had first brought me here. If so, I just needed to figure out where exactly I was and then go find her.

The entrance had brought me into a small corridor with doors on either side. I ignored them and headed forward, into what I was pretty sure was the main hallway that led to the rooms where Lisbet had been hiding before. Just like last time, the darkness in this wing of the palace was thick, pulsating like a living thing, its hot breath pressing in on me. I inhaled shallowly, trying not to let my terror get the better of me. The last time I'd come here, I'd sensed someone was following us — and I'd been right. Iker had been hiding in the shadows that night. Did tonight conceal an even more formidable adversary? It was hard to imagine anyone being more frightening than Iker, but Vera's and Rafe's ability to control other people made them worse, because they could turn even my friends into mindless enemies with a look and a word.

The whole palace was probably out for my blood by now.

Damian might even wish me dead, if she told him to feel that way.

Suddenly chilled, I quickened my pace. I had to find Lisbet *now*.

When my surroundings began to look a bit more familiar, I started trying doors. They all opened to reveal dusty, empty rooms. But finally, I tried one that was locked. It had to be hers.

Knocking softly, I stood back and waited. I couldn't stop myself from trembling — from exhaustion, from the wound in my back, from the devastation of Tanoori's admission, from my own fears. There was no answer. I tried again, knocking a bit louder this time, even though the noise made me cringe and glance over my shoulder, half expecting to see the palace guards coming for me with torches lit and arrows aimed at my heart.

Finally, finally, the door inched open. Then it swung wide to reveal Eljin standing there, holding a lit lantern, his eyes wide above his mask. He grabbed my arm and pulled me in, swiftly shutting the door behind me again.

"Where have you been?" he asked, his voice quiet but accusing.

I shook my head, the enormity of our situation suddenly overwhelming me and choking my words.

"She's injured," Lisbet pronounced from behind her nephew. The smaller woman walked around him and took my hand in hers. "Come, let me see what I can do for you. Then you can tell us what's happened."

I let her lead me to the bed, where she helped me lie down on my stomach, on top of my sword. I didn't even care that the scabbard bit into my stomach and legs. I was lying down, Lisbet was here — she was herself — and she was going to heal me.

"Fetch my basket," she instructed Eljin. I heard the sounds of both of them moving through the room and then felt her lift the nightgown, and the next noise was that of scissors biting through the material.

"It wasn't mine," I said.

"It was ruined anyway." Lisbet continued to cut the nightgown off, until it fell into pieces beneath me. Then I felt her tug at the binding Lenora had made around my back, cutting it away, and my ruined tunic beneath as well, to reveal my wound. She whistled softly.

"Alexa, what happened?" Eljin asked. "Where have you been?"

"Keep it down so I can focus," Lisbet admonished him.

"I found a trail left by the kidnappers and followed it with Rylan. Didn't he come and tell you?" I lifted my head slightly, but I couldn't see her. "We found him, Lisbet. We found Jax."

Her hands went still on my body; I could feel them trembling against my skin.

"And . . . is he . . . did they . . ."

"He's alive. For now. But I have to be back there before dawn tomorrow, or they will kill him."

"What do you mean?"

"I have to turn myself in. My life for his."

There was silence for a long moment, and then Eljin said, "You can't turn yourself in."

"I can't let him die, either!"

No one said anything, and then I heard Lisbet try to stifle a sob. "Yes. You can. You can't leave — you have to stop Vera. You're the only one left who can. You and Eljin together."

163

"I'm not going to let him die, Lisbet." I sat back up, even though my vision tunneled into hazy darkness for a moment. "I made a promise, and I will keep it. I have to get to Damian first, though. Can you heal me enough to get by? I have to find him before the sun comes up."

"You only have an hour, if that, before dawn," Eljin said.

"I can't do much in such a short amount of time." Lisbet looked into my face, her eyes full of pain and hope, emotions that tore at my heart.

"Do what you can," I instructed, lying back down. "And I will do what I can."

As she worked, I quietly relayed what I'd discovered in the jungle, at Rafe's camp, leaving out some of the details to spare Lisbet.

"So it is Dansii behind the attacks, as I thought," Eljin said when I was finished.

"Yes. It would seem so."

"I told you that there are no black sorcerers in Blevon."

We were silent for a long moment. "Eljin," I finally said, "you need to at least explain to Damian and General Ferraun why you are so sure. We'll need every bit of proof we can get that Blevon isn't to blame, so everyone will support us in whatever we must do to stop Dansii."

"You don't think sending some sort of sorcerer and sorceress we've never encountered before to put the king under their control is proof enough?" Eljin countered.

I had to admit he had a point, but *I* wanted to know why he was so sure — for my own personal reasons. Yes, we now knew that the Blevonese soldiers who had attacked the king were under Rafe's or Vera's control. But that didn't explain the attacks on our villages over the years, during the war with Blevon. It didn't explain the black sorcerer who had attacked my village with Blevonese soldiers and killed my parents.

"The reason he can be so sure is a strictly guarded secret," Lisbet said softly, as though she knew my thoughts. "Only Blevonese sorcerers or sorceresses are ever told the truth, and then they make a sacred oath to keep the knowledge they receive at *Sì Miào Chán Wù* in their hearts, sworn to never be revealed, except to another Blevonese sorcerer."

"*Sì Miào Chán Wù*," I repeated. "What does that mean?"

"Roughly translated, it means 'Temple of Awakening to Truth,'" Eljin said, his voice gruff. "It's where all Blevonese sorcerers go once they are of age."

"Why is it a secret? And if only the sorcerers know the secret, how can you be sure that part of the Blevonese army wouldn't work with a black sorcerer if they had the chance?"

"Because," Eljin explained, "even though not everyone knows the entire truth, our people know enough to not make that mistake. The consequences from taking such a risk are too dire."

"Please tell me," I begged. "I'm half Blevonese. Shouldn't I be allowed to know? I won't tell anyone. I promise."

"Shh," Lisbet murmured. "You need to relax so I can work. This is too distracting."

I begrudgingly fell silent as Lisbet worked on my back. Already, the pain was dimming; I could breathe deeper. But my willingness to remain silent didn't last long. After just a short time, I couldn't bear it anymore. I wasn't relaxed — I was burning with questions. If I couldn't be out in the palace searching for Damian, I could at least get some answers.

"Eljin, since you've suspected them the whole time, why do you think Dansii is doing this?"

"I think Armando wants more than just Antion," Eljin replied, his voice grim. "I think he wants to distract both our kingdoms, so he can sneak his way into the heart of Blevon, while we're busy tearing each other apart."

"If he wants Blevon, why doesn't he just attack you? Why go through us? Supposedly, we're allies. It doesn't make sense."

"Armando and his armies can't get into Blevon from Dansii — the Naswais Mountains that create the northern border of Blevon are insurmountable. The only way to our kingdom is through Antion."

"The what mountains?"

"You aren't familiar with the geography of Blevon?" Eljin sounded incredulous.

"Excuse me for not having time to study maps while I was doing everything I could just to survive," I snapped back.

"Enough," Lisbet interrupted us. "I need to concentrate."

I tried to lie still, but I was thrumming with tension — with the need to be doing something. Helping Damian, stopping Vera. And there was one more question that I *needed* answered, before it was time for me to go face them and possibly never get the chance to ask again.

"So my father . . . you believe he was a sorcerer, *and* he was Blevonese. Would he have known the truth — would he have known your secrets?"

Lisbet sighed, but it was Eljin who answered, "Yes, if he was a Blevonese sorcerer and had ever been to our temple, he would have known."

As I thought back on that day, the day my parents were killed, I suddenly saw his actions in a new light. From where he made us hide, I'd watched him prepare to fight the enemy. He'd seemed concerned, but confident — until the black sorcerer had started attacking. Then he'd been so shocked he'd stumbled. I'd never seen him stumble before. I remembered the look on his face — the way his eyes had widened when the man drew up the abominable fire in his hand. How anger and horror had been etched as the final expression on his face as he'd valiantly tried to save us.

I'd always assumed the anger and horror had been because he was afraid of dying — of all of us being killed. But maybe the true shock had been realizing a black sorcerer was fighting with the Blevonese army.

"Now is not the time for this discussion. We need to focus on the problem at hand." Eljin cut into my thoughts, and then he proceeded to fill me in on what had happened in the palace while I was gone — whether to silence me, distract me, or give me more information to aid me in whatever lay ahead, I wasn't sure. Probably all three.

Yesterday, Eljin had woken to find his door barred, and he'd spent the morning fashioning a rope ladder from his clothes and bedsheets, so he could break out of his own room. There were no secret passages in his quarters.

When he'd finally made it free, he found the grounds deserted. Eljin was able to locate Lisbet, and she told him that King Damian and Vera had called for a meeting in the great hall, asking every guard, servant, liveryman, messenger, and even the kitchen staff to be present. Lisbet didn't trust Vera, so she'd gone to hide instead. Eljin concealed himself using his sorcery and snuck in to see Vera going from person to person in the room, while Damian watched from his throne. Eljin had quickly snuck back out, before Damian could sense his presence, and gone to Lisbet.

"What about his guard? Are they all under her power?" I asked.

"At this point, we have to assume so. Except Rylan, if he came back during the night."

I wondered what had happened to my friend — if he'd had the same reception as I did. Was he imprisoned now? Had he been taken to Vera and put under her power as well? Or was he, too, hiding somewhere?

"Are you almost done?" I asked Lisbet, my body taut with urgency. I had to get to Damian, to see if it was possible to break Vera's control over him before things got any worse.

"Healing can't be rushed. It's a difficult process, especially when I'm exhausted and trying not to be distracted by all of your talking. I've managed to stop the bleeding, but it's going to take me hours before I can get all the layers of skin, muscle, and nerves completely knit back together."

Her words sent chagrin through me, but I didn't have time to lie there silently any longer. "I don't have hours. Wrap me and let's go. It'll have to do."

Lisbet didn't argue with me; she just took my arm and helped me sit up. "Your tunic and your vest are ruined. Eljin, do we have something we can give her to wear?" The remains of my uniform covered the front of me, but my back was exposed. I gritted my teeth as I moved.

When Eljin turned away to rummage in a trunk in the corner, Lisbet carefully helped me pull off my destroyed vest — the one with the insignia of the king on it — and then my tunic, leaving me half naked on the bed.

"We have —"

"Don't turn around." Lisbet cut him off, and Eljin froze with his back still to us, holding out a dark tunic that looked like it was made for him.

She quickly bound my back with clean bandages, then took the tunic from him and helped me pull it on. When I was decent once more, he finally turned to face me. With his mask on, it was hard to know for sure, but it looked like his olive skin was slightly pink along his hairline, as though he were blushing. I couldn't imagine the indomitable Eljin blushing, and for some reason, it made me smile.

"What's your plan?" he asked, and my smile died as quickly as it came. "How can I help?"

"Do either of you know the secret passageway that leads to Damian's outer chamber?"

"Yes," they both responded.

"I'll take you," Eljin offered. "Lisbet, you stay here — and if anything happens to us, flee the palace and go straight to my father. Tell him what's happened and that he must go to King Osgand and request the aid of the *Rén Zhǔsas*. If it comes to that, they may be Antion's only hope."

I suppressed a chill as Eljin picked up an unlit torch and held it up to the one in the bracket until it caught fire, doubling the amount of light in the room. "What are the *Rén Zhǔsas*?"

"The three most powerful sorcerers alive — they are the reigning sorcerers of Blevon. They live in *Sì Miào Chán Wù*, to protect it."

"Why haven't I ever heard any of this before?"

A dark look crossed Eljin's face, which was reflected on Lisbet's. "Because King Hector didn't want his people to know of it. And the threat of death was good enough to silence anyone who knew even a little bit about your supposed enemies."

I wanted to keep questioning him, but there wasn't time. I could only hope to make it through the next day and night, and maybe someday have the chance to get more answers to all of my questions.

Eljin crossed to the wall with wood paneling opposite the bed and began to feel along it. I watched him, wondering how the mysterious passageways worked. Finally, he pushed and the concealed door sprung open, revealing a narrow, pitch-black pathway.

"How do they work?" I asked, still unsure of how he'd found the lever I'd been unsuccessful in locating in Damian's room after Jax had brought me the letter.

"The mechanism is concealed as a knot of wood. When you push the right one in, it releases the latch and the door opens," he explained, pointing to a small, round imperfection in the wall that looked like any of the other natural knots in the wood.

That explained why I'd never found the way to open the secret door. I'd been searching for something sticking out, not trying to push part of the wall *in*.

"Stay close," he instructed, "and let's hope Vera hasn't figured out all of the palace's secrets yet."

I shivered at his words, despite the heat, and moved to follow him, but Lisbet touched my arm, stopping me. I looked down into her dark, somber eyes and swallowed past the sudden lump in my throat.

170

"Be careful" was all she said, and I nodded.

As I turned to follow Eljin, she called after me, "And thank you."

I didn't turn back around. She had nothing to thank me for. I hadn't saved anyone yet.

The pathway was stifling — the dank walls were too close and the darkness too complete, even with Eljin's torch throwing a small circle of light around us. It illuminated cobwebs hanging from the low ceiling and crisscrossing in front of us. I kept batting at them, trying to keep them from sticking to my face. The walls were layered with dirt, and the passageway was so narrow my shoulders occasionally brushed one side or the other, surely coating the arms of the tunic in grime.

We walked and walked through the damp blackness — turning corners, going up stairs, continuing down long stretches of endless dark, passing barely noticeable lines in the otherwise unendingly smooth walls that must have been exits from the passageway into other rooms. I wondered who was on the other sides of these walls, most likely sleeping, completely unaware of us walking past them.

At last, Eljin stopped and gestured for me to come closer. He pointed at a knot in the wall, similar to the one he'd pushed in Lisbet's room. He pantomimed opening it and that he would wait for me.

I nodded. Taking a deep breath, I unsheathed my sword, unsure of what awaited me on the other side of this door. My heart pounded beneath the cage of my ribs. Damian was so close. I'd finally reached him. But what would he do when he saw me?

Pushing away my fears, I stretched my hand and pushed the knot. The latch sprung, and the door popped open silently. With one last look at Eljin, the torch he held casting his face into alternating shadow and light, I slipped through the opening and into the king's outer chamber.

⇥ NINETEEN ⇤

*T*HE CHAMBER WAS dark. Only the dim illumination from the skylight above me offered the meager glow of the stars to reveal that the room was empty. I quickly strode across the familiar space, my blood pulsing through my veins, making my back hurt and my hands clammy. I'd never been so nervous to see Damian. When I reached his actual door, I twisted the knob, only to find it locked.

I stood there for a long moment, unsure of what to do. Normally, I would have knocked, demanding he let me in. But did I dare do that tonight? He never locked this door — why would he, when his outer door was already locked and guarded?

There was no other way to get to him. I'd just have to risk it.

I'd barely lifted my hand, ready to pound on his door, when I heard a voice from within his room — a female voice. I couldn't make out what she was saying, but I knew who it was. Vera. In Damian's room. Before the sun had even begun to rise.

My stomach twisted, sending a surge of acid into my throat, nearly choking me. *He's not himself,* I reminded myself. *He's under her control.*

But jealousy, white hot and unstoppable, suddenly burned through me. Jealousy and fear.

I pressed my ear to the door, straining to decipher her words.

"She's here, Damian. She's coming for us, just as I said she would."

"How will we stop her?" he responded, his voice so familiar and yet his words so wrong, making everything inside of me constrict.

"I'm taking care of it," Vera responded.

I spun around, my heart racing.

Maybe she hadn't been with him all night, if she was telling him about me coming for them. But whether she had or not, their words proved that my fears were true; she'd turned him against me.

What did I do now? Above me, the skylight was beginning to show the gray shades of dawn, slowly wiping away the stars, bleeding away the black night into morning. I had one day. One day to stop Vera — without hurting her — and get back to Rafe to save Jax.

My options were so limited. I could either pound on the door and demand to be let in or wait until they came out.

And then I remembered the passageway Damian had used to enter my room the other night. He'd said it led straight to his inner quarters. If I could find it, I'd have a way in without causing a huge scene. I didn't know what I was going to do yet; all I knew was that I had to get in there and at least try to talk to him. Without allowing Vera to look into my eyes and put me under her spell as well.

I hurried back to the passageway where Eljin waited, still holding the torch.

"The door is locked," I whispered. "And I could hear her in there with him. She's turned him against me."

"What are you going to do?"

"There's another passageway. I'm going to go straight into his room. You should hurry back to Lisbet and help her escape. Go to your father and get his help."

"I'm coming with you." He moved forward, stepping past me into the empty chamber before I could protest.

There were worse things than having a sorcerer next to me, if it came down to a fight. But it also put him at risk of falling under Vera's control. If we both failed, it left everything on Lisbet's shoulders. There was no time to argue with him, however. I knew Eljin well enough to realize that I wasn't going to change his mind.

We headed for the door to the hallway, away from Damian's room, but I held up a hand before we reached it.

"There will be guards," I said under my breath.

He nodded and pantomimed fighting. I swallowed the knot of dread that suddenly formed in my throat. I wasn't sure how much more fighting I could stomach tonight — especially against my fellow members of Damian's guard.

"Too much noise," I whispered, my voice barely audible, gesturing to my sword.

Eljin pointed to himself, and I nodded. He'd use magic to subdue them, hopefully silently. The last thing I needed was anyone else being alerted to our presence or drawing Vera's attention.

He met my eyes one last time, and then reached out and unlocked the door and turned the knob.

Deron and Mateo both stood outside the door, looking exhausted, until they saw us emerge from Damian's chamber. Deron's eyes widened for a split second, then narrowed again, and Mateo straightened up.

Eljin hesitated before lifting his hands — maybe hoping, as I had, that he wouldn't have to fight our friends — but Deron already had his sword out and moved to strike him down. It sickened me to fight my captain, but I had no choice. I lunged forward to defend Eljin, but before I could block Deron's intended strike, Eljin made a sudden gesture and knocked Deron back, slamming him into the wall, just as he'd once done to me.

But Mateo was still free to move. He lunged at me, and since my focus had been on Deron, I barely spun out of his reach in time, twisting my wound. I could feel it tear wide open again, undoing Lisbet's work. Mateo's sword sliced through the air where I'd been standing one moment earlier. They weren't just trying to stop me — they were fighting to kill.

Deron charged forward again, and Eljin slammed him against the wall once more with his sorcery, this time hitting Deron's head hard enough to make a loud crack. He slumped to the ground, unconscious.

At the same time, Mateo changed tactics and went for Eljin. I didn't dare shout a warning to Eljin, mindful of the open door behind us. Instead, I had to do exactly what I didn't want to do — I had to hurt a fellow guard and friend. My sword came down silently, until it met his arm, slicing through skin and muscle. I didn't cut hard enough to sever his bone, but it was enough. With a howl of pain, Mateo dropped his sword to the ground.

Eljin spun to face him, lifting his hand again, and Mateo's cry of pain suddenly cut off. I glanced into the darkness of Damian's quarters, but the door to his room remained shut. There was a strangled noise from behind me, and I turned to see Mateo drop to his knees and then fall face-first onto the ground.

Is he dead? I mouthed, horrified, but Eljin shook his head no.

I stared down at Mateo and the pool of blood growing around his arm. I couldn't just leave him there. If he was out too long, he might lose too much blood and never wake up. There were bandages in my room, long strips of fabric left over from when I'd had to bind my breasts every day. I turned on my heel and rushed to my room.

When I opened my door, I had to stifle a gasp. It had been ransacked, making me wonder what in the world Vera could have been looking for — if she was the one who had searched it. At least my basket of wrappings was still there, though upended and spilled out onto the floor. I grabbed a bunch of them and headed out to where Eljin still stood over the two unmoving bodies. There was no time to let myself think about what we'd done.

I knelt down beside Mateo and wrapped one bandage around his arm, tying it tightly to stop the bleeding. Then I used another one to tie his hands behind his back and a third to gag him. When he saw what I was doing, Eljin took the other strips of fabric and did the same to Deron.

"I'm sorry," I whispered, before standing up and waiting for Eljin to finish tying up my captain. When he was done, Eljin grabbed Deron underneath his arms and began to drag him into Damian's outer chamber, where no one would find him and sound the alert. I quickly did the same with Mateo. Once they were both in the room, Eljin shut the door behind them and turned to face me.

I gestured for him to follow me, and we hurried to my room. Once I had the door shut, I sagged against it for a moment. Pain throbbed across my back with each beat of my heart.

"You're bleeding again," Eljin whispered.

"There's nothing I can do about it now." I pushed away from the door, forcing myself to stand up tall. There was no time to rest, no time to wish that our situation was different.

"Have you ever heard of anyone like Vera?" I asked quietly, but Eljin shook his head.

"She's not a true sorceress, or else I would sense the magic in her blood, and I haven't felt a thing from her."

"Then where does her power come from? How do we stop her?"

Eljin shook his head again. "I wish I knew."

"She's going to do everything she can to put us under her control when we go in there. Don't let her look into your eyes."

"I'll try to gag her, so you can talk to Damian. I hope that you can succeed in breaking her control." Eljin looked down at me, straight into my eyes, his expression grim. "But what if you *can't* get through to him? Are you prepared to kill her? It might be the only way to stop her," he continued, when I tried to protest.

"We can't," I said with a scowl. "Rafe has commanded Jax to kill himself if I'm not back before dawn tomorrow — *or* if I hurt or kill him or Vera."

Eljin continued to look at me silently. "I love him, too," he began, making my stomach twist from fear of what he was about to say. "But it's one life, Alexa, compared to hundreds, even thousands

178

of people who will suffer and possibly die if Vera and Rafe turn Damian into their puppet. If you don't succeed in stopping her without violence, we might not have a choice."

"No," I said fiercely. "I can do this. There has to be a way. I'm not going to let him do that to Jax. I can't . . ." I broke off as an image of the fear on Jax's little face rose up. I swallowed hard, forcing the emotion down. I didn't have time to argue with Eljin.

Without another word, I turned away and strode over to the wall Damian had come through. As I searched for the knot that would open the passageway, I wondered yet again if things would have been different if I'd accepted him, if I'd let my heart guide me instead of my head. Would this have happened if Vera had shown up to find Damian engaged to be married? I wondered if that was what Tanoori had meant when she'd told me to stop being so stubborn. Did she mean to stop refusing Damian?

I forced the thoughts away as I searched along the wall, pushing every knot I found in the wood. Finally, one sunk in about half an inch, and the hidden door popped open with a gust of dank, musty air.

"If I have to, I will kill her myself," Eljin whispered from behind me.

I didn't turn around.

"You know I can't let you do that. I *won't*." And with that threat hanging in the air, I plunged into the darkness, feeling along the wall with one hand. I clutched my sword in the other, though I knew I couldn't use it — unless it was to stop Eljin. I prayed he wouldn't force me to hurt him as well.

The passageway wasn't long at all, since Damian's room was next to mine. It turned sharply left, then right, quickly coming to a dead end. If my guess was right, I was next to one of his windows and would come out beneath the thick drapes that hung in his room. I searched along the wall until I found the release. Taking a deep breath, I steeled myself for whatever lay ahead and then pushed it. The door popped open about an inch. There was no sound of voices, no talking.

I didn't dare wait, in case the door wasn't hidden like I thought, and they'd just seen the wall move. In the darkness of the passageway, it was impossible to know. Terror pounded along with adrenaline as I pushed the door open wide enough for my body and slipped past it and ran right into Damian's thick velvet drapes. We were hidden then — at least for a moment.

Eljin was right behind me; I could feel him standing so close that the warmth from his body filled the inches between us. I tightened my grip on my sword. I couldn't use it, but Vera didn't know that. Sometimes a good threat was all that was needed.

With my empty hand, I reached out and grabbed the drapes, yanking them aside, and rushed forward.

But when I saw Damian's arms wrapped around Vera — who wore nothing more than a silken shift, her dark auburn hair unbound and cascading down her back, and his mouth on hers — I ground to a stunned halt, making Eljin crash into me.

I must have made some sort of sound of horror, because Damian's eyes opened and he saw me standing there.

He broke away from Vera, and she made a pathetic whimpering sound. "What is it —"

"Alexa" was all he said, and she spun around to face me.

⊰ TWENTY ⊱

A LEXA," VERA REPEATED, her voice as honeyed as I remembered it. But now I knew that honey hid a venom more toxic than any predator's in Antion. I looked away from her, refusing to meet her eyes. "How kind of you to show up here."

Eljin came to stand next to me, and Vera giggled. She actually *giggled*. The sound made my stomach turn over. That wasn't the reaction I'd been expecting.

"Oh, how sweet. You even brought the resident sorcerer to me as well. You've been a sneaky one, hiding away where I couldn't find you." She lifted an eyebrow and wagged a finger at Eljin.

I stared at Damian, beseeching him with my eyes, silently pleading with him to come back to me. But he looked at me dispassionately, no sign of his former feelings evident in his expression or the stance of his body. His arm was still around Vera, who stood next to him, as though they were now a team. My nightmare came back to me all of a sudden, of the two of them towering over me, watching me fall and fall as they tore apart the entire world around us. . . .

Eljin lifted his hands, and I could feel the pull of magic, as I always did when I was close to a sorcerer using his power, but Vera just laughed again.

"Try all you'd like, sorcerer, but your power is useless against me. I'm impervious to your parlor tricks."

I turned to stare at Eljin in horror. "Is she telling the truth?"

I watched as his hands began to shake, and yet Vera continued to laugh, completely unaffected.

Finally, Eljin dropped his hands, his eyes wide. "What *are* you?"

Vera laughed again, the sound as clear as a bell, and yet it scratched down my spine like nails on steel. "Wouldn't you like to know. You'll have to pay my king a visit, if you want to find out. But, alas, I don't think that's in your future."

With a cry of frustration, Eljin yanked his sword out of his scabbard. "You might be impervious to sorcery, but no one is immune to steel!" he yelled, and charged at Vera.

"Eljin, no!" I shouted, dashing forward, but it was too late — he was too close to her. She looked directly at Eljin as he raised his sword to bring it down on her head and, with a smile on her face, said, "Halt immediately."

Eljin froze, his sword still in the air above her.

"You don't want to hurt me." Vera smiled at him. "The plan was to keep Alexa alive, but now that Damian has become so . . . *agreeable*, I don't think she's necessary anymore." The sweetness of her voice turned deadly cold. "Kill her. Kill Alexa. *Now.*"

Terror seized my lungs in an ice-cold grip as he spun to face me, his eyes empty above his mask. I'd *warned* him not to look into her eyes. In his anger, he must have forgotten.

"Damian, help me! Don't let her do this," I shouted as Eljin lunged at me.

I jumped back, out of his reach, and lifted my sword to deflect him when he jabbed again, his movements quick and lethal. My blade met the magical shield I'd spent weeks learning how to penetrate in Blevon, and I had to stumble back to avoid getting sliced in half. I was so shocked that he was fighting me, that Vera had taken control of my one ally, that I could barely bring myself to attack back. Instead, I concentrated on deflecting him. I spun away from yet another swipe of his sword. "Eljin, stop! You don't want to do this! *She's* your enemy, not me!"

But instead of responding, he lifted his arm, suddenly choking me with his magic. When my body began to burn with the need for oxygen, I finally realized he wasn't going to show me any mercy. He'd been commanded to kill me, and he was determined to do just that. I glanced at Damian to find him staring at me, his expression bemused.

He wasn't going to help me, either. He was going to watch me die.

I had no choice but to stop Eljin. Fighting the spiraling darkness, I lifted my sword and rushed at him. I refused to die. If nothing else — if I couldn't save Damian — I at least had to get to Jax in time. I had to ignore the fire in my desperate lungs as I swiped my sword at his raised arm. He jumped back to avoid my hit, but in so doing, he lost control of his magic, and the invisible grip on my neck disappeared.

That gasp of air was as exquisite as it was excruciating; oxygen surged back into my body. Without a pause, I attacked again. As hard and furious as I ever had in any sparring match in his father's castle in Blevon. I knew how to get past his defenses; I'd done it

183

many times before. He was good, but I was better, when it came to sword fighting. It was his sorcery that had given him the advantage in the past, and he had been the one to teach me how to beat him, despite that.

But I'd never intended to hurt him before, and we'd been using wooden swords for the most part. This time was deadly serious, and the sounds of our blades clashing echoed through Damian's chamber while he stood next to Vera, unmoving, watching us fight.

I jabbed and spun and lunged and ducked as fast and hard as I could, refusing to give him the chance to use his sorcery to fling me back against the wall and knock me unconscious. I had to ignore the blinding pain as the wound in my back tore more and more. Blood dripped, hot and sticky down my spine, soaking my tunic. Over and over, Eljin used his shield to deflect my hits, but I knew how to do this. I knew it. I just had to focus.

I got close, but he was always a split second ahead of me. It had been too long since I'd practiced against him, and I was rusty. If I didn't beat him soon, he was going to succeed in following her command. I was growing tired — from lack of sleep, from fighting again and again and again, from the pain and loss of blood. This was it. If I didn't beat him now, I knew I wouldn't have the strength to continue on, and he *would* kill me.

I would fail everyone.

Channeling all of my fear and anger, I tried one last time. With a cry of desperation, I spun and attacked, faking right and then lunging left in a lightning-fast move, and finally, *finally*, he couldn't get his shield up fast enough. My blade surged toward his body. At the last moment, I checked the direction so that it sliced through his side, instead of his lungs.

He stared at me in shock, the emptiness draining out of his eyes as his sword clanged to the ground. Then he dropped to his knees.

"I'm sorry," I whispered, still standing over him, my body trembling, my voice thick with tears. "I'm so sorry."

He lifted a shaking hand to his side and stared at the blood on his fingers in shock. "You . . . you . . ." His eyes lifted to mine again. "I'm dying."

"No! You're *not* going to die."

"It would appear that he is, actually," Vera supplied, sounding amused. "Not exactly the result I was hoping for, but I'll take it. For now."

I looked away from my friend to glare at her, remembering at the last second not to meet her eyes. I wanted to charge at her, to kill her right there. Rage churned through my body, hot and urgent. I couldn't hurt her or Jax would die — I knew that. But in that moment, it didn't matter anymore. Eljin's words came back to me: that as much as he loved Jax, we might not have a choice if we wanted to save Damian and Antion.

Maybe Eljin had been right. And because I'd ignored him, now *he* was dying. She'd hurt so many — and if I didn't stop her, she'd continue to do so. She'd turned our own men against me; I'd had to kill one and injure others to get here. She'd made me hurt Mateo, Deron — and now Eljin. She'd taken Damian from me, from all of Antion.

Vera *had* to die.

I'm so sorry, Jax, I thought as I lifted my sword, gripping it with both hands, and rushed at her. I stared at her heart — the place where I was going to embed my sword — instead of her lethal eyes. I swung my sword back and then began to whip it around as I took the last few steps —

And suddenly, it was Damian my sword was about to stab, instead of Vera. With a scream of rage and frustration, I forced myself to halt, barely stopping the forward progression of my sword in time to keep from impaling him on it.

"Why?" I cried out, backing away, staring at him with tears blinding me. He'd jumped in front of my sword — willing to *die* — to protect *her*. "How can you forget me so easily? I don't care how powerful she is — what we had was stronger than this. Wasn't it?"

I looked at him and clenched my jaw to keep the tears from spilling over. I refused to look weak, to let Vera see just how deeply I was hurt. A strange expression crossed Damian's face — his eyebrows pulled down low over his eyes as he stared back at me. Then his gaze moved to Eljin, who clutched his side with shaking hands.

"Damian, this isn't you. Eljin is your friend. And I . . . I am . . . I was . . ." My voice broke, and I swallowed hard, trying to regain control. "You don't want to let her kill me," I finally said. "Somewhere in your heart, you have to remember that."

"Aren't you trying to hurt us?" The uncertainty in his voice gave me a sudden surge of hope. Maybe there was still a piece of him in there. The strong, unyielding man I knew and loved couldn't be completely gone. Our only hope was that some part of him remained that I could reach.

"Damian." Vera's voice was sharp. She reached for his arm, turning him to face her, staring into his eyes. "You love *me*. You know you do. You can feel it, right?"

"Don't look in her eyes!" I yelled, but it was too late.

"I love you," he repeated.

"Yes, you love me," Vera practically crowed in triumph. "Damian, this guard is a rebel. She's trying to overthrow your kingdom. She just tried to kill me. You can't let her get away with this act of treason."

"No, I can't," he said. "We will have her tried and sentenced tomorrow."

The exhaustion and devastation were too much; my arm that held my sword trembled. And then Damian lifted his hand. Suddenly, my arm was forced to my side, and I couldn't move — bound by the sorcery he wielded.

"Please," I begged, my voice barely above a whisper, struggling against my invisible bonds, "remember me. Remember us. You don't want to do this."

"There's no time for a trial. She'll find a way to escape, to come and finish what she started. You know how lethal she is. *You* must kill her. Now." Vera glanced past him to me, a triumphant smirk on her face.

"Damian, don't listen to her," I pleaded desperately as Eljin collapsed onto his side, his eyes rolling in his head as he fought to stay conscious. "You love me, not her. Damian, *please*." I had to get Eljin to Lisbet immediately or else he *would* end up dying.

Damian's beautiful blue eyes met mine across the space between us and he grimaced, as though his head hurt. His hand faltered, and I felt the sorcery drop away, leaving me free to move again. "I . . . I love . . ."

"*No*. You love me. Look at me," Vera commanded. "*You love me.*"

"Fight it, Damian — fight her control. You know it, don't you? In your heart, you know you love *me*." I stepped toward them again, shouting now to be heard over Vera as she reached up and turned his face to hers again, telling him again that he loved her, that I needed to die.

Damian moved back from Vera, shaking his head. Was he fighting her — trying to figure out what was real and imagined? That was the only reason I could think of why he hadn't followed her order to kill me yet.

"She is a threat, Damian. Kill her *now*!"

"But, I . . . I love . . ."

"Of course he'd be in love with his disgusting, scarred guard," Vera hissed, her voice no longer holding any pretense of sweetness as she spun to face me. "You think you can stop me? You think your *love* is strong enough to overcome my power?" She sneered at me, and all the beauty I'd been so jealous of before seemed suddenly stripped away, exposing her true self beneath the alluring facade. "Once you're gone, it'll take less than a day before he won't even remember you existed. *I* will be his entire world."

I didn't dare continue to look at her. Instead, I kept my eyes on Damian, willing him to fight. To remember.

Vera suddenly stepped in front of him, blocking me, and pulled his face to hers, kissing him passionately. He didn't respond at first, but then he slowly softened, kissing her back.

"Damian, *please*!"

He didn't respond, continuing to kiss her until Vera finally broke away, her head still tilted up to his. He stared down at her, right into her eyes.

"Don't look in her eyes!" I lifted my sword, but before I could rush forward, Vera yelled at him.

"Go to your desk, get your dagger, and *kill her*! Embed it in her heart and finish this! Kill her, so you can get your brother back!"

Damian immediately spun on his heel and marched over to his desk as though he were a soldier following his general's command.

"She won't stop you; she can't bring herself to hurt you."

My grip on the hilt of my sword tightened as he grabbed a long dagger lying on top of his desk and turned to face me.

"Damian, you don't want to do this. If you kill me, Jax will die, too! I made a deal. . . ." My voice broke as he advanced on me, his expression cold. My entire body began to shake, and helpless tears burned in my eyes. "I made a deal to save him." The tears spilled out, running down my cheeks, but I didn't care anymore.

"You made a deal with my brother?" Vera laughed, the sound echoing through my mind, burning into my brain as Damian stalked closer, gripping the dagger, preparing to strike me down.

I stared into his face, into his eyes — eyes that had once glowed with love for me but now held nothing but deadly intent — and let my sword drop to the ground beside me. My blade clattered against the stone floor. Vera was right; I couldn't hurt him. I couldn't stop him. If he was going to follow her orders, I couldn't bring myself to fight back, to harm him. I was willing to do almost anything to stop her and her brother, to try and save Antion. But hurting Damian wasn't one of them.

He stopped right in front of me, so close I could almost feel the heat of him. My entire body shook. I wanted his face to be the last thing I saw before I died. Even if his heart was no longer mine and his eyes held no love for me, they were still his beautiful eyes.

Damian was still the man *I* loved.

I held perfectly still as he slowly lifted the dagger above his head.

"Damian," I whispered, wanting him — *needing* him — to know the truth before I died. I'd been lying to him for too long.

He paused, the dagger still above his head.

"Damian," I repeated when his arm began to tremble and the dagger dipped down slightly. "You don't love that woman. You love *me*."

"Don't listen to her! She's trying to trick you. *Kill her!*" Vera shouted, making my ears hurt, but I refused to be silent. My only weapons were my words — my love.

"You love me, Damian. I know you do. She can't take that from you — from us — unless you let her."

Confusion and pain flickered across his face, but then Vera screamed at him.

"*Kill her!* Now, Damian! Do it *now!*"

His expression hardened, and he lifted the dagger higher again, his grip tightening on the hilt. This was it. Vera was going to win.

"I love you!" I shouted over Vera's screaming. "I love you, Damian! I always have and I always will!"

Damian sucked in a sharp breath and stumbled back a step, as though my declaration had physically slammed him.

"*No!*" Vera howled. "Kill her now!"

Damian's eyes narrowed, and my whole body tightened, anticipating my death. He swung the dagger back, but as the blade began to arc back down toward my heart, he suddenly spun on his heel and threw it with perfect aim into Vera's chest — directly into *her* heart.

I stared in shock as her eyes widened; crimson blood bloomed around the hilt of the blade, spreading quickly to soak the front of her silken shift. Her mouth opened and then closed wordlessly. She tried to lift a hand to the dagger, but while we watched, the color in her cheeks drained away and her arm fell uselessly to her side. With a choking sound, she dropped to her knees. Blood bubbled out of her mouth as she crumpled to the ground, her eyes open. Unseeing.

She was dead.

My frozen horror gave way to panic that made my entire body shake. Damian turned back to me, and when our eyes met, I nearly collapsed in relief. His eyes were his own again. Her death had released him.

And then his arms were around me, holding me, gathering me into the strength and comfort of his body. "Alexa," he choked out, burying his face in my hair. "Alexa, what did I do? What did I almost do?" He trembled even as he held me. His arms tightened around me, and I couldn't keep from crying out in pain. He immediately let go and stepped back. When he saw the blood on the sleeves of his tunic, his eyes flew to mine. "You're hurt! What happened? We have to get —"

"Damian" — I cut him off, my eyes dropping to where Eljin lay on the ground unmoving — "Eljin needs Lisbet's help *now*."

"Eljin," Damian repeated, horror blooming on his face as he spun to face his friend.

He rushed to Eljin, with me right behind him. Eljin's face was ghastly pale above his mask. I dropped to my knees next to him and pulled the mask off, heedless of the scars he tried to hide. He needed to breathe, not to hide the evidence of a war we'd fought so hard to stop.

"Is he . . . ?"

"He's alive," I said, my fingers pressed against his neck. There was a faint pulse. "But not for long if he doesn't get help."

"Where is Lisbet?"

"Hiding in the same room as before."

I glanced up at him, and my heart constricted at the pain on his face. "Go — hurry!"

He gave me one last look, his eyes full of remorse, and then he turned and rushed to the door. Once he'd gone, I turned back to Eljin.

"You can't die — do you hear me? I didn't want to hurt you." I pressed my hands against the wound I'd given him, trying to slow the loss of blood. "I can't let you die."

Vera's body wasn't far away, but I refused to look at her. To look at her was to admit that she was dead, and what Damian didn't know yet was that if we lost Eljin, he wouldn't be the last one to die this day.

Jax was going to die as well.

⊰ TWENTY-ONE ⊱

WHEN I HEARD the door open again, I knew it was too soon for Damian to be back, and I glanced over my shoulder nervously, not knowing who — or what — to expect.

My captain walked in, rubbing his wrists, Mateo behind him, a little pale and his arm still wrapped in the bandage I'd tied around the wound I'd given him, but he was alive.

"Alexa," Deron said, and I tensed, unsure of whether he'd still be under Vera's power, even though she was dead. "What happened?"

I breathed a sigh of relief when he got close enough for me to see how clear his eyes were, though his expression was confused and troubled.

He stared first at Vera's body, then at Eljin's next to me.

"I need more bandages — something to help me stop this bleeding until Lisbet gets here," I said. "Can you find me anything to use?"

Deron nodded and turned toward the dresser where Damian kept his clothes. Mateo came and knelt down beside me.

"What can I do to help?" he asked, looking at Eljin in dismay.

"I don't know." I continued to press my hands into his side as hard as I could, but blood still pulsed between my fingers, over my skin, staining me with the life that was draining out of Eljin right in front of us. "I didn't want to hurt him. I didn't want to hurt any of you."

Mateo reached out and placed his hand on top of mine, adding more pressure to the wound. I glanced over at him and was surprised to see not only grief but also empathy in his eyes. "I know you didn't want to. You did what you had to do to save us all. Even if it meant fighting your friends to stop her."

I shook my head, unable to speak, afraid I'd break into sobs if I did. I had to look away from him, back to Eljin, who lay unmoving beneath our joined hands. Why did it always come to this? Hurting friends — sacrificing those I loved — to battle the evil that continued to besiege us?

"Here," Deron broke in, kneeling down on the other side of Eljin. "Will these work?" He held out some of Damian's shirts, and I nodded.

"Push one beneath our hands, and then tear off a long strip from that other one, so we can tie it around him."

Deron did as I asked. In just the brief moment that we lifted our hands to put the material beneath them, blood gushed with renewed force out of Eljin's body. I couldn't believe there was so much left. From the massive pool surrounding us, running over my hands, soaking my pants and boots, it felt as though he would run out at any moment.

We were just binding the strip of fabric around him, as tightly as we could, when I heard Lisbet's cry from behind me.

"Eljin!"

She rushed over to us and dropped to her knees beside me, heedless of the blood. "Give me room," she said, her voice urgent.

I did as she asked, pushing myself to my feet and stepping back. Mateo did the same, standing next to me. I was covered in blood — Eljin's all over my front and my own down my back. I could still feel it dripping out of my wound.

I couldn't bring myself to ask Lisbet if there was any hope. Deron still knelt next to him, watching as Lisbet ran her hands above Eljin, her whole body trembling from the sorcery she was using, trying to heal him, murmuring beneath her breath rapidly in Blevonese.

"Alexa." A voice from behind us startled me — a voice I'd know anywhere, and one that I'd thought would never say my name like that again. I turned to see Damian standing there, his eyes on mine, clear at last of Vera's control but filled with an infinite sadness that tore at my heart.

He moved toward me hesitantly. One step. Then another. I swallowed hard past the lump in my throat. I was so tired, so beaten down. Death stained me — my skin, my heart, my soul. And still he came closer, slowly, as though he were afraid of spooking me.

When he was near enough to touch, he reached for me, but I flinched and he froze.

"I'm covered in blood," I whispered, my voice thick with unshed tears and guilt.

"Did you mean what you said?" he asked quietly, urgently, his eyes unyielding on mine. His gaze stripped away all the defenses I had built up around my heart to protect it from him, until I was laid bare before him.

"Yes."

And then his arms came around me, gently pulling me to him, careful of the wound on my back.

"But the blood," I protested weakly.

"I don't care about the blood," he said, pulling back just enough to thread his hands through my hair, cupping my face, heedless of my scars, staring down at me. "All I care about is *you*." His hands trembled slightly, and a muscle in his jaw tightened. "I can hardly bear to think of what almost happened . . . of what she made me . . ." He trailed off, self-loathing in his voice, his eyes dropping from mine at last.

"But you didn't." When he still wouldn't meet my gaze, I repeated, "Damian, you *didn't* do it. You fought back and somehow you overcame her control. I don't know how, but you did."

He opened his mouth to answer, but Deron suddenly said, "Sire! You'd better come over here."

Damian's hands dropped, and he looked past me to Deron. "What is it?"

I turned around to see Deron staring at Eljin with wide eyes. When I looked down at my friend, I had to choke back a sob of relief. Lisbet was bent over him, her entire body shaking, but the makeshift bandages we'd wrapped around him were gone, revealing that his wound had stopped bleeding.

"Will he live?" Damian finally dared ask the question I'd been too afraid to voice.

Lisbet didn't respond right away, continuing to work on him. As we watched, the skin began to slowly inch together so that the wound shrank by half, the edges of red scar tissue starting to take form. She finally paused, falling forward onto her hands, so that she was on all fours on the blood-soaked ground next to his body. When she turned her head to look at Damian, her eyes were bloodshot and full of tears.

"He'll live," she said.

Relief hit me — so hard and strong that my legs went weak and I stumbled forward a step. Damian caught my arm, holding me up. He looked down at me sharply. "You're exhausted — and hurt. We need to get you to your room. Is there anyone who can care for Alexa's wound?"

"I need to have Eljin moved to my room so I can continue working on him. Then I can help Alexa." Lisbet pushed herself up onto her knees.

"We can take him," Deron said, gesturing to Mateo.

"But he's hurt, too," I said.

"It's not that bad." Mateo shrugged, flexing his hand as if to prove he was fine, though he had to conceal a grimace of pain.

"He's not —"

"If he says it's not that bad, then it's not that bad." Deron cut me off. He and Mateo bent down and lifted Eljin into their arms, Deron taking most of the weight. Lisbet stood on shaky legs and slowly led the way out of the room. Before we knew it, Damian and I were alone, with a massive pool of blood at our feet, Vera's body beside it.

"Where is the rest of the guard?" he asked.

"I don't know," I said. "I haven't had a chance to find out. I came straight here to try to stop Vera — and save you." I paused, then added, "Well, after going to Lisbet and Eljin to help me find the secret passageways. Vera had the entire palace searching for me to kill me or throw me in the dungeon."

Damian looked down at her body with disgust on his face. "I can't believe I let her . . ." He broke off with a shake of his head.

"You can't blame yourself. Their power is . . . well, no one can stop themselves once they take control." I cringed, remembering Felton's screams of agony the night before. And then with a sickening drop of my stomach, I remembered Jax huddling on the ground in fear.

"What do you mean 'their power'?" Damian asked as I said, "There's something I have to tell you."

He turned to face me fully, concern on his achingly handsome face. He knew how I felt now — he knew the truth. Had it somehow broken him free from Vera's control? Or had he done that on his own?

But Rafe still lived, and that meant, regardless of Damian's knowing how I truly felt, I had to leave him again. If I didn't, Rafe would come for me — for us. Felton may have already heard that Vera was dead and left the palace to go report to Rafe. Or any of her other men — including the man in the black and white robes. If that happened, Jax would be forced to kill himself, because I broke my deal with Rafe to keep him and his sister from harm before returning.

"What is it?" Damian reached out and gently took my shoulders in his hands. "Can it wait until you are healed and rested?"

I shook my head.

"Alexa, it can't be that bad. She's dead; she can't hurt us anymore. I'll have this mess cleaned up while you sleep, and you'll never have to see her again." Damian started to guide me toward his door, but I pulled free of his touch, my stomach churning. He tried to conceal his consternation, but I could tell he was frustrated. Oh, how I wished frustration was the worst of the emotions he'd ever feel toward me. But once I told him, I was certain there would be something far more terrible.

"Vera wasn't alone," I finally said. "The taster who supposedly died and then went missing?"

Damian nodded for me to continue, his eyebrow lifting.

"He was Vera's twin brother. He has the same power she does. He's not dead — he's the one who took Jax."

Damian stepped forward, reaching for my hand again, but I pulled out of his reach once more. "Stop it, Alexa! *Stop* pulling away from me. Nothing you have to tell me could make me not want to —"

"He's going to die, Damian," I blurted out, and Damian froze. "I made a deal with Rafe, and now that Vera is dead, my deal is broken and he's going to make Jax . . . he's going to force Jax to kill himself," I finished in a choked whisper.

Damian's face paled, horror twisting his expression. "No. He wouldn't do that. Jax is just a child. He wouldn't . . ."

"He's worse than Vera. I saw him," I admitted as the tears I struggled to contain managed to escape, slipping down my cheeks unchecked. "I saw what he can do, and it won't matter that Jax is a child. I promised that I would return before dawn tomorrow and that he and Vera would remain unharmed. If any of those stipulations aren't met, he has ordered Jax to kill himself."

Damian didn't move, didn't speak.

"I was trying to save him," I said, fighting to keep myself from sobbing. I didn't dare wipe the tears from my face, knowing my hands were still stained with Eljin's blood. So much blood on my hands, and more to come. Would it never end?

"You tried your best," he finally said, but he wouldn't look at me.

The sudden silence was weighted with my failure, with the impending loss of the only family he had left. And then a new, desperate thought occurred to me. A dim, but fierce, hope. "I won't let him die. I'm not going to give up, Damian." This time, *I* stepped toward *him*. He watched me, his eyes brilliant but unreadable in the pale light of the slowly brightening sky. The thought of the rising sun, signaling the start of a new day, seemed incongruous with the horrible events of the last few hours. With what still lay ahead.

"What hope is there?" he asked, his voice toneless, his hands motionless at his side.

I stopped right in front of him, staring up into his beautiful face. "When you killed Vera, it broke her control. That's our hope. I'm still going to go there, to that camp, as soon as possible. If I can kill Rafe in time, Jax won't do it. He won't have to die. If I can kill Rafe, his command will die with him."

"And Jax will live," Damian said, light springing back into his eyes.

I finally reached for him, taking his hand in mine, heedless of the blood on my skin.

"And Jax will live," I repeated.

⇥ TWENTY-TWO ⇤

THE SUDDEN HOPE on Damian's face was so exquisite it was almost unbearable. But I was determined to make this new plan succeed. I hadn't known before now that if one of them died, their commands died with them. I could do this — I could kill him in time. As long as we found Felton, the man in the black and white robes, and all of Vera's men, and imprisoned them before they realized something had happened to her and escaped to tell Rafe.

But if we wanted to kill Rafe, I had to do it on my own. If I brought a large force with me, he'd know what I was attempting, and he'd do something drastic to stop us. There was no question in my mind that he would stop at nothing to achieve his goal. He was even more ruthless than his sister.

As if he'd read my mind, Damian squeezed my hand tighter. "I'll come with you. You don't have to do this alone."

"You're right. She shouldn't be alone," a voice came from behind us, taking us both by surprise. I whirled around to see Rylan standing there, sporting a black eye but otherwise looking unharmed. "But you can't go with her, Sire. You have to stay here and protect your palace and kingdom, in case it goes badly. *I'm* going with her."

201

"Rylan!" I cried out, letting go of Damian's hand to run and throw myself into my friend's open arms. "You're alive!"

He caught me, holding me tightly. I had to suppress my cry of pain, but he noticed and immediately let go. "You're hurt."

"I'm fine." I brushed it off. "All that matters is that you're alive. I was so afraid —"

"Of course I'm alive." He scoffed. "Just got to waste a bit of time in the dungeon with the other guards not under Vera's power. But about twenty minutes ago, our jailors suddenly remembered we weren't the enemy and let us out." Rylan glanced past me to our king, his expression darkening infinitesimally. "As soon as I heard what happened, I came straight here."

"I'm very sorry for what you were put through," Damian said, coming over to where we stood, taking my hand in his again, as though he were afraid to let me go. Maybe he was. Rylan looked down at our hands and couldn't keep his eyes from widening.

"It wasn't your fault, Your Majesty," he said, his voice suddenly much more guarded.

"You don't have to call me that when we're alone, Rylan," Damian said wearily. "Not after everything we've been through together."

Rylan's eyes were still on our clasped hands when he nodded. "If you insist, *Damian*." There was a wry bitterness to his voice that I didn't like, but now wasn't the time for any of this.

"Could you go find Tanoori?" I asked Rylan. "Have her come to my room at once." She deserved to know what had happened to Eljin — and I was hoping she could help me sew up my back and bind it for me. There was no time to wait for Lisbet to heal me. She would most likely be working on Eljin for days, and be completely drained from the effort, I was sure. "And send some men to find Felton and that man in the robes, immediately. They need to be imprisoned and questioned." I quickly related what had happened to him last night, and my fears if news somehow got out and any of them fled the palace and reached Rafe before us. "We should also make sure all of Vera's men and attendants are imprisoned, to be safe."

Rylan finally looked away from our hands to meet my beseeching eyes.

"And you can tell me all about your imprisonment and how you got that black eye when we leave to find Rafe's camp together, all right?"

"You can't —"

I squeezed Damian's hand harder, and he cut off his protest.

Rylan nodded, giving me a sharp look. I knew he'd want to talk about me and the king, more than brag about his battle wounds. "I'll bring Tanoori to you, and I'll make sure Vera's men are all found before anyone gets away," he said at last.

I nodded gratefully, and without another word to Damian, he turned and left.

"He's not happy to see this, is he?" Damian held up our joined hands.

"No."

He lifted his free hand to brush a lock of my hair behind my ear and then let his thumb trail down my jaw. "Doesn't he wish for you to be happy?"

I shivered beneath his touch. Longing filled me, despite everything else that had happened and still lay ahead of us. Part of me wished to lose myself in Damian's touch and never resurface. To let the world fall apart around us while we kept each other safe and protected, hidden in each other's arms.

But that wasn't possible, and no one knew it better than I did.

"He doesn't think you'll make me happy." I couldn't meet his probing gaze.

"Why would he think that?" Damian gently tilted my face up to force me to look at him.

"Can we not talk about this here?" I was all too aware of the bloodstained floor and Vera's body nearby.

Damian glanced at her as well and winced. "Of course. We need to get you to your room anyway, so you can lie down."

Maybe he was right, though I didn't want to admit that I needed to rest. But now that I was sure Felton and the man in the black and white robes would be caught and that the other men who had been in the delegation with her would be taken care of, we had a little bit of time before I had to rush back into the jungle. Still, a part of me — the part that had trained to be Damian's top guard for so long — wanted to go to the dungeons and question them myself. Particularly the man in the robes. I still couldn't get the look that had passed between him and Vera at that dinner out of my head. My instinct told me that he needed to be interrogated, and I didn't want to entrust it to someone else.

But I ignored the instinct — for now — and let Damian guide me to the door. When we exited his chambers, one of the young women who had been at the dinner with Vera, the same one who had told her younger sister that I was vulgar, was standing in the hallway, talking to Jerrod. He looked rested and his uniform was clean — leading me to believe he'd been under Vera's control and not imprisoned. Even though it was early, the girl's hair was already coifed elaborately, and she wore a stunning, pale yellow morning dress. They both glanced up when we walked out. The young woman's eyes widened when she saw us emerging together from the king's quarters covered in blood. Her words in the hallway, her haughty glare that had been only partially hidden by her fan, and her laughter at the dinner rose up unbidden in my mind. But now, when her gaze dropped to our entwined hands, her jaw literally fell open for a split second before she snapped it shut again.

"Your Majesty." Jerrod bowed to the king after looking me up and down quickly, his eyebrows lifting. I'm sure he wanted to know why I was covered in blood, if he hadn't already heard.

"Your Majesty," the young woman echoed belatedly, falling into a hurried curtsy. She'd probably come hoping to steal a moment of time relatively alone with the king. I couldn't help but smile, just a bit, when her eyes dropped to our hands again before she clenched her jaw and looked away.

Damian inclined his head. "Jerrod, will you please see to it that the, ah, mess in my room is taken care of immediately? After you escort Miss Durand back to her rooms," he added, his eyes flickering to the girl in the yellow dress briefly.

"Of course, Sire." Jerrod bowed again, though he looked at me questioningly.

I was too tired and in too much pain to do anything other than shrug at him. He'd have to find out what happened another time — or from the palace gossip chain. Miss Durand stared at us openly, not even trying to disguise her shock and evident dismay at being dismissed so callously.

Damian turned, gently pulling me toward my room, and I walked away from them with relief. Before I knew it, he'd opened my door and led me to my bed. I sat down carefully but still flinched at the sudden pain that shot up my back.

"Will you let me look at it and see if I can help?" Damian knelt down in front of me, concern on his face.

I shook my head. "Tanoori will be here soon. She can help me." I didn't want him to see my body, not like this. Not bloody and torn.

He reached up to smooth my hair back from my face again, cupping my head with both hands, heedless of my scars. "I know it's probably a really bad time to tell you, but I love seeing your hair down like this. You truly are beautiful, you know."

I thought of the day Lisbet had stood beside me in his room, looking at my reflection in the mirror, telling me I was both fierce and lovely. I'd believed her then, but weeks of stares and whispers and worse had shaken my belief that I could still be attractive despite my scars. When Damian told me I was beautiful, though, for some reason I believed him. The truth was in his eyes, in his touch. In the way he looked at *me* — not just at the ruined skin.

The silence stretched out until the smile slowly slid off his face. "Alexa," he began haltingly, softly, "I don't understand why, after everything we'd been through . . ." He shook his head once, a sharp, jerking motion. The pain he'd buried, hidden away, seeped into his eyes. "Why did you push me away — why did you let me believe that you didn't trust me? That you didn't find me good enough for you? I truly thought you didn't love me anymore. That it had been nothing more to you than some sort of game."

His words — his accusation — sent a hot stab of regret beneath my ribs into my heart. I reached up to cover his hands with my own trembling fingers. "No," I breathed. "It was never a game. How could you even think that of me?"

He didn't say anything, just stared into my eyes, waiting. His unspoken answer hung heavily in the air between us. How could he not? With the way I'd been treating him, what other conclusion was there?

"I was — I *am* — afraid, Damian. I'm not fit to be your queen. You need to think of what's best for your kingdom — and that would be someone of noble birth. Someone who could help solidify one of our alliances. The people of Antion deserve a queen who is equal to their king. Not your scarred guard. If they saw me on the throne beside you . . ." I trailed off, remembering the girls' mocking giggles at that dinner, Miss Durand's look of disbelief just a few moments ago when she saw us doing nothing more than holding hands. "It would diminish your power to have me at your side. It was never about *you* not being good enough. It's about me. I don't deserve you. All I know how to do is fight — I don't know how to rule a kingdom at your side. *I* am the one who isn't good enough for *you*." Once I began to tell him the truth of my feelings, and my fears, it all came flooding out. The dam I'd built inside to protect myself — to protect him — had broken, and there was no holding it back now. "I led you to believe that I didn't care about you so that you would forget about your feelings for me and do what was best for you and Antion."

Damian's lips tilted at the corners, a wistful, sad smile. "How could you ever think such a thing? First of all, how many times do I have to tell you how beautiful you are? Your scars aren't something to be ashamed of; they are a mark of your greatness. And secondly, you know how to do much more than fight. You are a natural leader, and you love with your whole heart. I am the one who would be honored to have you at my side."

"I know *you* feel that way — but what of your people? What will you do when they mock me? When they laugh at you behind your back for marrying your scarred guard? I'm no lady from the court — or nobility from another kingdom. I am not what they expect you to marry."

"Oh, Alexa." Damian stroked my hair back from my face, his touch gentle. "Do you really think I care what anyone else thinks — if your fears were even valid? Which, by the way, I don't believe to be true," he continued, not allowing me to protest. "You can't judge the beliefs of our entire kingdom based on the immature reactions of a few girls at court or a couple of insecure men in the guard who don't like being beaten by a girl." His eyes suddenly took on a teasing glint. "But that brings up another point — I have never *actually* proposed to you. That's a pretty confident assumption to make."

My eyes widened and a sudden blush burned my cheeks. I dropped my hands into my lap. "I — I didn't mean to . . . it wasn't my intent to . . ."

"Alexa." He brushed my lips with one finger, silencing my stuttering attempts to dig myself out of the hole I'd apparently created. "Can't you tell yet when I'm teasing you?"

I opened and then closed my mouth. But when I finally met his eyes once more, I couldn't ignore the way they glowed — a glow that somehow warmed all of me.

"This isn't how I pictured asking you, but if there's anything I've learned from all of this, it's that we never know how much time we have. And I refuse to waste a single minute more."

Damian shifted so that he was kneeling on one knee in front of me. My heart felt fragile beneath my ribs, thrumming with tender hope as he took my hands in his, lifting the edge of his tunic and gently wiping the blood from them, until they were mostly clean. Then he pulled them to his mouth, pressing a kiss to my knuckles, first one hand, then the other. The pulsing of my blood through my body made my back hurt worse again, but I didn't care.

"Alexa Hollen, you have served as my most trusted and valuable guard for quite some time. You have saved my life, and my kingdom, over and over again. But even more importantly, you have given me a gift more precious than life. You've given me your love." He paused, his eyes as piercing as ever. "Will you marry me, my beautiful, indomitable Alexa? May I try to deserve you by cherishing you and showering you with all the love I possess for the rest of forever?"

The emotions I felt for him nearly overwhelmed me as I gazed into his face. My heart was so full it seemed impossible for my body to cage it any longer. I suddenly remembered Tanoori's words, and I decided she was right — I wasn't going to be stubborn anymore. I was going to seize my happiness and make it my own.

Tears stung my eyes as I nodded. "Yes," I said, unable to suppress a sudden grin. "Yes, I will marry you, Damian."

Joy suffused his face, making his eyes light up with such an intense happiness, I'd never seen anything like it before. In the warm glow of dawn trickling through my window, they shone like bright blue jewels. He kissed me once, hard, then pulled back before I even had a chance to reciprocate.

"I'm sorry I don't have your ring with me right now," he said. "But I know exactly where it is — I've kept it hidden for years. It was my mother's, a parting gift from her father before she came to Antion to marry. I think she'd be very happy to know I was giving it to you." He reached up and threaded his hand through my hair.

"I can't wait to see it." My voice came out breathy as his thumb stroked down the soft skin behind my ear. My gaze dropped to his mouth, and then he was pulling my face forward, slowly, so that I was weak with need by the time his lips met mine. I immediately melted into the gentleness of his touch. This was all I'd ever wanted and never thought I deserved. As his mouth moved on mine, all the longing and love I'd suppressed for so long surged up, urging me closer to him. Ignoring my back and my dirty clothes and everything else except Damian, I clung to his shoulders and pulled him toward me, until his body pressed against mine. He carefully wrapped his free arm around me, trying to avoid my back wound. But I didn't care about the pain — it was just part of me at this point. I kissed him harder, deeper, wanting *more*. The taste of him, the smell of him, the feel of Damian was everywhere. He was my everything.

And now I was his. Truly, officially.

Forever.

A knock at the door made us jump. Damian pulled away just in time for it to open and Rylan to walk in with Tanoori on his heels.

When he saw us so close together, his eyes narrowed. I'm sure he could tell we'd been kissing — my mouth throbbed from Damian's stubble, and my unscarred skin was probably red.

"Alexa, I brought Tanoori to help you. But maybe you have all the *help* you need right now." I could tell he was trying to control his anger, but bitterness still seeped into his voice, reminding me of the awful time when we were at General Tinso's castle in Blevon, and he'd practically stopped talking to me because of my relationship with Damian. I thought we'd moved past that; I thought he'd decided to be happy for me no matter what. But apparently that was only when he thought I wasn't going to give Damian a chance.

Tanoori also looked at me with raised eyebrows, but she stayed quiet. Seeing her reminded me of the horrible reality we were all facing — of the devastating news I had to deliver to her. But at least it wasn't as bad as it could have been.

"Well, do you want her help or not?" Rylan asked impatiently.

And then Damian finally spoke. "Rylan, I demand that you apologize to Alexa at once. That is no way to talk to my fiancée."

⊰ TWENTY-THREE ⊱

YOUR WHAT?" IN his shock, Rylan didn't even attempt to hide the half horror, half jealousy on his face or in his voice.

When I looked past him to Tanoori, I saw she was trying to suppress a grin. She winked at me with a slight nod. "I wish you both every possible happiness," she said.

I couldn't help but grin back, despite Rylan's glower next to her. I was certain now that this was what she'd meant earlier. She looked truly happy for me — for *us*. I was grateful to have her there, to counteract Rylan's dismay, which threatened to wreck my happiness mere moments after achieving it.

"The man in the robes was found sitting in his room, Your Majesty, almost as if he were waiting for us." Rylan stood stiffly now, having schooled his face into a mask of indifference as he stared at the wall above our heads. "We've taken him, Felton, and the rest of Vera's attendants and men to the dungeons for further questioning."

Damian stood up slowly, reluctance on his handsome face. There was no time to continue celebrating our engagement; reality and duty beckoned us both. "Thank you for seeing to that, Rylan. And Eljin — any word on how he's doing?"

"Something's wrong with Eljin?" The smile slid off Tanoori's face as her eyes widened in concern.

212

My own grin died as I also forced myself to stand, despite the exhaustion that weighed me down and the constant pain.

"It was my fault, Tanoori —" I began, but Damian cut me off.

"No, it was *Vera's* fault. She angered Eljin so much he attempted to kill her, but in the heat of the moment, he forgot to keep his eyes turned away from hers, and she took control of him as well — and then commanded him to kill Alexa. She had no choice but to fight him."

Tanoori gasped, fear on her face. "He's not . . . he's . . ."

"I didn't kill him," I said quickly, saying a silent prayer of thanks that Lisbet had reached him in time to save him. "I tried to only defend myself, but he wouldn't stop. He was going to do whatever it took to fulfill Vera's command. I . . . I didn't have a choice. I'm so sorry."

"He was going to kill you?" she whispered, horrified.

"I told you about what they can do."

"But now she's dead. And Eljin . . . ?"

"There's no word yet," Rylan supplied. "But he was taken to Lisbet's room and she's working on him. I'm sure he'll be fine." He reached over and squeezed her hand, and Tanoori smiled thankfully at him. My heart ached when I saw him looking at her with such kindness on his face. I was afraid I'd lost my friend for good this time. When he glanced over at me, the coldness returned to his eyes, confirming my fears.

"Do you think you'll be able to help Alexa?" he asked Tanoori, looking away again, the impatience returning to his voice. "We need to leave as soon as possible."

Tanoori nodded. "I brought my sewing supplies. I'm not offi-cially trained to do this, but I have seen it done before, and I am a decent seamstress. I think I can do well enough until Lisbet can help you."

I made myself smile, though inwardly I grimaced to think of the pain of having her sew my back together. I'd grown used to being healed by sorcery. It was much less painful and also a great deal faster than the traditional route.

There was a knock at the door, and when everyone turned to look at me, I belatedly called out, "Enter!" after remembering we were all standing in my room.

General Ferraun swung open the door and stepped in, with Deron on his heels.

"Your Majesty," the general said, bowing slightly, "I am so glad to see you well."

"As am I, to see you unharmed."

"However, because of the, ah, interruption to our normal schedules, another border attack went unnoticed yesterday, Sire." General Ferraun looked vaguely embarrassed.

"What border? What happened?"

"If you could come with me, Sire, I will show you the report." General Ferraun bowed again.

"Yes, of course. And you, Captain? What tidings do you bring?"

Deron also bowed to the king. "Your Majesty, Lisbet sent me to tell you that Eljin is doing much better, although he is still unconscious. She expects him to return to full health in two or three days."

"That is excellent news, thank you, Deron." Damian glanced at Tanoori, as did I. She smiled briefly, relief washing over her face.

"I also wanted to let you know that the body has been taken care of, and your room is being cleaned as we speak."

"Very good. Thank you."

Deron's eyes flickered to me and then back to Damian. I recognized the look on my captain's face — there was something else. Something he didn't want to say.

"What is it?" I asked. "What's happened?"

When Deron didn't answer right away, Damian reached for my hand, as though it was already an instinct to turn to me for support and comfort. Warmth spread through my belly at the thought, despite my concern over what else Deron was about to tell us. "Do you have more to report, Captain?" Damian pressed.

He reluctantly nodded. "Yes, Sire." Though he addressed Damian, he finally looked straight at me as he answered. "The Dansiian man who was found waiting for us has been . . . difficult to interrogate. He . . . he is *different*. There's something about him. . . ." Deron trailed off, looking uncomfortable. "He refuses to speak, no matter what we do — except for one thing. He keeps repeating the same phrase, over and over."

"And?" Damian prompted when Deron fell silent again. "What is it?"

" 'Bring me Alexa or everyone will die.' "

There was a horrible, pregnant pause as Rylan's eyes widened and Tanoori gasped. Then Damian surprised us all by laughing. "Is that all? It's an idle threat from a desperate man. I know that everyone is probably feeling very nervous after everything that has happened in the last few days, but I assure you, no one else is going to die. Especially now that Vera is gone and the rest of the

Dansiians are imprisoned. What does he intend to do? Kill us from his cell in the dungeon? I've been close enough to him to know he's no sorcerer." Damian laughed again, and some of the concern — the fear — in Deron's eyes lifted.

But I felt the way Damian's hand tightened on mine. He wasn't as certain that it was an idle threat as he was leading them to believe, and neither was I. A chill ran down my spine as Deron grimaced in embarrassment and then chuckled nervously.

"You're right, Your Majesty. There's nothing he can do to us, or he would have done it already. I'm sorry for letting myself get . . . superstitious," he finally finished, after searching for the right word.

"It's quite all right. Completely understandable, Captain." Damian smiled at him encouragingly, but I was close enough to feel the tension hovering around him. He truly was an amazing actor, because not a hint of his underlying concern was visible or detectable in his voice. But then his expression hardened. "However, you can inform this man that he'll rot in hell before he ever gets within ten feet of Alexa. Is that understood?"

"Yes, Sire." Deron pressed his fist to his chest and bowed to the king.

Tanoori had relaxed slightly, her expression much more calm, now that Damian had put their nervousness to rest. She looked at me and gestured at the bed.

"Alexa, why don't you lie down, and I'll get to work on you?"

Damian refused to let go when I tried to untangle our fingers and follow Tanoori's suggestion, pulling me gently toward him instead. Ignoring everyone else, he said softly, "Together, we can beat anyone. You believe that, right?" He stared down into my eyes. "Please . . . don't ever leave me again."

I wasn't sure exactly what he meant — did he mean physically? Or emotionally? He knew I had to go try to save Jax as soon as possible. And we needed to talk about the man in the dungeon — and his threat. But, with everyone watching us, I didn't dare ask him, so I simply nodded and shrugged. An ambiguous response.

He bent over to press a brief kiss to the corner of my mouth and then straightened again. My cheeks burned, and I couldn't bring myself to face the general or Deron. I could feel the shock radiating from them, even without seeing their faces.

"General, let's allow Tanoori to do her work on Alexa, and you can show me that report, all right?" Damian said, moving past me to exit the room.

"Of course, Your Majesty."

I heard the sounds of feet shuffling and people walking out, and only when the door shut did I dare turn around. Tanoori stood there alone, holding a basket of supplies, a smirk on her face.

"So, you and the king . . . ?"

"I —"

"It's about time," she continued with a wink.

I stood there, my arms hanging at my sides, unsure of what to say. It was still so new. I hadn't expected so many to find out what had happened so quickly.

"All right, go ahead and lie down, and we'll get you sewn up." She took pity on me by not pressing the issue. "I'm sorry if this hurts. Would you like to drink a bit first? I've heard it can help dull the pain."

I did as she asked, not quite meeting her eyes again as I walked over to the bed. "I can't afford to be drunk right now. I'll just have to grit my teeth and bear it."

After I was lying on my stomach, I turned my head away from her and closed my eyes. I'd hoped I was so tired that I could drift off, but as soon as my lids shut, all I could see was the red stain of blood — the life force of so many, flowing over my hands, soaking my clothes. I opened my eyes again and stared at the plain wall instead as Tanoori gently lifted and tugged at the tunic, trying to pull it free from where the blood had dried. I winced but kept myself from making any noise as the fabric came away from my torn skin with a rip of pain.

"I'm sorry," she murmured.

"It's fine," I grunted.

She gently pulled the destroyed tunic away from my back and then the bandage that was underneath it as I tried not to flinch or move. Once the humid morning air touched the bared skin, she paused. "I have to make sure the wound is clean before I sew it up. This will probably burn."

I nodded against my pillow, still staring at the wall. Even though I stiffened, I wasn't prepared for the instant fire when the alcohol she used hit my exposed flesh. My back arched almost against my will, and Tanoori had to reach out and physically push me back down on the bed.

"Hold still. I'm almost done."

I couldn't answer her; I was too busy closing my hands into fists and tightening every muscle in my body in an effort to keep from moving. Within a few moments, the burning had receded, leaving behind a vague stinging, along with the throbbing pain.

"All right." Tanoori took a deep breath and blew it out between her lips. The sound was that of someone steeling their courage. "This is going to hurt. I'm so sorry."

"Just hurry" was all I said as I clenched my sheets between my hands and ground my teeth together as hard as I could.

I couldn't see if she nodded or responded in any way, but a moment later I felt her cool fingers carefully pinching the skin of my back together once again. And then the needle pierced my skin. Only by sheer willpower was I able to keep from screaming out. I knew she was moving quickly: I could feel her deft fingers working their way up my wound, but it wasn't fast enough. Each pierce of the needle, every tug of my skin, pushed me closer and closer to the edge of what I could endure.

"Tell me . . . about you . . . and Eljin. . . ." I gasped in an effort to distract myself.

She paused, her hands going still on my back.

"Don't stop." I was practically panting in the short break from the torture. "I won't be able to handle it if you stop."

"Right. Sorry." The needle pierced my skin again. Tug, tug, pull. Pierce, tug, tug, pull. "I haven't really spoken about this with anyone. . . ."

I didn't respond, just continued to clench my teeth and nodded for her to continue.

"When he saved me, I couldn't believe it. I'd resigned myself to dying — and then this hero in a mask shows up at the very last moment. He was unbelievable. I'd never seen anyone do what he could do." She spoke quietly as her fingers continued to guide the needle over and over again. "Though I'd lived with the Insurgi, it hadn't been that long, and I'd never really seen any of the sorcerers do anything significant."

I focused on her words, pushed aside the unending pain, and let her story envelop me instead.

"You saw how he was on that trek to Blevon. Not exactly endearing. And when I found out who he really was — I was so upset I refused to talk to him. But once we got to his father's castle, something seemed to change in him. I'd catch him watching me, and I couldn't tell for sure with his mask on, but sometimes it looked like his eyes were smiling." Her hands grew still on my back. "That should do it. Let me tie this off, and then I'll wash your back and get a bandage on you." The bed creaked a bit as she bent over to retrieve her basket again.

I breathed a huge sigh of relief now that it was finally over. My entire torso ached, and every infinitesimal movement caused a jolt of pain, but now that the wound was closed, it wasn't as bad as it had been. "Go on," I urged as she began to wipe down my back with a moist cloth. It must have been alcohol again, because it stung a bit when she went over the stitches, but nothing like before.

"Things didn't truly start to change until we made it back to the palace and you defeated Iker. Once he decided to stay and Damian put me in charge of the displaced women and babies from the breeding house, he started seeking me out. For silly things mostly, and I began to wonder if he might be . . ." She paused, her hand going still again for a moment on my back. "But I convinced myself I was wrong. No one could ever want me; I was sure of it. Not after they found out I was damaged."

"Tanoori, no. You can't let yourself think that way."

She began to wipe my back down again and gave a soft, self-deprecating laugh. "How can I not? After what I've been through . . . it's hard to imagine any man wanting me . . . like *that*. Especially once he finds out I am barren." Her voice was so matter-of-fact it tore at my heart. But before I could speak, she continued, "And honestly, I wasn't sure if *I* could ever want a man like that, either. For a long time, even the thought of a man touching me in any way made me ill."

The wiping stopped, and the next thing I felt was a soft towel being used to dry my back. My heart ached for her, for what she'd been through and still suffered because of it. I wished I'd known she was there — so close, this whole time. But even as I thought it, I wondered if it would have made things even worse, because what could I have done to help her? Nothing, except expose us both.

"But Eljin was kind. He never tried to do anything inappropriate; he'd only come to talk. We are both outsiders because of the wounds we carry — even if mine are invisible to the eye. And that's how it happened. He found me crying one particularly difficult day when I'd spent hours trying to find my friend's baby with no luck. He asked if I would mind if he put his arm around me . . . and I wasn't sickened at the thought. His touch was the first that actually comforted me, rather than hurt me.

"After that," she said as she carefully helped me sit up so she could wrap a new bandage around my torso, "he began to ask me to go on picnics with him. He's surprisingly kind and understanding. We both have battle wounds. We understand each other."

I watched her as she looped the thick white cloth around me and tied it off. When she was done, she blew a strand of hair out of her face and finally met my eyes. I impulsively reached out and took her hand in mine, squeezing it. "He's going to make it," I said. "And I truly wish you both all the happiness in the world. No one deserves it more than you."

Tanoori squeezed my hand back, blinking hard. "You have to help Damian. Help him figure out what's really going on and stop it, so we can finally all live in peace."

"I plan on doing exactly that," I promised. But in the back of my mind, the threat the man in the dungeons had made lingered, along with the bitter tang of fear in my mouth from the looming fight with Rafe.

But Tanoori was looking at me with such faith in her eyes, and a smile on her face, that I couldn't bring myself to say anything that would ruin her hope for happiness. Forcing my worries down, I smiled back.

She let go of my hand to stand up. "You need to rest, at least for a couple of hours." She began to gather her things, putting the needle and thread and bloody pieces of fabric and cloth into her basket, as well as a dark bottle of liquid.

"I can't afford to let time waste."

"You also can't afford to collapse from exhaustion. I put a lot of work into those stitches. I don't want them going to waste if you run off and get yourself killed because you're too tired to fight." Tanoori pointed her finger at me with mock severity.

"All right," I relented. "But do you promise to come wake me in two hours?"

"Just two hours?" She lifted an eyebrow at me, but when I glared back, she finally nodded. "If you insist."

After putting the basket over her arm again, Tanoori turned and headed to the door.

Just before she opened it, I called out, "Tanoori — I — thank you."

"Of course," she said. "Now get some rest." And then she was gone, leaving me in solitude for the first time in hours.

After carefully pulling on a set of clean clothes, I slowly inched my way back down onto the bed. I thought I'd be unable to sleep after all of the horrible and wonderful events of the last day, but this time when I shut my eyes, blood didn't haunt me, and I was asleep before my head had fully sunk into my pillow.

A pounding on my door woke me after what felt like only a few minutes. Groggily, I forced my eyes open to gaze blearily around my room. The light from my window was brighter, the sun high in the sky. So it had been longer than a few minutes.

The pounding came again.

"Who is it?"

"It's Rylan," I heard my friend's voice through the wood.

"Well, come in already. What are you waiting for?"

The door swung open and he strode in, not meeting my eyes. He looked like a thundercloud ready to burst.

"What is it?" I pushed myself up in bed, feeling my new stitches pull but thankfully hold.

"We have to go. Now."

"All right. I was planning on leaving as soon as I rested a bit. I was ordered to catch up on my sleep." I stood up and waited for a moment as the blood rushed through my body, turning my vision temporarily dark.

"This isn't the time for joking," he spoke shortly, striding over to me to hand me the sword I'd dropped in Damian's room.

"I'm sorry," I replied, taking the sword and sheathing it at my side. "I wasn't really trying to be funny. I was only speaking the truth."

"Look, something's happened, all right?" Rylan took my arm when I walked past him to get my extra pair of boots, turning me to look at him.

"What?" My stomach dropped as I imagined all sorts of horrible scenarios. "Is it Damian?"

"No. Your *fiancé* is fine." He bit out the word. "For now. But the attack the general came to tell him about? It wasn't an ordinary raid."

I stared up into his eyes, relief and fear beating in time with the pounding of my heart.

"This time, the sorcerer burned the entire village to the ground, killing everyone, except one man. He was only left alive so he could deliver a message. That this is a declaration of war. And that this is only the beginning of what's to come for our people."

⇥ TWENTY-FOUR ⇤

THE BLEAKNESS IN Rylan's eyes matched the sudden horrible emptiness in my gut, the feeling that the ground was falling away from me.

"But . . . why?" I whispered. "They killed *everyone*?" Tears sprang to my eyes as I remembered another attack, another village, years ago, that left me standing alone next to my twin, staring down at the burned bodies of our parents. How could anyone — even a black sorcerer, as vile as they are — kill an *entire* village of people? Women, children, *babies* . . . My stomach lurched, and I was suddenly grateful I hadn't eaten in so long. There was nothing to come up except bile that burned my throat.

"King Damian wishes to see you before we go. But we must hurry and finish this and return with Jax. General Ferraun is pushing for retaliation against Blevon, but Damian is still clinging to the hope that it's not them causing this fight."

"It's *not* Blevon," I said. "We know the truth now — it had to be Rafe or Vera controlling the Blevonese soldiers that have been involved in the raids. We can't attack our allies. The real fight is with Dansii."

"No, it isn't." Rylan looked at me with pity in his eyes. "The man they sent to deliver the message had a sealed missive.

It held the declaration of war — and it was signed by General Tinso."

His words echoed in my mind, spiraling down into my body, where shock clutched at my heart. My mouth opened and closed, but nothing came out. It wasn't possible. We knew the truth now — the threat was from *Dansii*, not Blevon. They were our allies. Eljin had told Lisbet to go to his father if all else failed. General Tinso had done so much to help us —

"Damian won't listen to reason, though. He keeps claiming Eljin can prove he's right, and that there's no way Eljin's father really signed the declaration. But Eljin is unconscious right now, and the general doesn't want to wait for him to wake up before taking a course of action. He feels that too many lives will be lost if this continues. This is two attacks this week alone." Rylan paused and then said, "Alexa, you have to talk to him. You have to convince him to let go of his hopes and face reality."

My mind whirled as I hurried over to get my boots and pull them on. I couldn't believe it. General Tinso, declaring war on us? Less than two months after helping Damian take the throne — and with his son and sister living here? My stomach clenched as I quickly braided my hair back and bound it with a small leather strap, and then I pulled on a clean vest with the king's insignia.

Rylan watched me silently. When I finally faced him, his expression was expectant. "Alexa? Will you talk to him?"

I took a deep breath and then shook my head. "I agree with Damian. This doesn't make sense. Why would Blevon declare war on us again — and in such a violent, horrible way?"

"It doesn't matter if it makes *sense*," Rylan bit out, his color rising, "what matters is saving our people from further destruction. If we don't fight back, soon there won't *be* an Antion to save."

His words sent an icy finger of dread through my body. "Where is Damian?"

"He's waiting for you in his library." Rylan opened my door and gestured for me to precede him.

I rushed down the hallway, desperate to see Damian, to try and figure out what was really going on. Nothing added up. Why would Blevon declare war on us after working so hard to establish peace? Damian was one of their own — a half Blevonese king ruling a neighboring kingdom. They couldn't hope for a better ally. And after what Eljin and Lisbet had told me about Blevon and their sacred beliefs, I believed Eljin's claim that Blevon would never use black sorcerers for anything. But then why would General Tinso do this?

It had to be Dansii. They must have done something to him; they had to be forcing him to do this. *Dansii* was the kingdom that used black sorcerers. Dansii was the kingdom that would be furious right now at the death of King Hector. The kingdom that had sent the delegation with the intent to bewitch the king, turn him into a mindless slave, and take me for some reason. It all came back to Dansii. Somehow, King Armando was behind this.

Was it because he wanted Antion? Or was Eljin right, and he was only using us to get to Blevon and whatever secret was guarded there?

The threat from the man in the robes echoed through my mind again. His promise was coming true — people were dying.

I already knew that Rafe was one of King Armando's secret weapons. But were there more like him? Or others who had powers we couldn't even fathom? The thought was chilling. Particularly since regular sorcerers couldn't sense them.

My mind whirled around and around as I raced through the palace, running toward Damian.

"Alexa, slow down!" I heard Rylan call from behind me, but I didn't listen.

And then I ground to a halt.

"Alexa!" Rylan shouted, nearly caught up to me, but I ignored him.

Suddenly, I knew what I had to, even though it would make Damian furious. Turning on my heel, I ran the other way, toward the nearest door that would let me out into the courtyard.

I was going to the dungeons to talk to the man in the robes.

The dungeons were as dark and hot as always, but instead of Jaerom waiting at the bottom of the stairs with a smile and a teasing welcome, calling me Little Boss, a new keeper of the keys stood in his place, a tall brute of a man with eyes the color of night and a wide mouth. The reality that Jaerom was gone hit me all over again, the memory of Iker killing him on the steps of the palace surging up in my mind.

"What's a girl doin' down here?" the new man growled, pulling my focus back to the moment. "Get back up into the light where you belong."

Refusing to be cowed, even though the man was enormous and his arms were the size of both of my thighs put together, I straightened my shoulders and gave him my haughtiest look. "I am no mere *girl*. I am Alexa Hollen, guard to King Damian, and I'm ordering you to take me to see the prisoner from Dansii who wears the black and white robes."

The man's eyes widened slightly, and then he shrugged, indifference sliding back into place on his face. "Makes no difference to me if you want to get yourself hurt or killed. But I'm not cleaning up the mess."

"Alexa, what are you doing?" Rylan flew down the stairs after me, shooting a look between me and the keeper of the keys.

"She wants to go see the wailer back there," he said, throwing a thumb over his shoulder, toward the cells.

"Damian made us all swear to keep you away from him. You can't do this — you'll get us all in trouble, and you'll make him furious." Rylan paused. "Although, on second thought, maybe you *should* go talk to him. See what you can get out of the man. You always were the best at interrogations."

I ignored him and gestured for the keeper of the keys to take me to the man's cell. He lifted a torch out of the bucket, lit it, and strode down the black hallway into the belly of the dungeon. The smell of unwashed bodies, feces, and sweat hit me like a wall, and only grew worse the deeper in we went. Memories of my own time locked down here welled up, but I forced them away. I didn't have time for distraction.

"Here you go." The man handed me a key and gestured at the door in front of him. "Good luck." And with that, he turned and left, striding back the way he'd come.

"Alex, do you really —"

"Wait out here." I cut Rylan off. "I'll be fast."

Rylan held another lit torch, and in the flickering firelight, his expression was severe. Worry tightened his mouth into a line. "Here, take this so you can at least see what you're doing."

"And leave you in the dark?"

"Better me than you," he said. "I don't trust this man. Something's off with him."

Now that I was here, I was beginning to question the prudence of this idea. But it was too late now. I refused to turn around and walk away. He might have answers. And if there was one thing I needed right now, it was answers. There had been far too many questions for far too long.

Steeling my courage, I grabbed the torch from Rylan, gave him the key, and pulled out my sword. "Go ahead." I nodded toward the door.

He shut his eyes for a moment, and then with a shake of his head, stepped forward and unlocked the door.

When I stepped into the cell, the first thing I noticed was the chill. It should have been just as hot, if not hotter, in there as in the hallway, but instead, I had to suppress a shiver.

And then I saw the man, bound to a chair with chains, sitting as tall and proud as ever. One corner of his mouth was swollen and bloody, and his face bore bruises and other marks. Either he had put up a fight before his capture, or he had been interrogated with quite a bit of brutality.

But his eyes were as clear as could be in the torchlight, and he was looking straight at me. His pupils were abnormally large, making his eyes almost look black, except for a ring of silver where his irises were visible.

"Alexa, I knew you would come," he spoke in perfect

Antionese, with barely a trace of an accent. "You aren't the type to let a threat slide past you."

"I didn't come because of your threat," I lied. "What can *you* do to hurt any of us? You're locked in a dungeon." I turned and put the torch in a bracket on the wall, then faced him once more. "I came for answers."

"Never underestimate your enemies, Alexa. That's always been the first mistake of the conquered." His voice was soft, but it sent a shudder through me. And where was that blasted cold coming from? My fingers were icy on the hilt of my sword.

"Are you my enemy? I had hoped that in your present situation, you might change your mind about that." I stepped toward him, lifting my sword so that it was level with his throat, though not close enough to touch — yet.

But rather than backing down, he just laughed, a sharp, guttural sound that sent fingers of alarm down my spine.

"*I* am not the enemy. Those who block the way to victory are the enemy."

"What are you talking about? I want answers, not riddles. Are you talking about Blevon? Is that what Armando is after? Is he using our kingdom to get what he really wants?"

The man just lifted an eyebrow, looking at me impassively.

"If you aren't going to tell me what I need to know, I don't see any reason to keep you alive." I tightened my grip on my sword and took another step forward so that my blade was only inches from his skin. "Tell me why Dansii is framing Blevon. Why does your kingdom want us to go to war again?"

The man remained silent, a slight smile curling his thin lips.

231

"Fine. Then tell me this — who are you? What was your relationship with Vera?"

When I said her name, I finally saw a crack in his calm veneer. A shudder went through his body, and a flame of hatred flared in his eyes. The chill in the room evaporated into blistering heat. But as quickly as the change came, it was gone. The man smoothed his features back into placid indifference, and a waft of icy air encircled us once again.

So it *was* him; somehow the coldness was emanating from *him*. What kind of power did he wield — and how much danger was I in? He was chained to a chair, weaponless, harmless; I was the one holding a sword. And yet, fear itched beneath my skin, urging me to turn and run.

"You will pay for what you've done," he finally spoke. "You and your king. The destroyers of our most precious masterpieces deserve to suffer and burn. And so you shall. You shall watch your king suffer and die for his crime. For both of your crimes."

"Vera was no masterpiece. She was a demon. And don't you *dare* threaten Damian." I strode forward and grabbed his hair, yanking his head back to expose his throat. "I could kill you right now, and no one would care. Your life is nothing to us, unless you prove useful."

"Your love is weakness. And it will be your downfall." He spat at me, even with my blade pressed so hard against his skin that a trickle of blood ran down his throat, staining his white robe.

"Who are you?" I shouted. "What do you want from us?"

The fire of hatred burned in his eyes again, and his pupils dilated suddenly, enveloping his irises entirely. I stifled a scream, fighting the urge to jump back; my whole body trembled.

A gust of wind tore through the cell, and my torch suddenly guttered and went out, leaving us in darkness.

"What did y —"

"You think you know what game you're playing at, little girl." His voice was a hiss in the darkness, coming from everywhere, echoing through the cell, in my head, through my body. "But you have *no clue*. This is so much bigger than you could ever imagine. You or your pathetic lover who calls himself a king. *My* king, the *true* king, will crush your kingdom to the ground if that's what it takes to get what is needed."

"Stop it!" I yelled. "Rylan! I need you! Rylan!" I spun in the direction of the door but couldn't tell if I was even facing the right way, the darkness was so complete.

"I only allowed myself to be taken to deliver this message to you." The man's voice came from directly behind me, a burning whisper that made me scream and whirl around, swinging my sword wildly in the dark. It met nothing but air. My heart raced and I gasped for a breath. He couldn't be behind me. He was chained to a chair a few feet away.

"You want to know who I am?" his silky voice came again, this time from in front of me. I lunged forward blindly, only to have my sword hit the wall with a loud ping. I flattened my back against the damp stone, trying to orient myself by staring forward into the impenetrable blackness. Terror gripped my lungs until I could barely breathe.

"I am *Manu de Reich os Deos*." His voice became a roar. "I should kill you and everyone you love right now for the threats you made against me. For taking Vera from me. And I will — you will pay for what you've done. But not now. The time has not yet come for your death."

His voice grew louder and louder, until my ears ached and my head felt like it would burst.

"King Armando is the only true king, and he will rain fire and destruction down upon you and all those you love before he'll let a pathetic, grotesque little girl get in his way. He will take what he needs from you — you will serve your purpose."

"Enough!" I screamed, lifting my sword up higher and charging forward. He was there, somewhere. I would shove my blade through him before he could use the power of his voice to frighten me anymore.

"And then, when he is done, you will die, little guard. You will die when the time is right." I felt his lips brush my ear and I whirled, blindly striking into the darkness, and hit nothing.

"And I look forward to it eagerly."

There was another rush of wind, the ice in the air turned to burning, fiery heat, and in a blast of light that nearly blinded me, I saw the man standing right in front of me, his eyes burning into mine. Next to him stood Damian. I gasped and tried to rush to him, but I was suddenly frozen. When did he get here — and why? Damian reached out to me, his mouth forming my name, but no sound came out. Instead, blood trickled out of a corner of his lips, running down his chin. And then he began to crumble to the ground, his eyes falling shut. I screamed his name, but I still couldn't move. And then with a boom that shook the dungeon like thunder —

"Alexa!"

I blinked and the horrific scene was gone. I still stood next to the man who had called himself *Manu de Reich os Deos*, with his hair in one hand, his head tilted back, and my sword against his throat. He was still chained to the chair, his eyes on mine.

And we were alone in the cell. Damian was nowhere to be seen.

"Alexa — I thought I heard you call for me," Rylan said from the doorway.

I could barely catch my breath; my heart thudded beneath my ribs. A trick. Some sort of mind trick. As though he'd suddenly scalded me, I let go of Manu's hair and stepped back, letting my sword fall to my side.

"I've heard enough," I finally answered Rylan. "The man is insane. I got what I could out of him."

I strode out of the room, Manu's voice following after me, "Remember what you saw! That's barely even a shadow of what's to come. . . ."

His harsh laughter echoed after me as I rushed down the hallway, trying to escape the sound, the memory of what he'd done to me. Past the new keeper of the keys, faster and faster, practically stumbling up the stairs, until I burst out into the light of day once more with a strangled gasp.

"Alexa," Rylan's voice came from right behind me, as gentle as the soft breeze that now touched my cheeks — nothing like the preternaturally cold gush of wind I'd felt in that cell. No, that he'd made me *think* I'd felt. "What did he do — are you all right?"

"I'm fine," I said, brushing Rylan's hand off my shoulder. "But make sure everyone knows to never look directly into that man's eyes."

When I finally reached the door to Damian's library, it was shut. Deron stood to the side of it, his hand on his sword hilt; he was watching me.

"Good day, Alexa," Deron said. "I hope you are feeling better."

"Much, thank you," I lied with a nod at him. I didn't want to talk to him about what had happened. I didn't want to tell *anyone*. "Shouldn't you be sleeping? You were up all night."

"There will be time to rest later. Right now the king needs me."

I pursed my lips but didn't argue. Who was I to tell him he needed to sleep if he didn't want to?

Without another word, I lifted my hand and knocked on the library door, unsure of the etiquette now that I was the king's fiancée and not just his guard. Rylan was right behind me, his face unreadable.

"Are you going to tell me what happened in there?"

"Nothing happened," I said, glancing up at Rylan just as the door opened.

"There you are, Alexa." General Ferraun's voice wasn't what I expected to hear, and I hoped the surprise didn't show on my face as I turned to face him. His gaze flickered to my scars, then back to my eyes again. "The king is waiting for you." The frustration in his voice was all too evident.

Pulling back my shoulders and holding my chin high, I stepped past him. After Damian and I were married, the general would have to address me as "Your Majesty" as well. It was a thrilling — and terrifying — thought.

But when I saw Damian standing behind his desk across the expanse of the room, watching me enter, any other thoughts fled, and it was all I could do not to rush to him and throw myself into his arms. After the terrifying vision Manu had somehow forced upon me, seeing him standing there — healthy and whole — made my legs weak with relief. Sunlight bathed his dark hair with an amber glow. He had washed and changed into dark breeches, tall boots, a clean tunic and vest. His collar of office encircled his broad shoulders. The thin golden signet crown he preferred for everyday use rested upon his head. When his eyes met mine, the intensity of his gaze stole my breath.

"Alexa." My name sounded like a sigh of relief from his lips.

I stopped a few feet back, unsure of what to do.

"Maybe she can talk some sense into him," I heard the general say to Rylan behind me, but Rylan's response was lost by Damian asking, "Did Rylan tell you the news?"

I knew immediately what he referred to. The destruction of the village and the declaration of war. "Yes."

Everyone was silent for a long, tense moment.

"Why did it take so long to get her?" Damian finally asked, looking past me to Rylan.

I spun to face Rylan, hoping he could read the warning on my face. He met my eyes and his lips tightened. "I'm sorry, Sire. Something came up that delayed me. I tried to hurry as fast as possible."

"We are on the brink of war, and you felt that something else took precedence?"

"I am sorry, Your Majesty."

I didn't dare mouth the words *thank you* with General Ferraun watching, but I hoped Rylan could read it in my eyes.

"The point is that I'm here now," I said, turning back to Damian.

"Yes, you are," Damian murmured, then looked past me to where the two men were waiting. "You are both dismissed for now." His tone brooked no arguments, but the general still huffed from behind me.

"Sire, we really need —"

"What I *need*" — Damian cut him off — "is to talk to Alexa. Alone."

There was a second of silence, and then General Ferraun said, "As you wish, Sire," from behind me, his tone tight with anger.

"Yes, Sire," Rylan echoed. I didn't turn around to watch them leave. My cheeks burned, and I flinched when the door shut.

Damian stood stiffly behind his desk, staring down at an unfurled scroll of parchment.

"Is that it?" I asked.

"Yes."

"I don't believe it. He wouldn't do this; I know it."

Damian looked up, a tiny flicker of hope igniting on his face. "You didn't come to tell me it's time to fight?"

"No. At least, not Blevon. Your uncle is behind this somehow. He has to be. It always seems to come back to Dansii."

"I think you're right. But . . . why? I feel like a pawn in a game that no one ever bothered to teach me." Damian closed his eyes, pinching the bridge of his nose. "All I want is to protect my people. To give them peace, for once in their lives."

My heart swelled with love for him as I stood there, watching him in the glow of the morning light. He was such a good man. Such a great king. "We'll figure it out, Damian. Together, we can do anything. Right?"

There was a long pause, and then he looked up at me.

"Alexa . . ." This time, my name sounded like a plea, a half-formed prayer. Our gazes met across his desk; I could see the desperation lurking deep in his eyes. His shoulders were tense with the weight he held — the weight of a nation on the brink of war, or destruction. A muscle flexed in his jaw as he finally moved, striding around the desk toward me. I rushed forward, and suddenly I was in his arms, gathered against his body. I held in the gasp of pain as his arms enclosed me, but he must have felt me tense, because he released me just as quickly.

"Did I hurt you?"

"No, I'm fine," I said, stepping toward him again. I could suddenly feel my pulse in strange places in my body — like my neck and my belly. I wanted to take away all of his pain and fear. Manu's warning that my love for him would be my downfall prickled at the back of my mind, but I refused to listen to it. He was wrong. Our love made us *stronger* — not weak.

His eyes darkened as if he could read my thoughts. He lifted his hands to run them down my arms. "Were you able to rest?" His voice was low.

"Yes." Could he hear my heart pounding? How could he not? It was practically deafening me. His touch, innocent as it was, made every inch of my body burn. I tilted my head back, reminded once again of how very tall he actually was, so that I could look up at him.

"Did you know that this room was my mother's favorite place in the entire palace? She used to come here every day." Damian glanced around us, at the soaring shelves of books, and I realized at last why he, too, came here so often. "After she died, my father forbade any of us from coming here. He not only took her away, he took away her memory as well. Her garden . . . her library. He thrived on cruelty. He used fear as a tool to ensure his power."

He looked back down at me at last, and the profound sadness in his eyes struck me like a knife, deep in my chest. "I don't want you to go," he said hoarsely, his hands growing still, gently encircling my biceps. "I can't help but think . . ." He trailed off, shook his head. Then suddenly, in a rush, he said, "I'm afraid that if you go, you'll never come back. That you'll be taken from me like everyone else I have ever loved."

I swallowed hard. "You know I *have* to go."

Damian's grip tightened slightly, almost subconsciously. "Is he suffering?"

I considered my words. "They hadn't hurt him yet when I left," I answered cautiously. "They aren't going to do anything to him until tomorrow at dawn — if I don't show up."

He nodded, accepting what I'd told him as fact.

"But that's why I have to go. I can save him, Damian. I know I can."

He searched my eyes and smiled grimly, a bleak expression on his handsome face. "I know you can. I just wish I could go with you."

I hesitantly reached up to brush a lock of his hair back from his forehead. "You have to stay here and protect your kingdom. If something were to go wrong, the king can't —"

"*Nothing* is going to go wrong." His fingers squeezed my arms so tightly it almost hurt. "You have to come back to me — do you hear me? You have to. And once you get Jax and bring him home, I never want you to leave my side again." The fervency of his expression made my heart stumble in my chest, stealing my breath. "Promise me."

"That I'll come back?"

"*Promise me*, Alexa. Not only that you'll come back but that you'll never leave my side again. I can't bear to lose you. I can't bear to lose anyone else that I love." The fear in his voice hit me like a physical blow. I thought again of the little boy who had watched his mother being killed in front of him. Of the young man whose brother sent him away to hide before also being murdered. He'd had to kill his own father. Pain and loss had been his constant companion for so long. I couldn't bear the thought of adding to it.

"I promise." I reached up with both hands to cup his face. "I promise I will come back to you, Damian."

He was so close I could feel the warmth of his breath on my lips. All the grief he'd borne seemed etched onto his face, into the very sinews of his body. I felt bare, completely exposed before him as he stared into my eyes. Surely he could see past my hazel irises, past my flesh and bone, and straight into my soul. Straight into the most sacred, hidden depths of my heart that had long been his.

And then he was kissing me, with a fierceness that took my breath away. All the desperation we'd both lived with, the sorrow of loss, the joy of finally committing our hearts to each other, the fear of what still lay ahead, enveloped us as his arms encircled me, holding me against him. I stretched up on my tiptoes, pressing into him, aching to be closer. I held him as tightly as I could, wishing we had more than this brief moment to be together, to celebrate our engagement, before I had to go once more to face the enemies who seemed to continually amass on all sides, determined to tear us apart.

As his lips left mine, I made a promise to myself. I would do everything in my power to make him happy, to spare him from any more hurt.

He was mine, and I was his. The king and future queen of Antion.

But even more importantly, we were Damian and Alexa. Orphans. Survivors. And now, finally, we would be together.

We were silent for a time as I mustered the courage to walk away from him. But he spoke first. "I've been thinking. What could Armando have to gain by pushing us into war with Blevon?"

Eljin's theory came to mind, and I briefly told Damian what the sorcerer had told me. "But if his only goal is to get to Blevon, why would Armando send Vera here, to try and control you? Why do they want me? Why are they doing any of it?" I didn't dare tell him about Manu's threat — that King Armando needed something from me, and once he got it, *then* he would kill me.

Damian looked past me, out the window. "I can only think of one reason why," he said. "If he wanted to invade and take control of Antion for himself, and then move on to Blevon . . . he would do all of this. Perhaps he is hoping to take everyone's focus off of Dansii and reduce our strength by starting another war between our kingdoms." Damian paused and his eyes shut for a moment. "He *must* be planning to invade." His shoulders sagged infinitesimally as he spoke. "He's never met me; he obviously couldn't care less about my being his nephew. Now that his brother is gone . . ."

"He wants to create an empire," I finished with a sickening twist in my belly. "It makes sense."

When Damian looked back into my eyes, he stood taller again, his expression turning from dismayed to determined. He suddenly bent forward to press a kiss to my lips and then took my hands in his.

"If you can kill Rafe, his commands will die with him — correct?"

"Yes. That's what happened with Vera." I nodded.

"Then if we're right, and he's the one controlling the Blevonese soldiers, once he's dead, they'll realize what they're doing and stop."

"At least that will solve one of our problems. And we'll get Jax back."

Damian smiled grimly at me. "I don't want you to go, but there is no one to whom I'd rather entrust my brother's life than you." He took me in his arms again, gently reaching up to tuck a strand of hair behind my ear. "I think I made a mess of your braid," he said, a hint of a smile teasing his lips, just for a moment, and then fading again as he stared down into my face.

"I'll come back. By tomorrow morning, we'll be together again." I stretched up to kiss him. Once, twice. "And like you said," I said softly against his mouth, "together we can beat any-one, right? Whatever it is Armando is trying to do, we'll stop him. Together."

He sealed my promise with another kiss.

All too soon, I had to pull away. "I should go," I whispered.

Damian nodded, letting his forehead drop to rest against mine for a moment. Then he pulled his shoulders back and stepped away. "Yes. You're right." He still held my hand as he turned and began to lead me to the door. Just before we reached it, he stopped and pulled me in for one last kiss. I tried to fill it with all the confi-dence and love I felt, but I was afraid he could feel my desperation and fear as I clung to him. I had promised him I'd come back with Jax, and I was determined to keep my promise.

But part of me was terrified of what lay ahead in the jungle.

"I love you," Damian said softly as we broke apart for the last time.

I hoped he could see the truthfulness of my feelings for him in my face. "And I love you."

I wasn't sure how much time had passed, but I could tell it had been long enough when Damian opened the door and Rylan spun around with an ill-concealed glare.

"Are you ready now?"

"Rylan," Damian warned.

"Excuse me, my *future queen*" — he swept down low in a theatrical bow — "for any offense I may have caused."

"Rylan, it's fine. Yes, I'm ready." I squeezed Damian's hand and looked up into his eyes one last time.

Come back to me, he mouthed.

"I promise," I said softly. My heart was unbearably full with all the love I had for him, to the point of being painful. As I took a step away from him, a strange foreboding washed over me, leaving me suddenly chilled. I shook it off and made myself smile at him. My fiancé — the king of Antion.

Deron still stood next to the door as well, but General Ferraun was no longer in the hallway. Damian turned to his captain and began to tell him our theories about Dansii and King Armando's intentions.

I walked over to Rylan, but he would hardly even look at me.

Taking a deep breath, I said, "Well, let's go."

Without a word, he nodded and turned to march down the hall. I followed, glancing back at Damian once to see him still talking to Deron, but his eyes were on me.

I promise, I thought. *I'll come back to you.*

But for some reason, that same chill scraped down my spine when I turned the corner, taking him from my sight.

ᗒ TWENTY·FIVE ᗕ

After eating some food from the kitchen and packing a bit more into a knapsack, Rylan and I headed out together. We stopped to check on Eljin first, praying that he would be awake and could give me some more answers about Blevon, sorcerers, and his father. But he was still unconscious, healing. My only comfort was that he looked so much better that I finally believed he would live. As long as I survived the next day and night, I would return and get the answers I needed.

Tanoori sat by his bedside, bathing his forehead with a cool cloth. She stood when we came in and wished us luck. Lisbet had gone to collect more supplies, so we weren't able to see her before heading out. Tanoori promised to deliver our message that we would return with Jax by tomorrow at the latest.

The sun was hot on our backs as we stepped through the palace wall. When we plunged into the thick greenery of the jungle, the shade was a relief of sorts, but the humidity swelled even thicker, coating my skin and making my tunic stick to my stitches. I wore a bow and a pack of arrows across my back, and my sword hung at my hips. I even had a small dagger strapped to my left leg. Rylan was similarly armed. I wished we could take a larger group with us, but I knew if we did, Rafe would immediately grow suspicious, and who knew what he'd do.

It was up to Rylan and me to sneak into the camp and kill Rafe before he could do anything drastic. And then hope his men hated him as much as I suspected they might, if they weren't under his control any longer. Otherwise, we'd be fighting our way out, too.

We trekked silently for a long time, following the same path we'd used before, and the more obvious signs that an injured Felton had made on his way to the palace. I'd also purposely broken a few branches as I'd followed him, to help us find our way.

Finally, after an hour of tension-filled silence, I spoke. "Could we stop for a moment? Maybe we could eat a little."

Rylan turned to face me and shrugged. "Fine."

Although I'd eaten a bit at the palace before leaving, my stomach was still aching from being empty for so long. I found a fallen log, checked the trees around it for hidden snakes or other predators, and sat down to open the knapsack and pull out one of the rolls and the cheese the cook had packed for us. I bit into the flaky crust, relishing the taste of the yeasty bread, despite how dry my mouth was. Luckily, we also had a water flagon this time, full of cool water from one of the palace wells.

"So, are you going to give me the silent treatment from now on?" I finally asked, when Rylan continued to stand several feet away, his arms crossed over his chest, staring stoically out into the endless, shadowed jungle.

He glanced over at me, then away again. "No."

I took another bite and waited, but he didn't say anything else.

"Rylan, please don't be mad at me. You're my closest friend, and you promised that would never change."

"I'm not happy that I had to lie to Damian for you." He finally turned to face me, his expression still guarded, but after a moment, he softened slightly. "But I'm not *mad* at you. I've already told you that I could never be mad at you."

"Then why are you acting like this?" I stood up, holding my half-eaten roll, ignoring the discomfort from my stitches pulling.

He shrugged, his brown eyes hooded. "I'm jealous, all right? You want the truth? That's it. I'm jealous of Damian."

His words hit me deep in the belly. My mother had always told me that although the truth sometimes hurt, it was always best to be honest. She was right, but it didn't make this any easier.

"I'd begun to hope that maybe . . . with some time . . . you and I . . ." He trailed off and shook his head. "But that was just ridiculous. I knew how you still felt about Damian. I could see it every time you looked at him. I could hear it in your voice."

"Ry, I'm so sorry —" I began, but he held up a hand.

"I'm happy for you. Truly I am." He finally met my eyes, and the unmasked pain on his face cut me to the core, belying his words. "But I might not be able to continue on as Damian's guard after this. It will be too hard."

I swallowed past a sudden constriction in my throat. "We will understand your decision if you choose that, of course. But I know that I, for one, hope that you will reconsider."

Rylan rolled his eyes, and I paused.

"What?"

"You're already referring to you and Damian as 'we.'"

"Oh." I fought to suppress a blush. He was right. "Well," I continued, flustered, "the point is that there is no one I'd rather have protecting us from future attacks or harm. Especially since I'm not sure if the queen will be allowed to walk around the palace with a sword strapped to her side."

"Most likely not. I can't imagine it, though — you without a sword." Rylan shook his head, a wry smile turning up the corners of his mouth.

"Me, either," I agreed. In fact, the thought was unsettling. Now that the initial happiness of having finally revealed my true feelings to Damian and our sudden engagement had worn off, I was struck again by the absurdity of *me* becoming queen. "I'm going to have to wear a dress all the time, aren't I?" I spoke the realization out loud. Even I could hear the dismay in my voice.

Rylan laughed, a sound that made me smile despite myself. "Yes, I believe that is the expected uniform of a queen. Dresses and silks and jewels. It will be a trial, to be sure."

"Oh, stop." I swatted at him. "For me, it will be. You know I have no idea how to act like a lady, let alone a *queen*. This is going to be a disaster." I glanced up at the sun, already far past the zenith of midday, arcing back down toward the western horizon once more. "We'd better keep going."

Rylan handed me the water flagon that he carried, and after I took a long drink, I passed it back and we started forward again.

"For the record," he said as we pushed the huge leaves and vines out of our way, "I don't think you're going to be a disaster. Honestly, I can't imagine a more perfect queen for Damian, or Antion."

I paused to glance over my shoulder at him. "Do you really mean that, or are you just saying it because I could order you beheaded if you didn't flatter me?"

"Well, that sounds like a terrible punishment for the minor sin of refusing to flatter you," Rylan teased. "But in this case, I actually mean it. You will be a remarkable queen, Alexa. Whether you wear a dress or not."

"Thank you." I reached out to take his hand for a moment, squeezing it tightly. "You don't know how much that means to me."

He stared down at our hands, and I almost let go, self-consciously realizing it was cruel of me to touch him when he now knew I could never be his. But before I could pull away, he squeezed me back.

"Let's go save your soon-to-be brother and get you back to your fiancé already." Rylan gently pulled his hand free and started forward again.

With a rueful sigh, I followed him into the depths of the jungle, toward the camp where I could only hope and pray Jax was still unharmed.

We had almost reached the spot where Rafe's camp was when the sun set, leaving the jungle lit only by the hazy light of dusk. Clouds streaked the sky above us, threatening rain in the next couple of hours as a storm gathered. We stopped before we came within sight of the tents, needing to finalize our plan of attack.

We'd agreed that we should wait until it was dark before trying to sneak into the camp, but we couldn't decide for how long. As soon as it was dark or when they were all asleep? It seemed like the safer option to wait until they were all asleep, but I was nervous for

Jax. The longer we waited, the greater the likelihood that he would end up hurt in some way.

"I want to make sure he's okay," I whispered to Rylan as we crouched behind the cover of an enormous bush and some low-hanging branches with massive green leaves dipping toward the damp ground of the jungle floor. In the distance, I could hear the chatter of monkeys, and I suddenly thought of my little friend, who had probably saved my life last night. I hoped he was happy somewhere, enjoying a fresh banana. "Then we can decide how long to wait."

"But you could be seen. Chances are they have someone on the lookout for you, since you're supposed to be back before dawn," Rylan argued quietly.

"Then watch my back," I said and pushed out of our cover before he could continue to try and dissuade me. I had to know if Jax was still all right or not. Though I'd told Damian he wasn't being harmed, I was terrified of finding out whether that was still true or not.

"Alexa!" Rylan hissed my name, but I ignored him and slunk forward, slipping from tree to tree, stealthily working my way closer to the camp.

If they did have a lookout waiting for me, he was either the worst lookout ever or the best, because I never saw a single person until I finally crept close enough to the camp to see the tents again and a few men milling about, tending the fire and preparing for nightfall.

I didn't see Rafe. When I looked over to the ground where Jax had been when I left, there was no one there. My heart began to pound with fear as I frantically searched the camp for any sign of him. Only grown men were visible. They couldn't have killed him already — could they?

Rylan was right behind me; I could feel him hovering a few feet away. Without turning back, I whispered, "I'm going to climb up there to get a better view." I pointed at the same tree I'd used before, which I'd stopped by on purpose. I had to see if Jax was all right or not.

Without waiting for his response, I pulled myself up onto the first branch, careful to move slowly, getting a firm grip before moving on to the next branch and then the next. I couldn't afford to fall and attract their attention again. I noticed a branch a little bit higher up than the one I'd used before, which stretched out over part of the camp, right above the closest tent, and would afford me a better vantage point. I climbed up to it and lay down on my belly, carefully inching forward, until I could see most of the camp below me. In the indistinct light of the coming night, I had to squint to make out individual faces. The fire was burning low, almost as if they didn't want too much light. But there was no sign of the boy.

Panic nearly strangled me when I glanced straight down and finally noticed a small figure curled up on the ground in the shadow of the tent just past the one I hovered over. He was so *close*. If only he knew I was clinging to a branch in the air above him, desperately trying to work out in my mind how to find Rafe and kill him before Jax's own life ended — by his own hand.

Jax's arms were still bound behind him, and he was shaking as though he were shivering — or terrified. It was a stifling night, the oppressive humidity of a building storm pressing in on all of us. He couldn't possibly be cold, unless he was shivering because he had a fever. If they'd allowed him to catch a jungle fever and he —

My thought wasn't even fully formed when I heard the sound of boots crunching across the ground. I recognized Rafe, sauntering over to where Jax lay on the ground. I couldn't read the expression on his face, and my entire body tensed, worry and anger pulsing through me.

"Get up." Rafe kicked Jax in the ribs — not hard enough to injure him, but it still made my blood boil, and my hands tightened into claws on the branch, my nails digging into the hard bark as I stared down at them. "Time for some entertainment."

"What? What is it?" Jax whimpered, disoriented. He gazed around blearily, and when he saw Rafe, he stiffened. "What do you want?" If he'd been shaking like that in his sleep, he must be ill, I realized with a sickening drop in my stomach.

"Don't worry. I just want to have a little fun. It won't hurt this time. Well, not *too* bad." Rafe laughed, a sound that elicited sudden terror. What was he going to do with Jax? I pulled myself up into a crouch, my heart pounding.

"N-no . . . please, d-don't . . . n-no m-more . . ." Jax stuttered, frantically trying to sit up. He looked like a helpless beetle as he pushed his shoulder against the ground and tried to shove himself up without the use of his hands. The sound of his voice — the fear, the exhaustion, the weakness — tore through me like a knife.

"Look at me, and we can get this over with soon enough for you to take a nap before the big finale." Rafe grabbed his face and yanked him off the ground by his jaw. I couldn't tell for sure in the dim light, but it looked like Jax had his eyes squeezed shut. "Open your eyes, boy, or I will cut them open myself!"

Jax's shivering grew worse; his entire body was shaking like a leaf in the wind. "No. I'm not looking at you ever again!"

As I watched, Rafe reached back, into his boot.

I'd seen enough; we had to act now.

I scrambled back down the tree, ignoring the pain of the bark scraping across my skin, or the branch that slapped my face when I jumped the last eight feet to land in a crouch beside the spot where Rylan still squatted, his eyes wide.

"What are you —"

Before he could finish his sentence, I yanked out my sword and stood up. "We're saving Jax — right now."

And without another glance behind me, I bolted toward the camp.

⊰ TWENTY-SIX ⊱

*I*RAN AS FAST as I could, straight for Rafe. When I realized he was holding a knife in his hand, reaching for Jax's face, a savage scream tore its way out of my throat unbidden. He froze and looked at me, his eyes widening in shock. I lifted my sword, ready to slice his head clean off his body, so quickly that Jax wouldn't be forced to hurt himself.

But before I could reach him, two men jumped into my path, swords raised. My blood pounded hot through my body — desperation and fury in equal parts — as I spun mid stride, dropping down into a crouch and swinging my blade forward to slice into the first man's legs, tumbling him to the ground. I immediately threw myself forward and rolled, barely avoiding the second man's jab. His blade embedded in the ground next to me, and before he could pull it back out, I rocked back onto my shoulder blades and then launched my body up in the air, landing on my feet. He didn't have time to get his sword back up, and I impaled him in one smooth movement — in and out. There was no time to waste in a fight. No time to worry about injuring instead of killing. He crumbled next to his companion, but I didn't even pause, rushing forward for Rafe once more.

He stood watching impassively, holding his own sword loosely in his right hand. His dagger was lying on the ground beside him, like he'd tossed it aside. I only had seconds to kill Rafe or else Jax would be forced to kill himself because of this ill-fated rescue attempt. I heard the sounds of more swords clanging behind me, and I could only hope Rylan had my back.

"Alexa!" I dimly heard Jax cry out, but I couldn't turn to him. Not yet. First, I had to kill Rafe. *Now.*

Rafe stared at me with his unnerving green eyes and didn't move until I was almost close enough to drive my sword through his heart. Then he finally lifted his sword, and the sound of our blades crashing reverberated through the camp. He defended himself with surprising agility and skill, but I was the better fighter. He was no sorcerer — at least not one who could fight. There were no magical barriers. No invisible hands to choke me or fire to burn me.

Only our swords and strength.

"You might wish to rethink this," Rafe said, his voice surprisingly calm as he parried another strike. He didn't attempt to fight back; he only blocked my hits. "Unless you want him to die."

I stumbled, hardly daring to glance at Jax. His eyes had gone blank, and he struggled to free himself. But his hands were tied behind his back — he couldn't do anything yet.

Furious, I lunged at Rafe again, nearly slicing his arm, but he spun out of my reach at the last second, turning so that he was directly in front of Jax. Involuntarily, my eyes dropped to the boy to see that his hands were loose now, and he was bending down to pick up the dagger from the ground.

Who had cut him free?

Panic coursed through my blood.

Now. I had to kill Rafe now.

With another scream of rage, I lifted my sword and rushed at Jax's torturer.

"Rylan, defend me *now!*" Rafe shouted, hastily scrambling backward, past Jax. His words made me pause, but I shook my head and lunged forward. He wasn't fast enough. This was my chance. Channeling every ounce of strength I had, I swung my sword down, aiming for his head, but then somebody jumped in the way, blocking my hit with his own sword.

The impact jarred me. I glanced at my new attacker and faltered.

Rylan gripped his sword, glaring at me with his familiar brown eyes, but there was no recognition in them now.

"*Rylan?*" I stumbled back a step.

My friend began to attack, and I automatically defended myself, shock making me numb. When had Rafe even had a chance to put him under his control?

Our blades crashed together again and again. I'd sparred with him countless times, but this was different. Now his blade was real, not made of wood. This time he was trying to hurt me.

I ducked one of his hits and dared a glance at Jax. He gripped the dagger in front of his body with trembling hands, his expression contorted, as though he were battling himself. His eyes weren't as blank anymore — now that I was no longer attacking Rafe, Jax seemed torn, partially himself and partially under Rafe's control.

"Rylan, stop! We're here to save Jax, remember?"

Awareness flickered into his eyes momentarily, a look of confusion crossed his face, and he paused for an instant. But the blankness won, and he swiped at me again; I barely avoided being gutted by his sword.

"Rylan, don't kill her!" Rafe shouted, and Rylan paused, his head cocked. With a nod, he moved toward me again.

No, no, no. This was wrong. I blocked his hits, but I couldn't do it. I couldn't fight him. I couldn't hurt him. Our blades crashed again and again as I struggled to come up with a new plan to save everyone I loved.

It was impossible. The only way to rescue Jax was to hurt Rylan.

How had Rafe done this? How had he stolen *Rylan* from me?

"Please, Rylan, stop!" I pleaded.

He attacked relentlessly, the horrible blankness in his eyes making me shiver. Of everyone in the guard, he was one of the few who had come close to beating me — but he'd never succeeded. I could stop him, and I knew it.

"Alexa, help me!" I heard Jax's cry from behind me; he sounded near tears, tearing at my heart. If he had enough awareness to ask for help, Rafe's command must not have been in force because I wasn't fighting Rafe anymore.

My grip tightened on the hilt of my sword, and I clenched my jaw against the tears that threatened to blind me. "I'm sorry," I whispered, and then I finally attacked.

Our swords flashed and collided in a flurry of silver and movement. Left, right, left, high, low, over and over the sound of blade on blade reverberated through the camp. Just when I was about to go for the strike that would have seriously injured my friend — but put a stop to the fight so I could go after Rafe and save Jax — Rafe shouted: "Rylan, stop now! Go over there and wait for my men."

Rylan immediately lowered his sword and stepped back. I was barely able to check myself in time before slicing into his sword arm.

Rafe pointed to a spot behind me, and Rylan obediently re-sheathed his sword, the blank look in his eyes giving me chills as he walked away.

"As for you, Alexa, don't move or I'll have them shoot you."

I turned to see three men standing behind Rafe, with arrows aimed at my heart.

My mind whirled, still unable to comprehend Rylan's betrayal — or what was going on here.

"Don't think I won't have them shoot you. I need you alive, but I don't necessarily care *how* alive you are."

I made a show of sliding my sword into my scabbard and lift-ing my hands. But as soon as he smiled — a smug little smirk that made me want to embed a dagger into *his* eyes like he'd threatened to do to Jax — I threw myself to the ground, rolling into a somer-sault and simultaneously grabbing my own bow from across my back. As I came forward again onto my feet, I heard the whistle of arrows flying near me but missing in the rush of my movement. I grabbed an arrow, with a speed that Marcel had once claimed was blinding, nocked it, and let it fly with barely a glance at my targets. The first man fell before he could even lift his hand to reach for another arrow. In the blink of an eye, I grabbed another arrow and shot it and then another, and suddenly all three archers were on the ground, before any of them could get another shot off, and Rafe stood alone unprotected.

But he was still smiling. My stomach dropped.

"You might wish to turn around."

Dread coiled in my belly as I slowly backed up so I could turn without losing sight of Rafe. With him still in my peripheral vision, I turned halfway to see Rylan ten feet away from me, a knife being held to his throat, four men surrounding him with more swords pointed at parts of his body. *Why?* Why were they threatening him if he was on their side?

And then I realized I couldn't see Jax anywhere. Frantic now, terrified that the worst had already happened, I spun farther, losing sight of Rafe but not caring, because if I lost Jax after everything —

And then I saw him. He stood a few feet away, in the shadow of a tent, trembling all over, clutching Rafe's dagger in front of him. He stared at me, a strange combination of despair twisting his mouth and emptiness in his eyes. Damian's eyes.

"No!" I screamed. "I haven't killed him, Jax! He's not even hurt — throw the knife away!" I lunged for him, ready to force him to stop, when I was tackled from behind and knocked to the ground. Rafe's hot breath in my ear turned my stomach.

"Watch," he said, his voice low in my ear. He pressed a knee into my spine, into my stitches, and yanked me up by my hair. I could have thrown him off, but I didn't dare move for fear of what that would make Jax do. "Watch as he dies because of your stupid little stunt."

Jax's arm shook as he began to lift the dagger.

"I didn't kill you!" I cried out, desperate. "Make him stop! I won't kill you — I'm turning myself in. I surrender. I surrender," I repeated, my voice breaking on a barely suppressed sob. I'd failed. I'd failed them all. Jax was still lifting the dagger. Rylan was captured, under Rafe's power. My promise to Damian was broken. I wouldn't be coming back to him after all. He would be alone, once again, and I hadn't even warned him about the madman in his dungeon.

"Jax, you can stop," Rafe said, amused, climbing off me but keeping a hold of my hair, yanking me up to stand in front of him. Suddenly, cold metal touched my throat. When I glanced to the side, I recognized the hilt he gripped. He held my own sword against my neck. "As she said, I'm still alive. And my sister?"

"The king is engaged," I whispered. Technically, it was the truth, and I could only hope Rafe didn't have some special way to find out if she were alive or not. We'd made sure no one could escape to warn him. But now that Rylan was under his control . . .

Rafe laughed again, a triumphant sound. "You see? No one has any hope of stopping us."

I stared at my friend, swallowing past the sudden lump in my throat. How had I not realized he was under Rafe's control — how had he hidden it? What had Rafe said to him that had enabled him to continue to act so normally until now?

"Let them go," I said, standing stiffly beneath my own blade.

"I don't think I want to. Your friend over there — he is called Rylan, right? He makes a wonderful soldier in my ever-increasing army, don't you think? So obedient." Rafe laughed again, his breath hot on my skin. "But that doesn't mean that I'm not willing to have him killed. So you can forget any of the ideas that are running through that mind of yours right now, if you want him to live."

Everything in me screamed to fight back, to kill Rafe. But Jax still held the dagger, and Rylan had five men with swords on him as well. I couldn't save them both in time. Even if I did kill

261

Rafe quickly enough to break the control on Jax, Rylan would die. Tears burned my eyes as I stared at them, first one, then the other.

"At least let Jax go."

"I'm not sure I want to." Rafe pressed the sword harder against my neck, almost hard enough to break the skin, but not quite. If I so much as swallowed, it would cut me.

"You made me a deal," I said, my voice barely above a whisper, trying not to move. "I gave myself up to you. Now tell Jax your previous order is rescinded and let him go."

"You aren't really in a position to be making demands," Rafe said, his lips brushing my ear, making my stomach heave. "And you didn't exactly come here on the terms we agreed to — you did *try* to kill me. You just didn't succeed."

"I could still kill you, if I wanted to. If you're going to keep Jax and continue to torture him, I would rather kill you and let him die quickly to spare him the suffering." My blood surged through my veins. I was walking a very fine line. "Don't doubt me. I'll do it. I could kill you right now, even with you holding my sword against me."

Rafe was silent for a long moment. "Then here's my offer. You look into my eyes, and I will give you one command. That's it. Just one little thing. In return for that, I will free Jax from my control and let him return to the palace."

I stared at Jax, at the flush on his olive cheekbones and the bright sheen of fever in his eyes, and my heart lurched. Then I glanced at Rylan. The blankness was gone; he looked like himself again. He shook his head, his expression horrified.

"Don't do it, Alexa," Rylan said. "Don't worry about me. Kill him and save yourself. Forget about my li —"

The man holding the sword to Rylan's throat pressed it hard enough to draw blood, and his voice dropped off. A thin ribbon of scarlet trailed down Rylan's neck to his collarbone, and he clenched his jaw against the pain.

Helplessness tore at my heart. This was my only option to keep everyone I cared about alive.

"I'm sorry." I blinked back the burn of tears in my eyes. "Tell Damian I'm so sorry."

"No! Alexa —"

"All right," I said, cutting off Rylan's protest before they could hurt him anymore.

"You agree?" Rafe crowed in my ear.

I nodded, a short jerk of my head, unable to speak again.

"Turn around," he ordered, "and look into my eyes." He moved the sword away and stepped back.

I turned slowly, swallowing hard to keep the rising acid from burning my throat. Rafe's eyes were the same odd green as Vera's had been. I held my breath as I fought every instinct in my body that screamed at me to look away, to grab my sword and plunge it into his heart. I clenched my hands into fists at my sides to keep myself from doing exactly that and killing not only Rafe but Jax and Rylan as well.

Rafe's lips curled into a horrible mockery of a smile as he stared back at me, directly into my eyes. "Alexa, you will never again attempt to hurt me in any way. Instead, you will now protect me from *any* and all threats that ever arise. You will be my personal guardian to keep me from harm."

His command seared into me, through his voice, through his eyes. Everything burned for a bright, horrible moment — my body, my ears, my mind. And then, all at once, my anger drained away. I unclenched my hands. Why had I been thinking about stabbing him? I stepped back, horrified at myself. I didn't want to hurt him — I was supposed to protect him.

But why did I want to protect him when I hated him so much?

Rafe began to laugh, and I looked away in confusion. "Jax, come here."

When I saw Jax walk forward, my stomach tightened again. *That* was why I didn't want to hurt Rafe — it was to protect Jax. The boy stared at me with wide eyes — Damian's beautiful eyes that I loved so much — and something inside me crumbled. I would never see Damian again, I realized. I remembered him kissing me this morning, telling me he loved me, making me promise to come back to him, and I had to squeeze my eyes shut against the sudden, blinding pain.

"You are free from my previous command. Go home. Don't stop until you reach the palace, and tell your brother that I have what I wanted."

My eyes flew open to see Jax nod and immediately turn and head into the jungle.

"Rylan, help him!" I cried out as Jax looked back at me with wide, blank eyes, a hint of terror on his face, even as he continued to walk away. "He can't stop now until he reaches the palace."

"No, I don't think I want your friend helping the boy." Rafe made a gesture, and the men guarding Rylan tightened around him, keeping him from moving.

"That wasn't the deal!" I shouted. "He'll die out there! He's sick, and he has no idea how to get back to the palace — especially in the dark."

264

"That's not my concern." Rafe shrugged.

Fury rose in me, hot and uncontained. I grabbed my sword out of his hand and swung it up in the air, but even as I lifted it, my anger left me. My mind felt strangely blank, and I looked at Rafe in confusion. What was I doing?

He smiled placidly at me as I slowly lowered my sword again.

Once my arm hung motionless at my side, I remembered Jax again, and the anger rose once more. And then I realized what had happened. I'd gone to strike Rafe — and couldn't. His order. I could never try to kill him again. The moment I did, my mind went blank, until I wasn't attempting to hurt him anymore. Was that how it worked — why some people's eyes looked empty only some of the time? The specificity or broadness of the command. That had to be the reason. And the one he'd given me was very specific.

I could never hurt him again. Instead, I was now forced to protect him.

"Was there anything else? No?" Rafe answered himself before I had a chance. "As I think about it, I would really rather make sure that your king gets my message. You" — he pointed at a man standing a few feet away — "follow the boy and make sure he arrives safely at the palace. Give Vera my regards, and tell her the plan is moving forward as hoped."

The man nodded, bowing to Rafe, then turned and hurried into the jungle after Jax.

"Happy now?" Rafe smirked at me. "See how I keep my promises? He won't die. What a relief."

I swallowed hard, trying to control my rage. It was useless. I'd made a bargain with the devil, and now I couldn't hurt him, no matter how much he deserved it. *At least Jax will return to Damian. At least he'll have his brother back.*

"Everyone not on duty, go get some sleep and prepare to depart at dawn." Rafe lifted his voice to a shout, making my ears hurt. When no one moved, he sighed and repeated himself in Dansiian, then turned back to me. "There's someone who wants to meet you, and since you were so kind as to show up a bit early, we should make better time than I was hoping."

"Where are we going?"

The men guarding Rylan shoved him forward, so that he stood next to Rafe.

"Why, to Dansii, of course. King Armando has a keen interest in the girl who killed one of his most valuable sorcerers."

"What exactly is your plan — what are you trying to do?" I couldn't meet Rylan's eyes; I couldn't bear to see either the horrible emptiness or the helpless fury that I was sure was also etched onto my own face. "Is this all an attempt to take Damian's throne? You won't succeed. I won't let you hurt him."

"Oh no, Alexa. *I'm* not going to hurt your beloved king. *You* are."

I stared at him in horror and then remembered to look away before he could give me any other awful commands. "I'd never hurt him," I whispered.

"Yes, you will." He walked right up to me, so that he could lean over and whisper in my ear. "The next time you see King Damian, *you* will be the one to kill him."

"Never!" I shouted. Terror pumped through my body, pulsing in my blood, white hot and excruciating. "You can't make me do that. I won't let you!"

"My dear girl, I can make anyone do anything I want. It's marvelous." Rafe grinned, lifting his arms in front of me, making a show of his empty hands. "Does that make you mad? Do you feel that anger boiling in your blood? Go ahead, try to do something about it."

I yanked up my sword, wanting to impale him on it, but the moment I swung my arm forward, my anger drained away again, my mind going blank just long enough for me to lower my sword to my side. Once he was out of danger, my fury returned, but it was too late. My anger was useless. I screamed in frustration and tossed the sword to the ground, my entire body shaking.

Rafe's laughter echoed through the camp as he turned away from me. "Try to get some rest — at first light, we leave. And my men will attest to the fact that I don't tolerate anyone slowing me down." He paused and glanced back at me. "Oh, and don't even think about trying to escape. Your friend will be under guard the entire time. If you try to leave, I'll have him killed before you get ten feet away."

My stomach dropped, but Rafe wasn't done.

"And, Rylan, if for any reason she tries to escape and you aren't killed in the process, *you* will stop her. You may not leave this camp, and neither can she. Understood?"

Rylan nodded, absorbing his command.

"Excellent." With one last smirk at me, Rafe turned to walk away.

"You won't succeed!" I shouted, unwilling to let him have the last word.

He paused and glanced back. "I already have."

"Antion is stronger than you think — *Damian* is stronger

267

than you think," I insisted, helpless rage burning hot beneath my ribs, driving through my muscles and bones. He didn't know Damian had fought through Vera's control and won — but I did. "We will fight you and we will win."

"Are you sure we're talking about the same people? Damian — your king who is now under my sister's control? And the people of Antion — uneducated villagers who are terrified at the very *thought* of sorcery? *They* are going to stop us? The most powerful kingdom in all the world." Rafe burst out laughing, a harsh, cruel sound.

"Our people aren't afraid of sorcery anymore," I said, even though I knew it was a lie. "And Dansii isn't as powerful as you think."

"Your people will fear sorcerers until the day they die, crushed like the useless pests they are. Hector made sure of it. Fear and ignorance are the strongest weapons any ruler can wield. Your kingdom has been built on both. And they are right to fear power — to fear Dansii. No one will be able to stop us."

"Blevon will. They don't fear you."

Rather than vanishing after my declaration, Rafe's diabolical smile only grew wider. "Ah, but they *will*. They think they've kept their secrets safe from everyone, hoarding their knowledge and power. But they're sadly mistaken. When my king is finished, both of your kingdoms will grovel at our feet, begging to be allowed just to *serve* us. *We* are the future," he shouted, making me flinch. "*We* have the power. And now that we have you, nothing will *ever* stand in our way again."

With that, he spun on his heel and stormed off.

I stared after him, my fingernails leaving crescent-moon marks in the palms of my hands, my heart slamming against my ribs. His words drove a cold, terrible panic deep into my chest. Dansii knew Blevon's secrets? I had to get back to Eljin and tell him — I had to make him share his knowledge with us so we could find some way to stop King Armando before it was too late. Rafe seemed to think taking me to Dansii was a key to their success, and that only made me even more determined to figure out a way to escape.

"Alexa, what is he going to make you do?" Rylan's familiar voice startled me; I turned and he stood beside me, the blood on his throat dried into scarlet lines. A few of Rafe's men flanked him, a constant reminder of his threats. Rylan's eyes were his own — for now. But for how long? We were both under his control now. The thought made me sick. As did Rafe's threats. "Alexa, tell me what he said to you."

I couldn't say it out loud. If I said it out loud, it made it real. It made it possible.

Somehow, I had to find a way to break this man's control over Rylan and me. Damian had been able to break Vera's control, although he'd never answered my question about how he'd done it. Was it the love we shared? Or was it something more — was it because he was a sorcerer?

No matter what the reason, I had to be able to do it, too — I had to be as strong as him. I refused to let this be the end for us. Not now. Not like this.

Somehow, I had to figure out how to escape with Rylan and get back to Damian. I had to warn him about what Rafe had said.

I stared after Rafe's retreating back and finally answered Rylan. "It doesn't matter what he said. I'm never going to follow another order from him again."

No matter what happened, I would never, *ever* let him make

me kill Damian. I'd rather die first. Rafe might have thought he'd won for now, but I wasn't so easily beat. He'd soon find out. And I refused to let him and his king succeed in whatever horrible plot they had put into action.

I'd made a promise to Damian, and I was going to keep it.

Somehow, I would come back to him.

⫷ TWENTY-SEVEN ⫸

*T*HE GROUND BENEATH me was hard and damp as I sat stiffly, staring at the fire in front of me. The flames were mesmerizing, licking at the wood, devouring it in an intoxicating dance of orange and red figures twining together and coming apart with a pop and a hiss. Rafe's men had taken my sword, my dagger, and my bow and arrows, leaving me unarmed, and tied my arms behind my back. One of them had tossed a thin blanket at me and gruffly said, "Sleep," in a very heavy Dansiian accent.

But as exhausted as I was, I had no plans to sleep tonight. Rylan was only a few feet away, also sitting up, his ever-present guards trying to stay awake, their swords lying across their laps. It had been hours since everyone else had gone to rest, except for those on duty.

"What are you planning?" Rylan asked me at last, his voice quiet.

I glanced at him, at the shadows and light flickering over his familiar face. He looked at me with clear eyes, but I remembered the emptiness in them all too well — and the command Rafe had given him to stop me if I tried to escape.

"I don't know."

I wasn't worried about the guards overhearing us; they obviously spoke only Dansiian. But I hardly dared let myself formulate the thoughts that were in my mind into a plan, let alone speak them out loud. So much could go wrong. Rylan could be killed by his guards. I could be injured. Or worse — *I* might be forced to hurt my friend, now that Rafe had commanded him to stop me.

But I had to try.

I glanced back at the flames. For the fire to live, it had to consume the wood, turn it to nothing more than smoke and ash. But once the fuel was gone, the fire, too, would die. Iker, Hector, even Rafe were all like that fire, burning all the life in their path, destroying everything and everyone in their wake. I could only imagine what King Armando — the man behind it all — was like.

And when the fuel ran out — what then?

Rafe's words from earlier today, his confidence that Dansii had more power than any of us realized, sparked a stab of fear inside of me once more.

I finally lowered my body to the ground, feigning sleep. Even if I hadn't been planning an escape, there was no way I would have been able to relax enough with the fire so close, coating my body in its heat, adding to the oppressively humid night. With my arms bound behind me, I wasn't able to get comfortable, but that wasn't my goal. Laboriously, I rolled over, turning my back on the fire, facing the darkness instead.

One of the men murmured something in Dansiian, and the others laughed. I ignored them. They wouldn't be laughing soon.

The entire back side of my body burned from the heat of the fire, from the thick, wet air of the jungle pressing in on me, even in the dead of night. In the distance, a bird screeched. It was almost enough. My hands were beginning to grow damp. Soon, they'd be sweaty. Wet and slippery. The man who'd tied my arms back hadn't done a great job of it — he'd been distracted by my fake attempt at struggling. I hadn't really been trying to escape, only to keep him from being able to get the ropes too tight. That plus the fact that I'd been flexing the tendons in my wrists when he'd done it, gave me about an inch of wiggle room.

With some struggle, I would be able to slip my hands free eventually, if my skin grew slick enough.

"Alexa, are you still awake?" Rylan whispered suddenly in the darkness. "I — I didn't know. . . . I don't . . . I don't even remember talking to him. I don't know why he can order me to do things without even looking into my eyes."

I didn't respond, still pretending to sleep. Part of me wanted to tell him it was all right, but even if my plan didn't hinge on the guards believing I was no longer awake, I wasn't sure I could have said the words. I was still reeling from the shock of his betrayal, even if it wasn't his fault.

When had Rafe spoken to him alone? He must have also commanded him to forget the conversation. I refused to believe that Rylan had willfully kept it a secret from me.

"Alexa?" His voice was quieter now, mournful. "I'm sorry," he whispered when I still didn't respond. "I'm so sorry."

I squeezed my eyes shut even harder, tightening the muscles in my jaw to keep from responding.

How had it come to this? Rylan and I, both under Rafe's control, trapped. Jax, wandering through the jungle, ill and weak, trying to find his way back to the palace, where Damian was surely awake, pacing his room, anxious and unable to sleep until I fulfilled my promise to return to him.

It was that image — the thought of my king, my *betrothed*, waiting for me, fearing the worst, trying not to let the terror that yet another person he loved would be taken from him swallow him whole — that drove my own fear to the back of my mind.

I loved Rylan and I didn't want to leave him — but Damian had my heart. I would escape now to return to my king, and then I would come back for Rylan. As soon as possible.

My mind raced, and the anticipation of a fight warred with the exhaustion that weighed my limbs down. The heat of the fire pressed in on me; perspiration dripped down my spine and coated my skin with moisture. It was now or never. The guards might never drift off, or new ones could come to relieve them. There was no point in waiting any longer. I would either survive this or I would die trying.

If only you could hear my thoughts. If only there was some way to tell you how much I love you, in case this goes badly. As I began to slowly inch my hands back and forth, wriggling them loose from the bindings, I pictured Damian as he'd looked only a few hours ago, when he'd held me in his arms, the sunlight glinting off the signet crown in his dark hair, his fiery blue eyes full of love — impossibly, for *me*.

Time seemed to slow to a crawl as I fought to free myself with as little movement as possible. It would be too easy for a guard to notice my hands moving if any of them looked down at me. Pretending to moan in my sleep a little, I made a show of turning my head jerkily, then rolled over once more, as though I were having a bad dream. This time, I stopped with my hands partially beneath me. Now I could work them out of their binding quicker, out of their sight. But I had to hurry, before the sweat dried or absorbed into my clothes and the damp soil beneath me.

The rope burned, chafing my skin as I pulled as hard as I dared. An instinct that I'd long ago learned to trust warned me that time was running out. I heard one of them say something softly in Dansiian. No one else responded, but it made my heartbeat kick up another notch in my chest. Tossing my head side to side, as though assailed by a nightmare, to distract from any motion visible from my arms, I yanked even harder. Pain exploded along my hands where my skin tore open. But the added slickness of the blood was the final boost I needed. Finally, *finally*, my right hand slid free. I quickly pulled the rope off my left hand as well.

Tensing, I opened my eyes to a slit. One guard had nodded off, the closest to Rylan. The others were drowsy but still awake.

Please, let this work.

With a deep intake of breath, I squeezed my eyes completely shut once more. *Damian, I love you. No matter what happens, I hope you always remember that.*

And then I burst off the ground, lunging for the sword lying on the lap of the guard closest to me.

⊰ TWENTY-EIGHT ⊱

*H*E DIDN'T HAVE time to react before I'd grabbed the hilt of his sword and quickly slashed it up through the air. He fell back, dead, the blade of his sword coated with his own blood before he even had time to blink. I couldn't spare time on the way my stomach twisted — I had no choice but to kill them, or they'd kill Rylan.

The other two men had jumped up, and one was lunging at Rylan, who was unarmed, the Dansiian's sword aimed at my friend's heart. I leaped forward, bringing my blade up to stop him with a clang of metal on metal. I cringed at the sound breaking through the blanketed hush of night. Rylan sat perfectly still as I fought for his life, the blood on my hands making my grip slippery.

The second guard rushed forward, arcing his sword through the air toward my head. I ducked, simultaneously spinning, my movement so quick the first guard couldn't block me before my blade sank into his side, biting through skin, muscle, and more. He dropped to the ground as I pulled my sword free and brought it up just in time to parry a blow aimed at my neck, with a jarring impact of the second guard's blade on mine. I thought

Rafe didn't want me dead. Apparently, these men had missed his instructions.

He twisted, lunging at my side this time, but I spun away, whipping my sword around and managing to slice into his arm before he jumped back out of my reach. I rushed forward, pressing my advantage, feigning right, and then, when he took the bait, whirled to the left, embedding my sword. In and out. Another killing strike.

He dropped to the ground beside his fellow guard.

The entire thing was over in less than a minute. Breathing hard, I closed my eyes briefly, but then I heard a sound behind me, and I spun around to see Rylan standing now, holding a sword in his hands, his eyes blank.

"We can't leave this camp. You killed all of them. I can't let you go." His voice was devoid of emotion. My friend was gone, and in his place stood Rafe's puppet.

A puppet very skilled with a sword.

"I don't want to fight you," I said, even as I tightened my grip on the hilt of my sword once again. "Rylan, I know you have to be in there somewhere. You don't want to do this. Please . . ."

Instead of responding, his eyes narrowed and he sank into his fighting stance, lifting his blade.

I heard a voice somewhere deeper in the camp, and my heart rate ratcheted up, pounding a desperate cadence beneath my ribs. The sounds of the fight had woken others — possibly even Rafe. I had no time. But the only way to fight fast was to kill, and I couldn't kill Rylan.

He circled to my left and then lunged forward. I automatically brought up my sword to parry his attack. The sounds of our blades echoed through the night, too loud.

I had to knock him out — or incapacitate him without making him useless to Rafe. I looked for any opening as he lunged and spun and attacked again and again. I twisted and parried and grew more desperate by the second, dancing farther and farther from the camp, leading Rylan toward the darkness and away from Rafe's men. More voices shouted in the darkness. They were coming. And then I would never escape.

Tears burned in my throat like acid as I swallowed my love for Rylan and forced myself to attack him harder than I ever had before. I'd never let myself fight him full out with real blades, because I'd cared about him. But now I had no choice.

I was no sorcerer, but some thrill of magic seemed to flow in my blood — an echo of the power my father had wielded. I was his *zhànshì nánwū*. And I had to defeat my friend right now to save us all — including him.

Right, left, right, faster and faster, until there was nothing except the darkness, the clang of metal on metal, the heat of the jungle, and the pulse of blood roaring through my body. And then he stumbled — only a slight bobble of his control, but it was the opening I'd needed. And not a moment too soon, because on the other side of the fire, three more men were rushing toward us, even as I led us deeper into the jungle and away from the camp.

With a savage cry — a cry of fury, of frustration and agony — I drove my sword forward, into my friend's thigh, just above his knee to the side of where his artery ran. With proper care, he wouldn't die. But he would always limp.

Rylan's empty eyes widened in shock, and his sword faltered as his leg gave out and he stumbled back, nearly falling to the ground.

"I'm sorry," I choked out. And then I turned and ran.

"Stop her!" I heard the shout — Rafe's shout — but he was too late. The jungle welcomed me with thick, dark arms, swallowing me into the depths of black night. Tears as hot as the guilt and anguish in my chest burned as they streaked down my face.

I heard the sounds of pursuit behind me, but I refused to let them catch me now. I ran and ran, branches and leaves and vines grabbing at me, tearing at my hair, my face, slashing the tears off my skin with vicious fingers.

They would save him. They *had* to save him, or I'd have no reason to go after them. Rafe would know that — he'd know he had to use Rylan to get at me.

After what felt like hours of running, the sounds of pursuit disappeared, until there was only my own harsh breathing and the noise of the jungle — the cry of birds startled out of sleep, of monkeys howling their outrage at the moon, of insects humming to life once more as the black sky melted into gray. And still I ran. My legs burned, my eyes burned as the blood on my hands dried. There was even more blood on my soul now, but I had escaped. *I had escaped.*

And then, just as the corners of the eastern sky began to streak blue with the oncoming dawn, the wall surrounding the palace soared out of the never-ending green canopy in front of me.

Someone stood atop the wall, staring out at the jungle. At first glance, I thought it was only the usual watchman — but something caught my eye as I burst out of the jungle, into the clearing before the massive gate. His head turned down to where I stood, and I saw him stiffen. His dark hair blew in the wind that rustled through the trees, touched my face and my bloodstained hands. His mouth opened, and I could see my name on his lips as our eyes met, but his shout was torn away by the force of the wind. He turned and ran for the stairs that would take him off the wall, back to the ground where I stood.

With a strangled cry, I stumbled forward toward the door that would bring me back to him, just as I'd promised.

I'd barely lifted my hand when the massive door began to grind open, and then Damian was there. He crushed me to him, his arms wrapped around me, holding me up. The sobs I could no longer hold back tore through me, and I clung to him, my bloody, battered fingers clenched in the folds of his tunic.

"You came back," he whispered, one hand stroking my tangled hair. "You came back to me."

The image of Rylan's eyes widening, my sword slicing through his leg, of his blood coating my blade burned in my mind, and I shuddered. "I promised I would," I managed to choke out.

Damian pulled away slightly, lifting his hands to cup my face, his eyes brilliant and sharp in the growing light of a new day. "But at what price?" he murmured as he stared down at me.

I shook my head, unable to tell him. Soon. Soon I would tell him everything. About the man in the dungeons, what I'd done to Rylan — and what had happened in the jungle. What Rafe had said about Dansii's power and Blevon's secrets and their plan to crush us all. But not now.

"Jax?" I asked, hardly daring to hope.

"He's with Lisbet; she's already begun to heal him. The man who brought him is in the dungeons."

Relief made my legs weak, and I sagged forward into Damian again. He wrapped an arm around me, holding me to him. "He's going to be all right, then?"

"Yes, he'll be just fine." Damian pressed a kiss to my temple and drew back just enough to look into my face again. "You did it. You saved him *and* you came back." He smiled at me, his eyes bright with hope and happiness.

But I could do nothing except stare into his beautiful face, my stomach churning. He didn't know I'd returned to him broken, under Rafe's control, and that I'd —

"Where is Rylan?" he suddenly asked, glancing past me into the jungle.

I met his questioning gaze, and my throat constricted.

"Alexa — where is he? What happened?" Concern and an underlying thread of shock strained his voice.

"I . . . I . . ." How much did I tell him? What would he do if he knew the truth — the whole truth?

"Is he —"

"No." I cut him off, not even wanting him to speak the words out loud. Rylan had to be alive. He *had* to be. "He's alive. But he's hurt. I . . . I had to fight him to escape. He's . . . Rafe . . ."

"Oh, Alexa." Damian's arms tightened around me. "I'm so sorry."

"I — I didn't have a choice. . . ."

"We'll go after him, of course — we won't let Rafe hurt him anymore. Now that I have you and Jax back, there's nothing stopping us from sending the army after him. And I'll let you have the pleasure of disposing of him however you please, my warrior bride-to-be." He reached up to softly touch my cheek. His finger came

281

away stained red, and I wondered how bad I must look. Cut, dirty, bloody, half out of my mind with guilt.

And Damian didn't know — I could never do what he'd offered. I could never hurt Rafe. He'd made sure of it.

Did I tell Damian now?

"Come on, let's go into the palace. I'll ring for a hot bath and some clean clothes for you." Damian turned me toward the palace, guiding me away from the jungle. "I'll send our best men out to find Rylan. We'll get him back — I promise."

"No, you can't. Don't send any more men. They'll die. Everyone is going to die. Rafe has control over Rylan! If more men come after him, I don't know . . . I don't know what he'll . . ." Hysteria built up in my chest, constricting my throat until I couldn't get the words past the knot of terror that choked me.

"Okay, okay." Damian's eyes widened, and his voice took on a soothing tone. "I won't send any men right now. It's all right. Ssh . . ." He stroked my hair, his touch slowly pushing the sudden anxiety back down. "For now let's just get you to your bed, so you can rest and heal. Then we'll make a plan to save Rylan. All right?"

"Fine." I tried to catch my breath, to force myself to calm down. There was nothing we could do right this minute. I could only pray Rafe would keep Rylan alive long enough for me to be able to think clearly again — to be able to figure out a solution to this mess. I needed to tell Damian the truth. He needed to know everything. But not now. Not with the panic only a hairsbreadth from consuming me. I could tell him later, after I'd rested — after I was back in control of myself — I reasoned as I let him lead me toward the palace. When I wasn't covered in blood and dirt.

Just before we walked through the gate, Damian stopped and looked down at me again. He lifted one hand to gently tuck a strand of hair behind my ear. His thumb trailed down my jaw, sending a shiver of want through me, despite all the worries and pain crowding my heart.

"Were you watching for me?" I asked, forcing myself to focus on Damian. To stare into his eyes, trying to ground myself in the reality of being here — with him.

Damian nodded, his expression still concerned. "When you didn't come back with Jax, and he said that Rafe told him to say that he'd gotten what he wanted . . . I was afraid that . . . that you . . ." He trailed off with a shake of his head, and I saw a ghost of the terror he must have felt rise up in his eyes. "I've been standing there for hours, unwilling to give up hope."

My heart pulsed painfully beneath my ribs as I gazed up at him.

"I love you, Alexa. And I never want you to leave my side again."

Before I could respond, his mouth was on mine, his lips hungry, all of his fear and love bleeding through his kiss into me. His arms crushed me into the hard planes of his body, but I didn't care. I held on to him as though I were drowning and he was my only hope of reaching the sky again. He was my air, my heart, my everything.

I pulled back reluctantly, wishing I could go on kissing him forever but knowing we needed to stop. Especially since we were standing in full view of anyone who happened to pass by. "Sorry, I just —"

"No, you're right. This isn't the place to get carried away. I couldn't help myself." Damian smiled at me, a wicked glint in his eyes. "Our people will have to get used to these types of displays, I'm afraid, with you as my wife."

A little thrill ran through me. *His wife.*

"Even covered in dirt and blood?"

"Even if you'd just *rolled* in the mud."

"You must be joking."

Damian chuckled. "Care to find out? I think there's an excellent patch of mud over there." He pointed as we both turned and slowly began to walk toward the palace. The perimeter guards had politely turned away to afford us privacy, but now, as we walked past them, they hurried to shut the gate and return to their posts.

"No, I think I'll just take your word for it." I shook my head.

"Ah, there's a hint of a smile at last." His eyes still held an edge of worry as he glanced down at me.

I tried to keep smiling, but the weight of all I had to tell him pulled it down, until I was near tears again. Damian stopped and turned to me.

"I'm sorry," I whispered.

"Don't apologize. You're exhausted — you've been through a terrible ordeal. And I'm sure you're worried about Rylan." His gaze was searching. "After you get cleaned up and rest, I promise you'll feel much better."

"I'm sure you're right." I forced a small smile, and that seemed to satisfy him. He had no idea that I was apologizing for much more than just not being able to smile easily at the moment.

But I still couldn't bring myself to tell him the truth.

I sat on my bed an hour later, staring at the dormant fireplace, where the ash of previous fires lay quiet and cold in the stone enclosure. My hair was still slightly damp, and the cuts on my face and arms stung from the soap I'd used to scrub myself clean. The scars on my face and neck ached, and the stitches on my back burned, but at least they'd held throughout the entire ordeal.

However, no amount of soap could erase the curse Rafe had put on me or the stain of guilt on my soul for what I'd done to Rylan.

A knock at the door made me jump, and I hurried to stand up. "Who is it?"

"It's Damian. May I come in?"

"Of course," I called back, tugging at my tunic, pulling it down lower over the breeches I wore. I was still barefoot, and I didn't have my vest on. But there was no time to do anything about it as the door opened and Damian strode in, leaving the guards on duty — Asher and Leon — in the hallway. When it had shut again, leaving us in privacy, he crossed to where I stood and took me into his arms.

"You were right," I mumbled into his shoulder, where I'd buried my face.

"As always," he responded, "but in what way, in this particular instance?"

I didn't have to see his face to know that he was probably smirking with one eyebrow lifted — the look that made my stomach do strange flips when he aimed it at me.

"I do feel better now that I'm cleaned up."

"I'm glad." He pulled back enough to look down at me.

And thankfully, it was true. The hysteria that had nearly pulled me apart was under tight control now. Sunlight streamed in through the window, coating my room in a golden hue. Damian didn't wear his crown or anything else to signify that he was king this morning. He was just my Damian — painfully beautiful and somehow in love with me. A man who had endured enough heartache to break anyone and somehow survived it. As if he'd read my mind, the light dimmed in his brilliant eyes and a shadow crossed his face. "I'm still not quite sure if you're really here. When I let you leave yesterday, I had this sinking feeling that I would never see you again. And when Jax came back without you . . ." He trailed off, a muscle tightening in his jaw.

I reached up to brush his hair back from his forehead and let my hand trail down his face. "I'm really here," I said, my voice low. "I promised you I would come back." And suddenly, regardless of everything that had gone wrong, I was intensely grateful that I had made it back. Despite the cost.

Damian closed his eyes and turned his head, pressing a kiss into the palm of my hand, sending fire up my arm to warm my body. "I love you," he whispered against my skin.

I gently turned his face back toward mine again, and he opened his eyes to look straight into mine. As always, I felt as though he could see more than just my face — scars and all. I'd always had the feeling that he could see past all of that, into my heart. Into my

286

soul. And as he stared down at me, bathed in the warm sunlight, I felt it yet again.

"I love you, too," I said, my throat tight with emotion.

He closed the gap between us, pulling me to him and pressing his lips to mine. His kiss was a sigh, a release of fear and worry, and also a test — to make sure we weren't actually dreaming. I clung to him, desperate to lose myself in his touch. To try and forget everything except him — except *this*: his body against mine, his lips on my cheeks, my jaw, my mouth, leaving a trail of fire on my skin, his hands on my back, urging me closer and closer. But at the back of my mind was the dark memory of Rylan, hurt, trapped. And my own awful secret.

I had to tell him. Now, before I lost my nerve.

Mustering all of my willpower, I pulled away.

Damian groaned as I pushed gently against him, forcing space between us. "Now I *know* you aren't a dream," Damian murmured, his voice low.

"Why?"

"Because in my dreams, there's no reason for us to stop."

My cheeks grew hot with my blush, but I couldn't let him distract me with his mischievousness. "I'm sorry, it's just that —"

"It's all right. I'm only teasing. I actually had another reason for coming to see you." He lifted one eyebrow. "Even though *that* was certainly reason enough."

I couldn't return his smile, as my heart beat with fear. Once I told him, would he want to kiss me anymore? Would his eyes still be lit with the happiness that was in them right now?

"Jax is awake, and he wants to see you. I promised him I would bring you right away."

"He is? He's all right?" Relief warred with the desperation lodged in my heart.

"He's almost better. Lisbet worked a miracle on him."

"I'm so glad." I managed to smile at last, but Damian's eyes narrowed.

"What is it — is everything okay?" He took a half step toward me, but I nodded, forcing a true smile to my face. I'd spent years acting; I could do it again. I didn't have the heart to tell him right now. Later — after we'd seen Jax. After he'd had at least a couple of hours to believe that I had returned to him whole and unharmed.

We had a huge battle looming ahead of us, and once I told him my secret, I had no idea what he'd do with me. Or feel toward me.

And we still had to come up with a plan to save Rylan.

But for now I wanted to just enjoy this — to be with him.

I reached for his hand, and the worry that had sprung up in his eyes faded again. "Let's go see Jax."

He squeezed my hand and turned to lead me to the door.

There was time enough to tell him the truth. Right now the only important truth was this: I'd done it. I'd brought his brother back to him, and I'd kept my promise.

Soon, we'd have to deal with Rafe — we would have to figure out how to save Rylan. Eljin would wake in the next day or two and would have to answer all the questions I had for him. The fates of both our kingdoms depended on it. I dreaded telling him about the missive we'd received from his father — that for some reason he was being coerced into betraying our peace treaty. We needed to find General Tinso, to figure out what was truly going on, before Blevon and Antion's alliance was destroyed forever.

And soon, we'd have to fight the imminent war against Damian's uncle, King Armando.

But for now, all that mattered was the feel of my hand in Damian's and the hope in his eyes. Hope that somehow — *together* — we could conquer everything ahead of us.

⊰ ACKNOWLEDGMENTS ⊱

Once again, I am so grateful for the many wonderful people who have helped bring this book into the world.

"Thank you" isn't sufficient for my agent, Josh Adams, for your wisdom and guidance through all the ups and downs, your hard work on my behalf, and your continued support. You always go above and beyond (what agent flies to their author's launch party in the middle of winter in UT??) — and for that I will always be grateful. Pretty sure I have the best agent ever.

Again, there aren't words adequate to express my gratitude to my brilliant editor, Lisa Sandell. I feel so privileged to be going on this journey with you. Your thoughtful feedback and guidance that make my books the best they can be, and your kindness and support (even when I'm being way too needy) mean so much to me. Thank you. Thank you, thank you. (Maybe if I repeat it enough, it'll mean more.)

To the rest of the incredible team at Scholastic, thank you for everything you do to bring my books to life and into the hands of readers — you are all rock stars. Especially my amazing publicist, Sheila Marie Everett; I can't thank you enough. You really are the best, and I'm so grateful to be working with you! And to Katie Grim and Elizabeth Starr Baer for your keen eyes and thoughtful copyedits that make all the difference! Thank you to all of the awesome people who make Scholastic the wonderful publishing company that it is. I'm so glad I'm a part of the Scholastic family! Thanks also to Bess, Emily, and everyone else in publicity, marketing, and sales who have spread the word about *Defy*. And to the design team that keeps giving me such gorgeous covers. You are all amazing!

Thank you to all of the librarians, booksellers, and book bloggers who have shared their love of *Defy* with others, and helped this series find readers. You are the true, unsung heroes. What you do is what gives us authors a chance to do what we love. THANK YOU. I wish I could personally thank every wonderful person who has supported *Defy* and helped spread the word — but that's just not possible. However, I do have to give particular thanks to Katie Bartow of Mundie Moms for all of your help in setting up events and promoting my books! And to Jaime and Rachel with Rockstar Book Tours — thank you for EVERYTHING! And to Windy and Andrea, thank you for your help, as well.

Huge squishy hugs to my amazing CPs for *Ignite* — Kathryn Purdie and Anne Blankman. Thank you for being willing to read on such short notice and for your insightful help. And above all else, thank you for being true friends. I'm so grateful to have you both in my life.

And the YA Valentines — you have all helped me survive this crazy ride. You've jumped up and down with me, talked me off ledges, and believed in me. I love being a part of this crazy-talented group of fabulous authors. Thank you for letting me be one of you! #Vals4Evah

Madi Brown — this book wouldn't have happened without you. Thank you for stepping in and taking such good care of my kids while I disappeared to the library to try and meet my deadline. (Especially on your summer break!)

I accidentally left out some important people in my previous acknowledgments, and I refuse to make the same mistake twice. To Caleb Warnock, Janiel Miller, Stephanie, Meghan, and everyone else from the American Fork Arts Council class — thank you. You helped me through a hard time on my path to publication. Thank you for all of your support!

I could have sworn I thanked Mr. Thomas in *Defy*, but apparently, I didn't — so I am rectifying that right now. When he gave his fifth-grade class an assignment to write a "story" for class, I'm sure he didn't expect me to show up with fifty handwritten pages — and then decide it wasn't good enough and write a different one that ended up being even longer! You had me read the whole thing to the class, and you told me I had real talent and that I should pursue my writing. You were the first person who made me believe I could actually be an author someday. Thank you for giving me that encouragement and for giving me the gift of hope!

Thank you to Marie Lu, James Dashner, Jen Nielsen, Meg Spooner, Veronica Rossi, Ally Condie, Erin Bowman, Jessica Spotswood, Natalie Whipple, and so many others who have supported *Defy*, or helped me navigate the murky waters of being a debut author. What a lucky person I am to have such wonderful friends and authors in my life!

I can't leave out the musicians whose brilliance helps inspire me. Hans Zimmer, as always — without your music, I'm not sure I would ever finish a book. For *Ignite* in particular, M83's "Oblivion" was absolutely pivotal to some of the scenes I wrote. Atli Örvarsson, Imagine Dragons, One Republic, Emeli Sandé, Sleeping at Last, and Josh Groban. Thank you, all. Music is integral to my writing process, and I can't thank you enough for creating such amazing songs for me to write to!

Thank you again to my parents, Henri and SuZan, for your excitement, support, and love. Dad, thanks for continuing to buy my books and talking to everyone about it. You rock. Mom, thank you for always being willing to read for me and for your thoughtful feedback. You help me be a better person in so many ways! And to my sisters, Elisse, Kerstin, Kaitlyn, and Lauren: thank you for your support and love. It means more than you know! Every time any of you post about my book, or come to an event, it makes me so happy! And of course, the part that makes me the happiest of all is when you tell me you love my latest book! And, Elisse — a special thanks for always being my first reader, for reading multiple drafts of all of my books, and for helping me be the best writer I can be. I couldn't do this without you.

To Robert and Marilyn, my in-laws, thank you for all of your excitement and support, and for your help with my kids so I can sneak some extra writing time. I'm so grateful for both of you!

And, as always, I saved the best for last. Brad, Gavin, and Kynlee . . . I love you more than words can express (which is saying something for an author). Thank you for putting up with Mommy when I have to work, and for being so excited about Mommy's books. You three are the joy of my life! Trav — my biggest fan and supporter and my best friend, I couldn't do any of this without you. Thank you for everything. It would take an entire book to thank you for all that you do. I am, without a doubt, the luckiest woman in the world. I love you.

And finally — the readers. Thank you for loving my characters and going on this journey with me and Alexa. Thank you for letting my dreams become reality through the pages of these books.

⊰ ABOUT THE AUTHOR ⊱

Sara B. Larson can't remember a time when she didn't write books —
although, she now uses a computer instead of a Little Mermaid
notebook. Sara is the author of the young adult novel *Defy*, and
she lives in Utah with her husband and their three children. She
writes during nap time and the quiet hours when most people are
sleeping. Her husband claims she should have a degree in "the art
of multitasking." When she's not mothering or writing, you can
often find her at the gym repenting for her sugar addiction.